KIRSTY MCKAY

UND

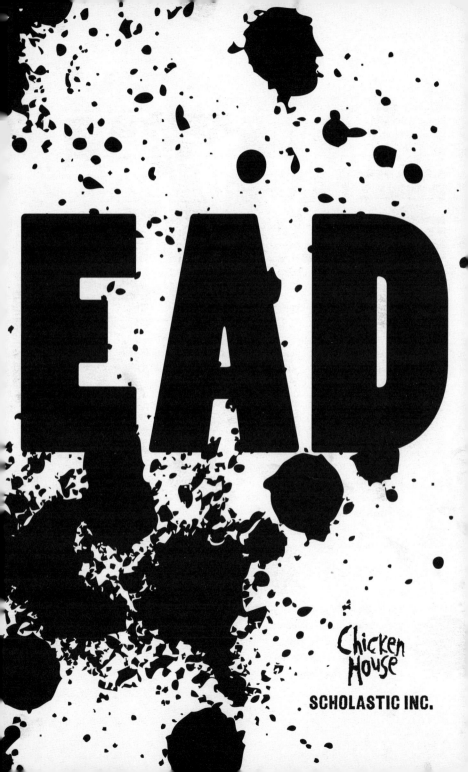

EAD

Chicken House

SCHOLASTIC INC.

ISBN 978-0-545-38189-5

12 11 10 9 8 7 6 5 4 3 2 1   13 14 15 16 17 18/0

Printed in the U.S.A.   40
First Scholastic paperback printing, August 2013
The text type was set in Alisal.
The display type was set in Alisal Bold.
Book design by Phil Falco

For John
Gobble, gobble, gobble

I would rather die than face them all again. Die horribly. In a messy, fleshy, blood 'n' guts kind of way. It is a total no-brainer.

I'm leaning my forehead against the cold glass of the bus window as we draw into the parking lot of the roadside café, earbuds in place. The music died long ago, but this way I maintain the illusion of invisibility. I'm perfecting my thousand-yard stare out into the desolate Scottish countryside, and the weather is doing the whole pathetic fallacy thing. (As in, it's crappy, and it echoes my mood. Just in case you nodded off during that particular English Lit class. Hey, I make no judgment.)

Another couple of minutes and I'll be alone. My dear classmates will all be going to lunch, and nothing and nobody can force me to go with them.

This would be the School Trip from Hell, if it wasn't so stupidly freezing. Cold and damp — the kind that seeps lead into your bones and slows your will to live. Compared to the wilds of Scotland, even hell has its perks.

"A skiing trip before the start of school, Bobby?" my dad had enthused all those months ago, when we were still back in the States and the England move seemed like a foggy half idea that was happening to someone else. "Perfect! What better chance for you to get to know your new classmates?"

"You can impress them all on the slopes!" my mum had chimed in, ever-so-helpfully.

Yep. So that was settled, then.

What my parents had failed to figure was that Aviemore, Scotland, was hardly Aspen, Colorado. And that trying to make new friends by showing off my souped-up skiing skills would be the very best way to get my butt kicked, UK-stylee.

Bum, not *butt*.

Butt marks me out as different, like *sidewalk, cell phone,* and *soccer*. When we moved to the US six years ago, they thought I sounded as British as the Queen. Now that I'm back in the motherland again, I'm like some weird hybrid, a freako chimera with an ever-changing accent. I need to relearn my own language. And fast. I've had enough of the snickering, the rolling of eyes, and the throwing of hard snowballs when my back is turned. American high school can be brutal (song and dance routines in the cafeteria? Meh . . . not so much), but the British version is just as cruel. Every meal at the ski resort this past week had been torturous. Looking for a space at a table. Hoping for Just One Friendly Face. Praying that Mr. Taylor and Ms. Fawcett didn't beckon me over to eat with them *again*, knowing that it would be social suicide to be marked as teachers' pet.

But the horror is nearly over. That thought has kept me going for the last twenty-four hours. Just the journey back to school to endure.

Everyone troops off into the Cheery Chomper café for lunch, but I'm staying right here on the bus. I've prepared for this, for sure; squirreling away a quickly made peanut butter sandwich at breakfast. As I hid it in my bag with an apple, that reality-star skank wannabe Alice Hicks caught my eye, and one of her cronies started singing "It's Peanut Butter Jelly Time." Whatever. Stupid girls with their pastel-colored skiwear and pink glitter nail polish. This lunchtime they'll have to find someone else to throw their fries at.

Gah! *Chips*, not *fries*.

My appetite is zero, but that's hardly the prob. Truth is, I have been dying to pee ever since we left the ski resort . . . but *come on*, only a fool would use the bathroom on board. Pete Moore dropped a deuce on the trip up, and they gave him hell about it for two hours straight. How could he have been such a goob? You'd think he'd have enough to worry about already with that whole Class Geek Extraordinaire thing he has going on. Some people even call him "Albino Boy" on account of his white hair and see-through skin, which is probably borderline racist. He smiled at me once, early on, but it was the kind of smile that someone gives when they recognize an easier target. He'll soon learn I'm not going to put myself in harm's way to save his plastic-wrap skin. And if that means crossing my legs for the next few hours, then so be it.

I wipe the condensation off the window. Wow. The snow is coming down thick and fast now. Typical. No fresh powder for five days at Aviemore, and now that we're heading back to civilization we have major dumpage. I watch my classmates snake their way through a channel in the snow across the parking lot and up the steps to the café. As they reach the door, squeals ring out.

A huge, furry carrot is standing at the entrance, waving at them. For a moment I think I'm hallucinating with carbon monoxide poisoning from the bus's engine, but no, it's a huge, furry carrot all right. The squeals quickly turn to laughter and derision. The carrot is some poor, unfortunate soul, dressed in an enormous orange suit and green tights and gloves. He's waving and handing out samples from a small cart, little cups of something. My fellow students grab the freebies greedily. I squint at a banner pinned to the wall above the door:

▶ CARROT MAN VEGGIE JUICE! ◀
PUT SOME FIRE IN YOUR BELLY!

Carrot Man stomps his carrot feet in the snow. He must be freezing his onions off. Suddenly I feel kind of lucky to be me. Ms. Fawcett shoos everyone inside, and Carrot Man is left to clumsily pick up all the discarded cups of Veggie Juice and tidy his cart.

"Smitty, you'll be staying here with me."

I peek between the seats. Mr. Taylor is barring the exit from an ink-haired indie kid in a leather jacket. Rob Smitty: rebel without a pause, freak show, and dropout in the making. But the best snowboarder, definitely. When I first clapped eyes on him, I was convinced he'd be the head of the underage drinking club — and he is — but dude knows how to throw himself down a mountain, too. He was the only other member of my class crazy enough to tackle the double-diamond black runs. Respect due, in spite of the try-hard guyliner and bad attitude.

"Mr. Taylor, you can't keep me on this bus," Smitty drawls. "It's against my rights."

"I can and I will." The teacher pulls a wry grin, the effect of which is lost when he sneezes violently into a large, checkered handkerchief.

"You lost all your rights with me when you deemed it necessary to buy vodka and cigarettes with a fake ID. Now sit down and shut up, and pray I don't give you this flu."

Smitty throws his arms in the air and stomps back down the aisle. "I warned you, Mr. Taylor. Don't know what the school board will think when they hear you wouldn't give me any food. That's deprivation, that is."

"Big word for you, Smitty," Mr. Taylor jokes, but I can see doubt in his glassy eyes. He puts on his ill-advised neon ski jacket. "OK, I'll get you a sandwich. But do not move from this bus." He jabs a finger. "Under any circumstances. Or there'll be hell to pay. Believe me, I am in no state to be trifled with." He sneezes again as if to prove his point. As the driver releases the door for him, a flurry of snow flies inside.

"Don't forget I'm allergic to nuts, sir!" shouts Smitty. "You wouldn't want my parents to sue if I drop down dead!"

The door swings shut. I huddle into my seat. The driver turns up the radio and this insanely happy song assaults my ears, something about the sun shining every day, how lucky we are to be in the sun. Lucky, riiight . . . The driver opens a flask of coffee, steam funneling into the air as he pours a cup. Why does coffee always smell so much better than it tastes? Not that I could drink a thing. I cross my legs and think of arid landscapes . . .

Useless. Gotta pee, gotta pee.

"Oi, mate."

I flinch — mortifyingly — as Smitty hangs over the back of my seat. He isn't talking to me, though, but to the bus driver.

"Let us off for a bit, will you?"

The driver glares at him. "Sit down, lad. You heard what your teacher said."

Smitty strolls back up to the front of the bus. "Come on, geezer. Just want to get some fresh air."

"Ha!" The driver says. "Catch your death of cold, more like."

It's now or never. While they aren't paying attention, I remove my earbuds, shuffle out of the seat—keeping low—and make my move down the bus, bathroomwards.

"Hey you, lassie!" Driver's seen me. "Toilet's closed when the bus is stopped!"

"But . . ." My cheeks are hot. Smitty is looking.

"Company policy!" the driver shouts. "Use the facilities in the café."

I linger in the aisle. There is no way I can hang on for another four hours; I might *damage* something. I have to face the mob in the café.

"I need to go, too!" Suddenly Smitty is hopping on one leg, the other crossed in front of him. The bus shakes as he jumps in time to the song on the radio. What. An. Ass.

"Sit down!" the driver yells, then turns to me. "And you—"

Something slaps the windshield.

We all jump, and the driver swears robustly. A streak of coffee is now adorning his white shirt.

There's another smack on the glass.

A fat pink hand waggles away the snow from a patch on the window. Then it's gone.

"Damn kids!" the driver mutters, leaning forward to put his cup on the dashboard. "Clear off!" he shouts, thumping the windshield. As he does, something slams hard into the side of the bus. I grab at a seat to stop myself from falling.

"All right, you asked for it!" Rubbing his head where he banged it on the steering wheel, the driver stands up and pulls on his coat. "Stay here!" he shouts at us as he pushes the lever that opens the door, then clomps down the steps and off the bus. The door shuts behind him with a hiss.

"I won't tell, Newbie." Smitty is smiling at me. I frown back, and he points behind me. "If you wanna go potty."

I give him my snarkiest eye-roll.

Suddenly the bus shunts violently forward, flinging us both to the floor. I gulp for air, the wind knocked out of me, waiting to see if anything is hurt other than my pride.

After a moment, Smitty speaks. "You OK?"

"Yeah." Rubber matting, sticky in places, against my cheek. Gross. I push myself up to a sitting position. "What was that?"

"Dunno." Smitty is already on his feet. "We were hit." He leaps over me and runs to the back of the bus. He rubs his hand against the back window. "Can't see anything."

I get up, trying not to cling too noticeably to the seats as I walk, and clamber onto the seats beside him. I peer through the back window. Whiteout. The snow is now filling the air, dense and whirling in a kind of violet light, obscuring everything.

"I'm going to look." Smitty bounds back up the bus.

"No!" I don't know why I don't want him to, but I really *don't*.

"Someone could be hurt." He's almost at the door, silhouetted by the brightness outside. I pull myself back up the aisle.

"We should stay here until the driver comes back."

"What if the bus explodes because something crashed into us?" Smitty says.

I blink. "Yeah. That *so* doesn't happen in real life."

"Says who?" Smitty makes a scream-face at me. He pushes the lever and the door clatters open with a rush of cold air. "What if driver dude is stuck in the wreckage?" He affects what he presumably thinks is my semi-American accent, and flutters his eyelashes. "I could, like, *totally* save the day." He launches himself down the steps to the door, stops with a jolt. "Whoa."

"What's wrong?"

Slowly, he points into the whiteness. I squint past him.

There in the snow is a large puddle of red.

"What is that?" I cautiously descend the steps until I'm right behind him. Flakes of snow fall through the doorway onto my face.

"Nothing good."

A crimson trail leads from the puddle to the front of the bus. Together, we lean out and peer around the doorway.

A screech, like a fox caught in a trap, comes from the direction of the café.

My head whips round.

"What the . . . ?" Smitty backs up into me.

The screech comes again, closer this time. I stare into the snow, eyes straining. A vague shape is moving in the whiteness.

"Move!" Smitty is behind me now, at the driver's seat. He slams the lever and the door unfolds shut, missing me by a hair's breadth.

"Hey!" I protest, then fall back in shock as the screech appears at the door, slapping hard and fast, trying to get in. Through the glass I see baby blue and yellow, a bundle of blond hair, and shiny pink nails scraping the glass.

"Open the door!" I shout at Smitty.

"Are you crazy?"

"Now!"

When he doesn't obey, I scrabble up the steps and hit the lever myself before he can stop me.

The door opens, and a manic figure propels itself into the bus.

"Shut the door!" it screams.

I go for the lever but Smitty is way ahead of me this time and the door slides shut again.

The figure lies panting on the steps. It's Alice Hicks. She lifts her head, black mascara dripping down her pretty face.

"Dead!" she screams. "Everybody's dead!"

2

Alice Hicks looks good even when she is lying on the floor crying. When *I* cry — which admittedly is about twice a century — I look utterly destroyed. Beet-red face. Tiny little pig eyes and runny snot nose. It's a genuine talent, looking pretty while traumatized. So if this is for real, I won't just be shocked, I'll be *impressed*.

"Dead?" I say. "What are you talking about?"

"Your friends are dead?" Smitty leans back casually on the driver's seat. "Have you only just noticed?"

"It's true!" Alice's voice trembles through the sobs. "In the café. Go and look if you don't believe me!"

"All right." Smitty springs up from his seat.

"No!" Alice says, raising herself to face him. "You can't go out there!" Her legs buckle and she collapses onto the steps again.

"Why not?" Smitty won't be put off.

"Get back!" she screams.

Smitty holds his hands over his ears, his face in exaggerated pain.

But there's something about the way she's slumped on the steps — the dirty, wet steps — wearing her rah-rah red pep squad skirt. This is genuine — at least, *she* believes it.

I nudge Smitty out of the way and offer her a hand. "Come and sit up here. Did you hurt yourself?"

"Keep him away from the door!" Alice wails, bracing herself in the stairwell, looking surprisingly immovable in spite of the flow of tears and the baby blue ski jacket.

"OK, he's sitting down over there." I point at a seat a couple of rows back and look at Smitty.

"I am?" Smitty says.

"You are." I grit my teeth, like some kind of genuine hard-ass. Smitty makes a face but — remarkably — obeys. Even more remarkably, Alice lets me help her into a seat. "So take a breath" — I take one of my own — "and tell us what you saw."

"I told you, everyone is *dead*," she repeats, jaw clenched. "I was in the café, I went to use the ladies' room — yes, even *I* have to go sometimes, Smitty," she snarls before he has the chance to say anything. "I came back and everyone was sort of lying across the tables . . . like they were asleep. At first I thought it was some lame joke" — her brown eyes flash with scorn — "I mean, hello, *très embarrassant*, but then I went up to Libby and Em and Shanika, and I shook Em and she fell onto the floor." Alice's face crumples and here come the tears again. "She wasn't breathing. No one was breathing!"

"Are you sure?" I have to ask.

"Of course I'm sure!"

"How did it happen?" I crouch down beside her. It looks like I'm being sympathetic, but really my legs suddenly feel wobbly. "Were they sick or something?"

"I'm supposed to know?" Alice yells. "They were all just lying there, the whole class!"

"What about everyone else? The waiters, other people in the restaurant?"

"All dead." She shudders. "On the floor, on the chairs, behind the counters."

"Mr. Taylor and Ms. Fawcett?" I turn to Smitty, like he's suddenly the sane one. "We have to find them."

"No!" screams Alice. "Mr. Taylor was there, I saw him, standing by the sandwiches."

Phew. World order is restored. "Has he called for help?"

Alice shakes her head. "I ran up to him. He turned around . . . his face was *yuck*. His eyes were weird, all red . . ."

"He has pathetic Man-Flu," Smitty says.

"More than that!" She pauses for effect. "He was dead, too."

"What?" I say.

"He grabbed at me," Alice says. "I ran . . . out . . . he tried to get me."

"You're so full of it!" Smitty squeals with laughter. "What's today's date, April Fools'? We're supposed to believe that everyone's tombstoned from instant food poisoning, and Mr. T has risen again and is trying to kill you?" He jumps up and holds out his arms, moaning.

"Believe it!" Alice thumps her fists on the armrests. "Do you really think I'd even bother to speak to you two unless everyone else was dead?"

I raise an eyebrow. "She has a point."

"She has a nerve, more like," Smitty says, his head shaking.

"Fine." Alice stands up carefully, her pretty retroussé nose in the air. "Go and check. But don't blame me if you end up dead."

Smitty steps up.

"Wait." Before I know it, I've planted myself firmly between them. Not a great place to be, but right now, very necessary. "We need to call the police, an ambulance, don't we? We should stay here until they come."

Alice's face widens in horror. "My phone . . . it's with my stuff! Oh my *god*!" Fresh tears. "I left my Candy Couture bag on the table!"

"Oh, the tragedy!" Smitty joins in, girlying it up. "The dead people might be . . . touching it!"

"Shut up! You know nothing!" Alice cries. "It's one of a kind!"

Enough of this. I have a damn phone. I rush to my seat and snatch my backpack down from the shelf. The phone's in the inside pocket. I've barely used it since my mother bought it for me when we arrived in the UK. What was the point? No friends to text me in this dumb, damp country.

Now it might just save my life.

Searching for signal . . . the screen reads. I hold it up to the window.

"Not working?" Smitty bounces past. "When did you get it, the Dark Ages?" He pulls a smart phone out of his back pocket. Nice. He probably stole it. "Now, this little baby will pick up a signal on the moon." He stares at the screen. For a little too long.

"But not here?" Alice is triumphant.

"Give it a minute," he says. "We are in the middle of Nowheresville." He presses a few buttons, like that will help. "Shiznuts. What's wrong with it?"

"No reception." My teeth are gritted again; I'm going to grind them down to pegs at this rate. I toss my phone-a-saurus onto the seat. "We have to find the driver. He's probably got a radio." I turn to Alice. "Did you see him when you were outside?"

Alice cocks her head to one side in a way she clearly thinks is super-cute. "What, you mean when I was running for my life through a snow blizzard? Er, that would be a *no*."

I don't bother with a reply—mainly because I can't spare the brainpower—and rush down the bus to the back window. The snow has eased off a little. I can just make out the shape of a car. "We need to go check behind the bus. I think that's where the driver went."

"See ya." Alice sits in a seat halfway up the aisle. "I'm not moving."

"I am," says Smitty. He's at the door before I can react. "You stay," he shouts at me. "In case *Malice* here gets the idea of shutting me out." He hits the lever for the door and runs lightly down the steps.

"Be careful." I reach the top of the steps.

He grins and grabs at his own neck, like some ghoul is dragging him off. The snow crunches as he disappears around the front of the bus.

"Shut the door!" Alice hisses.

"Give him a second. He'll be right back with the driver."

Fat flakes of snow are falling rapidly again. The wind has dropped and the air is so full of silence it almost hurts. The patch of red *whatever* on the ground is still there, but it's diluted pink now, with new snow beginning to cover it. My ears strain, and my hand hovers over the door lever, ready to push it shut if anything leaps out of the whiteness.

"Hey!"

I jump and bash my knuckles against the steering wheel.

"Give us a hand, Newbie!"

Smitty's voice. I climb down the first step. "What's the matter?"

"Come here!"

"Don't." Alice rises in her seat, but doesn't step into the aisle. "Stay!"

"He needs help." I linger on the steps.

"Oi!" Smitty appears at the door, and I jolt back onto the top step on my behind. *Stylish.* He looks up at me. "It's the driver. I can't carry him on my own."

"Carry him?" I stand, resisting the urge to rub my tailbone.

"Quick!"

And he's gone. I fix Alice with my steeliest of steelies.

"Do not lock us out."

"You've got two minutes," Alice shouts back.

I step out into the white, onto the path trodden in the snow by my classmates. Avoiding the pink, I step off the path and immediately sink up to my knees. Awesome. It's just snow. Steadying myself against the side of the bus, I place my foot in the first of Smitty's footprints, following them. The snow is shallower on the road and I move more easily along the length of the vehicle and round to the back, where a Mini Cooper with a British flag–painted roof is wedged against the bus's bumper.

"Here." Smitty's head pops up from behind the car. "Help me drag him."

I get closer. *Oh god.* The driver is lying motionless in the snow, his legs underneath the car.

"Is he OK?" Stupid Question.

"Not a scratch on him," Smitty says. "Except for his hand."

He holds up the driver's right wrist. There's a deep gash, and syrupy blood is pumping slowly down his arm. A hot, giddying wave of adrenaline flushes through me.

"We need to bandage him — quickly." My hand shoots up to my neck for my scarf. My mother's best cashmere scarf, actually. Pale lilac with blue stripes. She'd tucked it round my neck the morning we left, in place of a hug. I don't even like the scarf, but the look on her face was so out of character — like she was actually going to *miss* me for once — that I'd kept it on. But there are other things at stake now. I unwrap it quickly and wind it around the driver's forearm as tightly as I dare. I have nothing to fasten it with.

"Here." Smitty drops a small, black circle into my hand. It's a pin — a badge — with a laughing skull and the words *Death Throes* on it. The name of a band. I hope. I fix the scarf in place.

"Should we move him?" I look up at Smitty, and my eyes fill with snowflakes.

"Yeah. He'll freeze otherwise." He hunkers down and starts pulling the guy up, somehow. "Luckily for us he's a short-arse. I'll hoist him and you get under his other arm."

We shuffle upright, and suddenly the driver's heavy on my shoulder and I'm breathing in the uncomfortable warm, sweet scent of middle-aged-man sweat. He lets out a moan.

"Good, you're awake," says Smitty. "Mister, we need to move you. Just put one foot in front of the other and we'll do the rest."

We stagger forward, like an odd, three-headed monster, lurching and sliding through the snow. Finally, we make it back to the door of the bus.

It is closed.

"Malice!" Smitty bangs on the glass. "Let us in, you bloody moose!"

"Come on, Alice!" I cast a nervous glance toward the café. The falling snow is thinning, and I can make out the entrance again. There are dead people in there. I can't see them, but I don't want to. "Hurry up and open the door!"

Alice does not appear. The driver grunts, gesturing to a small, metal flap on the side of the coach. With numb, wet fingers I open it, and push the button I find there. The door opens with a *swoosh* of relief.

"I'm gonna kill her," growls Smitty.

"Get in line," I tell him.

Between us we manage to half push the driver to the top of the steps and help him into his chair, where he punches the door lever closed with his good hand and passes out.

"Is he dead?"

A voice from on high. For a reason that I cannot immediately fathom, Alice is standing on top of two seats halfway down the aisle, holding a pair of binoculars.

"You shut the door, you cow!" starts Smitty.

"Be grateful," Alice says. "Found these in Ms. Fawcett's stuff." She waves the binoculars at us. "I was being lookout." She points to the roof of the bus. There's an escape hatch. "You can see into the café," Alice says. "No one's moving."

Smitty is down the aisle pronto. "Here, gimme." He snatches the binoculars from her and scrambles up to the hatch.

"Ew, your hands are all sticky," Alice says. "Oh my god, it's blood!" she squeals, jumping down and wiping her hand on a seat. "Get it off me!" she screams. "Is it his?" She points to the driver.

"Yep." My voice is hard. "He hurt his wrist and he's unconscious. We need to get him some help. Like now."

"Heads up!" Smitty shouts from the hatch. "Here comes Mr. Taylor."

"No way," Alice says.

"For real?" I climb up on the seats, using the storage shelves on either side to pull myself up to the hatch. I poke my head out into the cold air and vie for space.

"He's coming out." Smitty holds fast to his position in the hatch. "He's heading this way."

"Don't let him in!" says Alice, trying to climb up, too.

I squint in the direction of the café. No need for the binoculars to see

Mr. Taylor now. The snow has stopped, and through the strange pale purplish light I can see the teacher stagger out of the door of the café.

"He doesn't look right," I state the obvious.

"Duh, you think?" Alice appears in the hatch. "I told you he tried to grab me and his eyes were all screwy."

"And the rest." Smitty shoves the binoculars at me. "Take a look."

I hold them up to my face and the eyepieces balance heavily on the top of my cheeks as I turn the dial to bring the scene into focus. Mr. Taylor's head sways in and out of view. I steady my wrists against the roof and stare. The teacher's face looks bruised and greenish-brown, his eyes are blackened and screwed tight, and his mouth is open like a trapdoor on a slack hinge. Worse, there is something running down his chin. *What is that?* I blink and look again. It's blood, dripping from his jaws and plopping onto the white snow. I slowly pass the binoculars back to Smitty.

"I don't think he remembered your sandwich."

"Let me see!" Alice tries to elbow me out of the way, but loses her footing on the seat below. With another squeal she slips and almost falls, saving herself at the last moment by shooting out a hand and grabbing at the hatch lid. It rises off the roof for a split second, then crashes down again with a thump.

Mr. Taylor's head snaps up. He sees us. Letting out a long groan, he stretches his arms out and heads directly toward the bus.

He looks . . . hungry.

3

I can only grip the side of the hatch and watch as the thing formerly known as Mr. Taylor lurches down the café steps toward us.

"He doesn't seem very happy," I say, overly casually, because it's either that or flat-out panic. "Maybe we don't let him in, huh?"

Beside me, Alice starts to whine, not unlike one of those little handbag dogs that she probably aspires to own.

"He's coming for me — didn't I tell you he tried to grab me?"

Smitty thrusts the binoculars at her. "Watch him. Scream if he gets close. You can do that." He turns to me. "We need to barricade the door somehow, now!" He's down off the seats and through the bus like a mountain goat. I follow, a little less cleverly.

"Oi, dude!" Smitty shakes the driver. "How do you lock this door?"

The driver's head lolls to the side, and Smitty slaps him on the cheek.

"Don't!" I say. "You'll hurt him."

"He's out cold." Smitty's looking for something on the dashboard. "Nope, doesn't look like these doors lock."

I search for a button, a lever, something — but he's right. The door is in four long vertical sections that fold in on themselves like a paper fan when they open. An idea comes to me. "If we had something to put across, like a piece of wood —"

"Got it." Smitty calls down the aisle. "How we doing, Malice?"

Alice's blond head ducks down into the bus momentarily. "Do not call me that, you total freak."

"Is Mr. T still heading for us?" I say.

Alice sticks her head out again. "Yes!" she shouts down to us. "Slowly. He's sort of staggering around the parked cars, but he's coming this way. Oh my god, he's horrible. He's completely *dribbling*."

"Lovely-jubbly." Smitty grins at me. "I'm going to get my snowboard. Shut the door behind me, won't you?"

"What?" My jaw drops. "Outside?"

Smitty reaches under my chin and closes my mouth, which makes a kind of *clop*. Before I have time to recover, he pushes the door lever and jumps into the snow.

"My board's stowed under the bus. Shut the door!" He disappears around the side of the coach, and I pull on the door lever and race back down to Alice, my face aflame.

"Where is Mr. Taylor now?"

"Past the cars," says Alice from the hatch. "Have you locked the doors?"

"Smitty's gone out to fetch his snowboard so we can barricade them."

Alice drops down from the hatch. "Tell me I didn't hear you right."

"Don't worry." I smile halfheartedly. "He'll only be a second. You said Mr. Taylor was moving really slowly —"

"Oh my god oh my god oh my god . . ." Alice runs blindly to the front of the coach. "Smitty's outside? We can't lock this thing?" A loud *clank* comes from underneath the bus and she screams. "He's going to get in! He's going to kill us!"

"That's just Smitty." I pull myself up to the hatch to make sure. Mr. Taylor is still on course. He's not fast, but fast enough to make it to the bus if Smitty lingers. "Open the door and help him!"

Alice looks up at me. "Are you totally mental? If you think I'm opening that door, you are living on Planet Crazy."

"Yeah?" I jump down and push past her. "Is that the planet where everyone randomly drops down dead and teachers go all monstery? Because I think we're already living there." I'm at the door lever before she can answer back, and I thump it. It doesn't move. I try again. No damn diff. There's a bashing noise at the door. Alice screams again. It's Smitty, waving desperately from the other side of the glass.

"I can't get it open!" I shout at him, trying the lever again. It refuses to move. I look at Alice. "Help me!"

"No way!" Alice backs down the bus aisle.

Smitty is kicking the door now; then I see him bend. He's trying to push the Open Sesame button on his side of the glass. My stomach flips as a dark shape looms into view behind him. Mr. Taylor has arrived. I lift my snow-booted foot and with an almighty force, kick the frickin' lever like it's responsible for every goddamn crappy thing that's ever happened to me. The doors open and Smitty falls inside, snowboard first.

"Shut it!" he cries, but my attention is not on him. Mr. Taylor is filling the space behind him, roaring, fingers clawing toward Smitty, his bloody eyes straining from their sockets. I pull the lever back with all my might, but it's bent. I must have broken it.

"I can't move it!"

Smitty turns and whacks Mr. Taylor over the head with his board. Frankenteacher's monster stumbles back from the door momentarily. I kick the lever again. Still stuck. With a deathly moan, Mr. T shakes himself—blood and saliva flying from his mouth like water from the fur of a wet dog—and attacks a second time. Blocking his way with the snowboard, Smitty tries to reach across and pull the doors shut, but it's no good. I abandon the lever and, against every instinct in my body, hurl myself down the steps and tug at the doors. Smitty is holding Mr. Taylor at bay, but the teacher is a breath away—and I smell it, like rancid, rotting fish-sick. Suddenly there is a rush of wind above. Alice appears over the front seat barrier rail like some kind of avenging angel, whirls the binoculars around her head on their strap, and thwacks Mr. Taylor full on and fabulous in the face.

"That's for the double detention, you moron!"

He is still and perfectly upright for a second, then he pirouettes away from us, an arm and a leg making a graceful arc to the side, and falls softly into the snow and out of sight. The doors, finally free, slide deliberately into place. Smitty slots the board across them and collapses, panting.

"Woo-hoo!" Alice punches the air with her manicured hand.

The bus starts up with a jolt.

The driver, awake now and rolling in his seat, reaches for the hand brake with his bandaged hand, and revs the engine violently.

"Stay behind the line, kids!" he gurgles.

I cling on to the rail and the bus lurches backward into the Mini with a *thud*. The driver cranks the gear stick and we leap forward. There is a crunch, the bus stalls, and the driver passes out again and slithers out of his seat.

I realize I'm huddled on the floor, my arms still clinging to the rail above. Like a nervous crab, I tentatively crawl sideways out of my space and crouch by the driver. He's still breathing.

"Everyone all right?" I call out.

"Been better." Smitty is curled below me in the stairwell, rubbing his head.

"Where did Mr. Taylor go?" I peek through the windshield. Carefully. This is when they come back. In the movies, this is when they jump out at you and smash through the window. It always happens. If you look though a keyhole, you get your eye poked out; if you look in a mirror, the killer's behind you. It's like the law or something.

"Did you see how I hit him?" Alice skips up behind me, oblivious to all laws and full of glee. Her blond hair sticks out at a weird angle. *Ha! So she's not always perfect.*

I pick another window and peer out again. "Oh. I think I see legs. Sticking out from under the bus."

"What's he doing there?" Smitty shoves in beside me at the window. I can feel the heat radiating off his body. It's oddly comforting. Then he's off again, climbing over the seats.

"Is he moving?" Alice says.

"I'll just open the doors and peek out . . . ," Smitty says.

"No!" we both cry.

"*Very* joking." Smitty clambers up through the hatch. I listen as he walks carefully across the roof of the bus, pauses, then returns to the hatch and lowers himself down again. "Think we just ran over our teacher." He grins. "Do you think that'll get us expelled?"

I gasp. "You're kidding me?"

"Yeah, I am," Smitty says. "Under the circumstances, I think they'd only suspend us."

"You know what I'm talking about."

He gives me his most sincere smile. "Mr. T is pavement pizza."

"Oh, gross!" Alice curls her lip in disgust. "Still, he totally had it coming."

I'm taking a moment. I'm trying to look busy, tending to the driver, but really, I'm taking a moment. We all are. Smitty's back up pacing on the roof, Alice seems to be looting the overhead compartments — but actually, we just need a few seconds to calm the hell down.

We've left the driver where he fell. It's not very dignified — or even practical, as he's blocking the aisle — but it'll have to do for now. I check his pulse on his good wrist, like my dad taught me. It's weak, but regular. I adjust his bandage and make sure he's breathing OK, and I even place a sweater under his head to cushion it. There's a bulge in his jacket pocket; I only hesitate a moment before I fish for whatever lies within. A phone. The screen is blank: no reception.

"See if you can get this to work." I throw the phone to Alice, who catches it deftly.

Hopping over the driver's body, I shimmy under the steering wheel into the driver's seat.

I turn the ignition one notch and gingerly press the radio's ON button. Static blasts out of the speakers, making me jump.

Following my lead, Smitty switches the TV on. White fuzz fills the screen.

Snow on the outside, snow on the inside. So much for technology.

"What about the CB radio?" Smitty points to a small black box, partially hidden under the armrest. "My uncle had one in his basement. It's how they used to hook up with total strangers before the Internet." He winks. "Hand me the mouthpiece."

I'm guessing he means the black round thing attached to the small box by a long curly wire. I oblige.

"Now flick that switch to turn it on."

A small button on the side. I do so. A static sound hisses out of the box and the number 14 appears in red on a little display.

Smitty presses something on the side of the mouthpiece, and there's silence. "Hello?" he says into it. "Is there anyone on this channel? Breaker-break, Breaker-break?"

I look at him questioningly. He shrugs.

"Saw it in a movie," he mutters. "Try twisting that knob and changing the channel."

As I turn the knob, the red numbers click up to read 15, then 16, then 17. Still nothing but static. Then 18, 19 . . .

"Stop!" Smitty shouts. "I can hear someone."

There are voices — quiet and distorted, but voices all the same. I hardly dare breathe.

"What are they saying? Can you speak to them?" Alice shouts.

"Mayday, Mayday," says Smitty.

The voices continue, as if unhearing.

"Help us, somebody!" Alice shouts.

"You have to press the button, Malice," Smitty sneers. He demonstrates. "Is there anybody there? We need help. Repeat, we need help urgently! Come on, people! This is no joke!"

We listen hard. The voices keep talking, undecipherable.

"Attention!" shouts Smitty. *"Au secours! Au secours!"*

I shoot him a look. "What, we're in France suddenly?"

"Anything's worth a try," he says, clicking the button on the mouthpiece over and over. "I think I can do Morse code for SOS, but then again I might be ordering takeout."

I crack a smile. "I'll skip the pavement pizza."

He grins back.

"Look," says Alice, leaning in, "I'm sorry to break up your special weirdo bonding moment, but we need to get help." She dangles the driver's phone between her finger and thumb. "The only thing on this phone is the driver's ear cheese, and Einstein here can't even figure out how to use the radio." She bats her eyelashes at Smitty. "We should find a landline and call the police or the army, or something. Get them to come and rescue us. *Très* quick."

Smitty gestures to the door. "Be my guest and lead the way, Malice. I'll be right behind you."

"Loser," spits Alice.

Smitty puckers his lips. "Ooh, call me another name. I love it."

Alice hurls the driver's phone at Smitty, who ducks and drops the radio mouthpiece. Both phone and radio smash against the window, and the voices coming from the receiver stop.

"Great job, guys!" I delve for the radio and try to make it come to life again. A crack now runs down the length of the mouthpiece, and a blue wire is sticking out. *Shit.* I thrust it into Smitty's hands. "You're a boy, aren't you? Go on and fix it."

Alice is right. Action is needed. I head down the aisle, picking the binoculars off the floor where one of my feckless pseudo-buddies has thoughtfully thrown them. Climbing up to the hatch, I hoist myself up to the roof as Smitty did. My arms burn with the effort, but I'm not going to let them see me struggle. The snow is holding off, but it won't be too long before the light starts to go. Scrambling up onto the slippery surface and standing carefully, I look all around the parking lot and peer through the binoculars into the café.

I can just make out the shadows of people slumped across tables.

My breath shortens. One thing to hear Alice tell it; quite another to see it myself. I scan for any signs of life — and spot a building, lights shining through a line of trees to the left of the café.

Bingo.

I shout down, "There's a gas station — they'll have a phone! We just need to make a run for it." I lower myself back into the bus and struggle to close the hatch.

Alice is slumped in a seat looking bored, and Smitty is fiddling with the radio.

"Time to move." I get my coat from the rack above my seat. "We need a phone."

Smitty looks up. "Yeah, and who knows if Mr. T has any dribbling friends out there, eh?"

"We don't know that. Everybody else is still doing dead in the diner."

"Hah!" Alice sits bolt upright. "But for how long? Do you know *nothing*?" She stares at me like I have the mental capacity of a potato. "They die, they come back to life, they eat our brains!"

"Maybe they have food poisoning. Maybe Mr. Taylor was kind of sick or rabid or something, and was coming to us for help?" *Oh, the lameness.*

"Are you *blind*?" Alice narrows her glare. "That was *not* Mr. Taylor anymore, that was a zom —"

"Stop!" I shout. "Do not say . . . that word."

"Why not?" She gets out of her seat and walks right up to me, head cocked. "Because that's what he was."

I want to slap her. Because she's right — again. That in itself is as bad an omen as a bunch of Shakespearian horses eating each other and the dead rising from their graves. The latter of which it would seem we already have.

"How come you know so much about them, eh, Malice?" Smitty is in her face. "You're working up quite a froth there." He points to the corner of her mouth. "Maybe we should put you into quarantine before you *turn*."

Alice yelps and slaps his hand away.

I stomp to the door. "We go — now."

Smitty is behind me. "Are you sure you want to risk it?"

"I'm sure *you* do." I'm also counting on it. "It'll be getting dark soon. And real, real cold. So we go while we still can."

"*I'm* not going anywhere." Alice, newly triumphant — glowing, even — returns to her seat.

"Good." I'm at the door. "We need someone to stay here and play nurse." I point to the driver. "And keep trying the phones and the radio. We'll be back as soon as we can. Barricade the door behind us, but be ready to let us in." I'm gambling that she won't lock us out indefinitely, if only because that'll mean she'll be on her own permanently. Like I said, gambling.

Smitty and I step out into the snow. As I hear the doors close behind us, there's a sinking feeling in the pit of my stomach. We immediately forge ahead, no nonsense. Smitty's legs are longer and he can get through the deep snow much faster.

"That way." I point to the left of the trees, although Smitty doesn't turn around. "Let's follow the road down."

He shakes his head. "We should cut through the trees. More direct route."

My stomach clenches. The spooky quotient is off the hook. At least on the road, nothing can jump out at us. And the snow on the road is less deep, making it easier to run if something does appear. I glance back at the bus. Alice's face is pressed up against the window, pale and ghostly. Suddenly I know with absolute certainty that if Smitty and I are ambushed, we are on our own.

We reach the trees and pause beside a large sycamore, silent and laden with whiteness.

"Lights are on." Smitty points past the gas pumps to the store beyond. "No movement. Think they're all dead, too?"

I can't stop a shiver. "Only one way to find out."

We move carefully toward the front of the store, low and quick, then up to its glass doors. I reach for the handle.

"Wait!" Smitty rasps. "There's someone by the counter!"

I look. Sure enough, I can see a man's head over the top of the cash register. His face is pale and moist, and there's a tuft of dusty black hair. A cigarette sticks out of the corner of his mouth, a twist of smoke curling into the air as he stares at us. For a moment I wonder if it's a floating head, then a hand snatches the cigarette away from the mouth.

Thankyougod. A real live grown-up person to make everything better.

"Piss off!" A voice crackles over a loudspeaker. "The door is locked. Get lost!"

Smitty bangs on the glass. "Let us in, mister! Come on, we need help!"

"No!" the man shouts. "Go away!"

"Sir, we're just kids!" I shout back. "And our bus driver needs a doctor. You've got to help us!"

"If you know what's good for you, you'll sod off now!" the man yells, and disappears behind the counter.

"We need a phone, you tosser!" Smitty kicks the door.

I spot a sign, CUSTOMER TOILETS, with an arrow pointing around the corner. "Come on," I call to Smitty. "Maybe there's a way in at the back."

Sure enough, there is.

"In here." Smitty runs ahead and pulls me through a door, like it was his idea. It's dark inside. There's a short corridor with two doors on either side. One is marked TOILET, the other PRIVATE. We try that one.

It's darker still inside. I reach for the switch. Yellow light blinks on. Thankfully, nobody's home. It's a janitor's closet, with a second door at the other end.

"There's our way in." Smitty tries the handle. "Locked. Bet we can force it open with something in here." He starts to search the shelves.

I know the time has come. I've been putting this off for way too long.

"I'll check out the bathroom," I tell Smitty. "I'll be right back." I leave the room and quietly open the door marked TOILET. Three stalls and a single basin. I duck into the first cubicle, silently lock the door, unzip my jeans, and sit down with a shudder. Life-endangering situations or not, when you gotta go, you gotta go.

Afterward, everything seems better. I sit for a moment, take a deep breath. It will all be OK. We'll get into the store, we'll call the cops, and get out of this hellhole. I'll be back home in a few hours, eating my mother's microwaved food and dodging her annoying questions with a comforting and familiar irritability. I rub my face, shake my shoulders, and allow myself to let out a deep, heartfelt sigh.

Something in the next stall answers me with a terrible, death-rattling moan.

4

For a second, I wonder if I imagined the moan. I only do this because I *want* to have imagined it. I want it so badly.

I saw a bear once. I was peeing then, too. We were hiking in the mountains back home in the USA — one of the last trips Dad took me on before he got sick. Anyway, I snuck off to take a pee, because I was freaked beyond all perspective that my dad might see me squatting. Like he'd look. Like he'd care. So anyway, there I was, and as I was pulling up my pants, there was the bear, too. Perhaps ten feet away. Beautiful, glossy, and fat, looking at me with molasses eyes. I crouched low, back down into the grass that was wet with my pee, and looked around for a rock or a stick. Any kind of weapon, but there was nothing. When I glanced up again, the bear was gone. Later I convinced myself it had never been there. I hadn't seen it. Who sees a bear?

Likewise, just now, I imagined the moan. Clearly. Or it was a gurgling pipe, or Smitty. Yeah, that's it — the toad has followed me in here and is trying to freak me out.

The moan comes again.

It's not a pipe, it's not Smitty, and it's not a damn bear.

I brace myself against the cubicle walls and slowly climb up onto the toilet bowl, ever-so-quietly pulling up my jeans and the zipper.

Whatever is next door cries out again, the noise wobbling and building to a wail.

Panic squeezes my throat. I glance at the door. *Locked.* Phew. Still, there's a gap below big enough to crawl under. Not to mention that whatever is next door might simply vault the wall or bash the door down.

Definitely not safe here. Definitely have to move. Before terror freezes me to the spot.

It's panting now: panting, wheezing, and moaning.

How quick can it run? If it's a thing like Mr. Taylor was a thing, then probably not very quickly. But there I go, gambling again. I shut my eyes tight and visualize unlocking the latch, sprinting to the bathroom door, flinging it open, then slamming it behind me — maybe finding a way to jam it shut — and shouting for Smitty, who has hopefully found a way into the store by now.

Probably, maybe, hopefully. Not good words.

Silence. I open my eyes and ready myself to move, glancing down at my feet bridging the toilet bowl. It's a tad gross that I haven't been able to flush, but if it's yellow, let it mellow . . . and run like hell-o. I have to make a move for the door, and fast.

As I prepare to leap, there is a new noise.

A familiar, rasping noise.

Last time I checked, the Undead have no use for an inhaler.

Leaning against the wall, I straighten up until I can almost see into the next-door cubicle. *Think brave.* Standing on my tiptoes, I force myself to peek.

A boy, crouching on the toilet, his hands covering his face. The white wispy hair is unmistakable. It's Pete Moore. He of the see-through skin

and bus trip stink bomb. Seems he likes to check out the bathrooms anywhere he can. My heart beats a little slower.

I whisper, "Hey!"

"Whaa—!" Pete unfurls like a falling kitten, legs and arms spread,
butt sinking into the toilet bowl.

"It's OK, it's just me!" I hiss.

Pete looks up at me with wild eyes.

"I'm in your class, remember?" I try to sound reassuring. "Are we
alone in here?"

"Pah!" Pete scuttles into the corner of his stall. "I don't know . . . Why
are you asking me? Where did you come from anyway?" He's babbling.
"Were you in the café? Because if you were, then you should stay away
from me. Go back there and don't come anywhere near me . . ."

"You were there? Did you see what happened?"

"Of course I saw it!" he snarls. "I saw the death come!" Then he starts
to wail.

"Shh!" I urge him desperately. "Unlock the door and let me in, OK?"

"Let me in, she says!" Pete laughs hysterically. "Let me in so I can
chew on your arm! Would you like fries with that?" He cackles to himself,
wicked crazy. "I don't think so."

Trying not to examine the grimy floor, I jump down, drop to all fours,
and shimmy under the partition. As I arrive on Pete's side of the wall,
his manic laughter turns to shrieking, and he kicks out at me. He's slow
and I dodge the first strike, but the second lands on the top of my arm,
deadening it.

"I'm trying to help you, you nut job!"

No choice but to crawl on top of his legs to try and subdue him,
but he's still screeching, and wriggling like a worm in a puddle.

"Be quiet already! If there are any more of those things around, you'll bring them right to us!"

By some miracle, Pete falls quiet, his arms across his face. He stares at me, head twisted, one pale green eye unblinking and bloodshot. He nods.

"Good." I allow myself a tiny dot of relief. "That's good. Just stay calm. It's all gonna be OK."

There's a bang and the door flies open. Pete and I nearly shed our skins.

"Found a boyfriend?"

Smitty is standing in the doorway, a screwdriver in one hand. "Got the shop door open, if you're interested. Or you can stay here on the floor with Albino Boy."

I pick myself up, and Pete instantly retracts his legs into himself like a hermit crab.

"He was hiding in here," I say. "He was in the café and knows something, but he's not making any sense."

"Ha!" Smitty laughs. "No change there." He leans down to grab Pete's arm and hoists him up in a single movement. Pete springs back against the wall of the bathroom stall, trembling violently. "I'm not the enemy, numbnuts," Smitty sighs. "Let's motor."

We head out of the bathroom and through the janitor's closet to the door leading into the store, which is now ajar. Pete lingers, wheezing again, and muttering.

"The death came, and it will come again. The death came, and it will come again. The death —"

"Shut him up, will you?" Smitty says to me.

"Like he does anything I say."

"You found him," he says. "We're going in."

Gripping the screwdriver firmly, Smitty slowly opens the door. The fluorescent light of the store spills into the small room. He listens for a moment, gives me a thumbs-up, then slips inside.

I turn to Pete, who glares at me. I sigh. *Fine. Stay here and wait for the death to come and come again.*

I follow Smitty, creeping behind shelves of chips and cookies and cigarette lighters, making for where we'd seen the man's head disappear behind the cash register.

Smitty leaps onto the counter, brandishing the screwdriver.

"Surprise, surprise!" he screams.

A battle cry sounds from under the counter and the man springs up and swipes at Smitty's feet with a bat. Who knew they had baseball in Scotland? I step back abruptly and the edge of a shelf bites into my back. Smitty has dodged the first swipe, but here comes the second. He jumps into the air as the man's bat clatters air fresheners, breath mints, and bottles of motor oil onto the ground.

"Stop it!" I know the words are futile before they've even left my mouth.

Smitty hurls himself away from the third swipe of the bat and falls against a cabinet of hot pastries. The man hurdles the counter and brings the bat down. Glass and doughnuts fly everywhere as Smitty ducks and skitters backward on his hands through a slick of motor oil that is fast filling the floor. I see my chance. I fling myself at the back of the man's knees, forcing him off balance and making him skid in the oil. He falls hard, and there is a smack as his head hits the floor. The bat flies out of his hands. I stretch out an arm and make the catch. Dad would have been so proud.

"I said stop!" I hold up the bat, threatening to swing. "Or I'll flatten you both." Spit flies out of my mouth in a really attractive way.

From behind the shelves, there is laughter. "She's not kidding." Pete pokes his head out.

"Shut it, Albino!" Smitty shouts.

"You shut it!" The man on the floor jabs a finger toward Smitty. "Crazy kid attacking me with a knife. You deserve to be locked up!"

"It was a screwdriver, sir." I grit my teeth. "And I'm sure he didn't mean it. He apologizes — don't you, Smitty?"

Smitty grimaces.

"Don't you?" I grip the bat tighter.

Smitty rolls his eyes and nods.

"There you go. We're all friends." For the first time, I notice a name tag on the man's shirt, hanging askew, which reads GARETH. I turn to the man, keeping the bat held high just in case. "Gareth? I'm Bobby, this is Smitty, and that's Pete. We need your help. There are people injured and dying; we don't know what's going on and we have to call the police."

Gareth sits up and rubs his head. "Psycho teenagers are all I need. But if you've come looking for a phone, you've come to the wrong place." He pulls himself up against the counter. "The line's dead."

"He's lying!" Smitty is up again.

"Why would I?" Gareth says, not unreasonably. "Think I want to be stuck here, either?" He throws the receiver at Smitty. "Check it yourself. We're all shafted." He walks around the counter and sits down on the chair, holding his head in his hands as if checking for cracks.

I figure I can lower the bat. "Do you know what's happening to everyone?"

Gareth smiles nastily. "The phones died. My boss went up to the café to check what was going on. He comes back and passes out, and I try to help him. I think he's had a heart attack, don't I? He's out cold and not breathing. Dead as a doornail. Next thing I know, he's grabbing at me and trying to bite." He gestures to my newly acquired weapon. "He kept the bat under the counter for late-night trouble. Never occurred to him that *he* might be the trouble. I smashed him to hell and back."

I look closely at the bat for the first time. There's a red patch and a clump of hair stuck to the end. My gut twists.

"What did you do to him?"

Gareth taps a cigarette out of a packet. "Hitting him only made him angrier. Nothing much I could do . . ." He lights the cigarette, pockets the lighter, and exhales deeply. "Until I found this." He picks up an object from the counter. It's a metal spike attached to a small block of wood, with small pieces of paper skewered to it. Sales receipts. Gareth chuckles. "He never did like balancing the books . . . said they used to do his head in." A gloop of blood drips from the spike. "Well, they did this time."

I gulp. "What happened?"

Gareth fixes me with his dark stare. "He fell on it." He thrusts the spike. "Up through the eye, popped like a grape."

"Cool!" Smitty says.

"No," I mutter. "That's horrible."

"Hey, it's not so bad," Smitty says. "We just ran over our teacher, remember?"

"Which one?" Pete asks.

"Mr. Taylor," I say, numb.

"Yes!" Pete claps his hands in delight.

I look at Gareth. "So what did you do next?"

He shrugs. "Tried the phone. Line was dead. Went up to the café.

Everyone was dead. Didn't hang around to see if they'd come back to life. Came back here and locked the body in the storage cupboard." He flicks a finger at a door in the corner. "Just in case."

"Didn't you even think to look for a phone in the café?" Smitty's face curls with scorn.

"Yeah, I hung around to go crazy like my boss," Gareth says. "Great idea."

"So we just wait here, right?" I say. "This is a gas station; people must be in and out all the time."

Gareth laughs. "This isn't your average day, lassie."

"He's right," Smitty adds. "Have you seen anyone arrive since we got here?" He looks up toward the café. "Either it's the snow, or —"

"Or whatever's going on here is going on everywhere."

Nobody speaks. I think we're all ignoring what I just said, but it's out there all the same.

I chance a smile. "Gareth, I'm thinking you're about the same age as all of us added up. Do you have a car?"

Gareth shakes his head. "Not today." His face reddens. "I got a lift."

I brighten. "Fine. So they'll be back to pick you up at the end of your shift, won't they? We wait."

"Or we hot-wire a car," Smitty says. "Or drive the bus."

Gareth looks exasperated. "Have you seen the weather?"

"Let's at least try!" Smitty shouts.

Before Gareth can answer, an engine roars into life outside and a large shadow lurches around the trees, heading toward the gas pumps. It's the school bus.

"Score!" Smitty shouts. "Hello, Mr. Mean Machine All-Terrain Bus Driver!"

We scramble to the window and watch as the bus leaves the road and mounts the bank. Narrowly missing the last of the sycamores, it careers down toward us.

"He's going too fast," I say. "Why's he going so fast?"

As the words come out, I see why.

Following the bus are people, stumbling through the snow. Arms out, heads lolling, feet dragging . . .

"And to complete the introductions, Gareth," says Smitty, holding out his hand toward the approaching mob, "may I present to you the rest of our class from All Souls' High School."

It's them all right. Some more animated now than I've ever seen before.

The bus is at the entrance to the gas station. Skidding on the icy ground, it heads past the pumps and directly toward the store.

"Slow down!" I scream.

Smitty grabs me. "He's not going to."

As the bus roars toward us with a sickening inevitability, I'm only aware of Pete's white hair ducking behind a shelf and Smitty's hand in the small of my back, pushing me to the ground. There's an almighty crash and everything collapses, burying us in an ocean of chips, cookies, and cheap store shelves.

I close my eyes and wait for the death to come.

5

For a lovely moment time is suspended and all is still under the debris. Quiet, dark, warm, and strangely comforting, like a cocoon.

I can smell motor oil, sugary doughnuts, and a sharper, sweeter scent. Raspberries? Something tickles my nose . . . I open my eyes and blow a straggle of hair out of my face. Not my hair, *Smitty's*. His head is buried in the crook of my neck, and he's out cold. He uses raspberry shampoo? *What a girl.* I chuckle to myself. Kind of embarrassing how he's lying across me, though, trapping one of my arms. His weight is heavy across my chest, and one of his arms is almost cradling my head. Lying but not moving. That isn't good. I feel a flutter of panic and fling out my free arm.

The pile of debris groans threateningly, a shaft of light cuts through the fug, and the world comes rushing back into focus. Someone is shouting, there's glass breaking, and an alarm is shrieking loud enough to wake the dead. I try to move but I'm pinned to the ground, partly by Smitty, and partly by something heavier with a sharp edge that is causing a throbbing pain across my legs. At least I can still feel them.

"Smitty!" I try to shake his shoulder with my free hand. "Are you OK?"

"Eh?" He wakes with a jolt, gasping for air like a beached fish. "What's happening?"

Before I can answer, he springs backward off me like I'm on fire, causing a tumble of items to clatter around me. The cocoon is truly breached.

"Quickly!"

I twist my head and see Pete, standing above, his clothes oddly shredded, as if he's been dragged through barbwire, his hand outstretched. He has a silver halo, like an angel. Then, as something catches his attention and he turns to the window, I realize it's a piece of shelving unit sticking out of his head. Blood is seeping through his white hair.

"They're coming!"

I follow his frantic gaze. Through the dust, I see dark shapes moving on the other side of what used to be the store window, arms reaching in a horrible welcome . . .

"My legs," I mutter.

In a second, the weight is lifted and I am being dragged from the debris by Smitty. The place looks like a bomb site. There is the bus, its front end wedged into the store like a dog with its head stuck down a rabbit hole. It's covered in glass and doughnut and detritus. The driver is slumped at the wheel, and Alice's white face is at the windshield, silently screaming at us, drowned out by the alarm.

We scramble around to the other side of the bus and there's Gareth, the end of the cigarette still hanging out of his mouth, baseball bat in hand, swinging blindly at dust.

"Come on!" he shouts at the approaching shadows. "Show me what you've got!"

The bus engine revs and Alice appears at the open door. "Hurry!" she screams, beckoning frantically.

We dodge the deranged Gareth and clamber onto the bus.

"Wait!" Pete says. "I'll be a second. Don't leave without me." He leaps off the bus and scampers back into the store.

"Sit down and hold on tight," the driver shouts — slurring like he's drunk — and revs the engine again.

"He woke up," Alice says. "They started coming. He woke up just in time to drive away." She stares into the distance behind her. "Oh my god, it's Em . . ." She moves to a window. "Em is out there — Em!" She hits the glass with the palm of her hand. "Over here! Libby's out there, too! And Shanika . . . Oh god!" She turns back to me. "We have to help them before those monsters eat them."

I stare at the shambling figures. "I think they *are* the monsters, Alice."

Alice slowly faces her frenemies. Em is clawing the air in front of her as she makes her way toward us, stamping each step like a runway model trying to extinguish a cigarette. Shanika's eyes bulge out of her face as she gnashes her teeth and clumsily climbs over a freezer cabinet that has rolled out into the driveway. Libby's head lolls to one side, and black blood oozes out of the sides of her mouth. Not exactly class portrait worthy. But like the rest of the mob behind them, they have a direction, and they keep on coming.

"It's horrible!" Alice cries. "They want to kill us!" Her eyes narrow. "And Shanika's got my Candy Couture bag, the bitch! Drive!" she says to the driver. "Run them over!"

"We can't go without Pete!" I shout. "Or him!" I point at Gareth, who is looking less sure of his batting skills the nearer the mob gets.

"One's useless and the other's crazy," says Smitty, throwing me into a seat. "Put the pedal to the metal, mister!" he shouts to the driver and lunges for the door lever.

"No!" I cry, forcing myself out of my seat again. The doors close, but as they do an arm sticks in the doorway and pulls them back. Pete, still with metal halo and now carrying a flat black box, flings himself onto the steps.

"You mentalist!" Smitty shouts. "Get up here!"

Gareth appears behind Pete and jumps on board. "Drive! Drive! Drive!"

The driver puts his foot down as Gareth and Pete scramble down the aisle. I dive back into my seat, wedging my knees up in front of me, and say a silent prayer to anyone who happens to be listening. The bus surges backward through the store window the way it came in, then stops in a screech of metal against metal. I clench my eyes closed and will us to keep going, but I am obviously praying to the wrong god. *Come on, come on.*

A thumping begins, like a sardonic hand clap for the driver's efforts. *Thump, thump, thump,* all around us. I open my eyes and dare to look. Hands are slapping the bus: small hands reaching up, adult hands smacking the windows. The bus jolts once more, there's a crunch of gears, and we're reversing again, then edging forward, nearly free from whatever is holding us back.

"You hit a pump, you idiot!" Gareth shouts, a few rows behind me. "There's petrol everywhere."

Sure enough, behind us there is now a fountain of gasoline spurting twenty feet into the air, spraying the shambling figures.

"Hold it!" Smitty snatches the glowing cigarette butt from Gareth's lips.

"Hey!" Gareth protests.

Smitty leaps up to the hatch in one easy movement.

"What are you doing?" I yell after him.

"Wait for my call!" Smitty is up on the roof before anyone can stop him. I'm close behind, hands scrabbling for a hold on the hatch, feet slipping on the seats below.

"Are you totally whacked?" I shout. I know what he's going to do, and part of me needs to stop him. But only part of me.

"Always wanted to do this." He winks, takes a drag from the cigarette, and flicks it into the air. I watch as it falls, slowly, beautifully, to the ground below.

"Move!" He shoves me back down the hatch, practically falling on top of me for the second time that afternoon. "Go!" he cries, and the bus jerks forward, wheels spinning, engine roaring. There's a *whoomp* as the air pressure changes. Glass flies in from the back of the bus, and flames are all around us. I stay low and cling to the seat as the bus races forward with new life. Out of the corner of my eye, I see figures dancing in the fire, balls of flame stumbling, falling to the ground, and staying there. As the bus rounds a corner onto the road, a huge explosion shakes the earth. The light is too bright to bear. I bury my face in the headrest. *Keep driving, keep driving.*

The engine screams as the road inclines. We're slowing. I peep out between shaking hands; there's a steep drop to our right. As we reach the brow of the hill, the bus almost seems to hover.

"The wheels are spinning!" Gareth shouts.

The driver's body collapses over the steering wheel. The engine cuts and, slowly, the bus starts to slide backward.

"He's fainted!" I yell, turning to Gareth. "Take the wheel!"

"Take it yourself!" Gareth shouts back, bracing himself against a seat.

From the back, Alice starts to wail. "What's wrong with you?" she shrieks at Gareth. "We're going to go over the edge!"

"I don't drive, all right!" Gareth shouts.

Smitty lunges at him. "You don't drive? What kind of shit adult doesn't drive?"

He rushes to the front and pulls the driver off his seat. For some totally unknown, insane reason, I jump into the seat. I can't drive a car, let alone a bus. *You don't have to,* my dad's voice says to me. *You just have to stop a bus. Brake pedal in the middle, remember?*

I shoot out a hopeful foot and stamp the pedal to the floor. The bus skids on a patch of ice, veering close to the edge of the drop. Dangerously close.

"It's not working!" I cry.

Smitty grabs the wheel and begins to twist it helplessly.

Alice screams as the bus picks up momentum. I'm thinking we are toast.

Suddenly Pete is at my side. "Let me," he says.

"What?"

"I can do it," he urges. He's still wearing the shelf-unit halo, but a piece has broken off and now it looks like a wafer planted in a scoop of vanilla ice cream.

I slip out of the seat, and Pete jumps in and turns the keys on the dashboard.

"Brakes are a no-no in these conditions," he shouts, as if this is just another day in driver's ed. He pushes a lever and presses down on the accelerator, carefully. The bus's slide downhill slows. "Trick is to get into a low gear initially"—he forces the gear stick and the bus stops—"then shift up into a high one as quickly as possible. The less traction the better." The bus starts to move forward uphill. "Nobody move!" he shrieks. "Cross your fingers we make it up, and don't move an inch!"

Subdued as much by Pete's all-out personality flip-flop as our impending doom, we all hold our breath. The bus creeps up toward the brow of the hill, slowly, slowly, every now and then giving a little judder and making the panic rise in my throat again. Eventually, *un-frickin'-believably*, we make it.

To the right, overlooking the café below the hill, there's a small parking lot marked OVERFLOW. It's carpeted with pristine snow. Pete expertly steers the bus into it, turns the key in the ignition, and the engine shudders and dies. He sits back in the chair and lets out a deep breath. Hunkered down on the top step and clinging to the barrier rail, I do the same.

"Keep going, White Bread!" Smitty says. "Why are we stopping?"

Pete reaches into his pocket and brings out his inhaler. He takes a long hit. "Go where, exactly?" he says, spookily calm. "The road continues up the hill." He points with the inhaler. "And there is no way this thing is making it up there." He takes another long drag.

"Um, well, I was thinking . . ." Smitty is feigning dumb. "How about the *exit*?" He grabs Pete and shoves him up against the window.

"Hey!" I protest, but Smitty's not listening.

"See that road down there?" He points to the turn we didn't take, the turn leading away from the gas station, back past the Cheery Chomper and out onto the main road, which is hidden by a line of trees. "Remember the way we came in? Now would be a really good time to go back out again."

Pete shrugs him off and sits down again. "Wasn't my call, remember? I wasn't driving at the time."

"So let's go now!" Alice steps into the aisle. "You can drive! Drive us out of here!"

"Great idea," Pete says. He taps the dashboard. "Except we're running on empty."

Alice's face drops. "We're out of fuel?"

Smitty swears. Gareth adds his own choice of word.

Pete sighs. "And it's safe to say Smitty may have taken away our chance to fill 'er up." He gestures to the gas station inferno, his hand as graceful as a ballerina's.

Gareth turns to Smitty with crazy eyes.

"Stupid kid—"

"Yeah?"

Gareth and Smitty puff their chests and muscle up to each other like a pair of over-excitable roosters.

"So we stay!" I shout. "For now." I get between them. Always the peacemaker. "Make the bus safe, wait for someone to come!"

They glare at each other for a few seconds, neither wanting to back down, then Smitty punches the back of a seat and flings himself onto the top of the dashboard, where he crouches, gargoyle-like and shaking his head. Gareth flounces to the back of the bus.

Pete winces. "I think I hurt my head." He flutters a hand around his halo-wafer.

"Uh, yes." It's probably best not to let him know he has shelving stuck in his skull.

"Here." Smitty leans over from his perch on the dashboard, grabs the halo-wafer, and yanks it out of Pete's head. "That better?"

Pete stares at the bloodied triangle of aluminum in Smitty's hand. "That was in me?"

"Only for a minute." I'm quick to retrieve a clean handkerchief that my mother thoughtfully placed in my jacket pocket for just such an occasion. (One of her token gestures to make up for never actually being there, I guess.) I hover over Pete's head. There's a perfect triangular mark in his skull, with a flap of skin sticking up like a tufted carpet. It's bleeding, but not too badly, and I can't see any brains leaking out. "Hey, it obviously didn't impair your driving." I give him the handkerchief and press his hand to his head. "But maybe sit down for a while?"

I crouch down beside the unconscious bus driver, feeling for a pulse. My own hand is shaking so much I can barely locate a vein. Eventually I find the beat, irregular and weak but present.

"He's alive," I say. "He probably saved all of us. We should make him comfortable."

Smitty hops off the dashboard and helps me drag him carefully down the aisle. We lever him onto the backseat and put him on his side: the recovery position. His face is slack and gray. It doesn't look like he'll be doing any recovering real soon.

"Are the doors secure?" Smitty bounds to the front of the bus.

"It's OK," Alice shouts from the window, holding the binoculars to her eyes. "No one's following. I think you got them all, Smitty. Burnt to a crisp."

"Yeah, that was a dangerous stunt to pull, you psycho," Gareth sneers. "You could have incinerated the lot of us."

"But he didn't," I say. My leg is beginning to pound. I'd almost forgotten I'd hurt it.

"I didn't," Smitty repeats, pushing past me and squaring up to Gareth again. "And if it wasn't for us, you'd have been munched by her BFFs" — he jabs a finger at Alice — "a fate worse than death. Shortly to be followed by actual death. So try a little gratitude for size."

"You little—" Gareth snarls.

"Hey!" Pete shouts from the driver's seat. "We have a signal!"

That gets our attention. Pete's hunched over the square, black object that he brought onto the bus with him—a laptop. "This was by the register."

"It's the boss's," Gareth says. "Uses it for stock. It's a pretty crap machine. Can't even go online."

"I beg to differ." Pete holds it in front of him and stands up gingerly, eyes fixed on the screen. "It has wireless, but it was disabled. Presumably to stop the employees from downloading boobies—"

"Shut it, kid!" Gareth roars.

"Luckily for us, I enabled the disabled." Pete smirks. "We're web-worthy."

"Internet?" Smitty rushes up the aisle toward Pete. "First he's Speed Racer, then he's the geek that saves us all. Aren't you just racing from zero to hero?" He makes a grab for the laptop.

"Back off!" Pete moves the laptop out of Smitty's reach. "Low battery, teeny-*weeny* signal. Not so much a signal, just the name of the provider, but it proves there must be Wi-Fi somewhere. I just need to find it." He moves through the bus like a water diviner, tilting the laptop at various angles, holding it above his head. After two lengths of the bus, he sits back down in the driver's seat.

"Well?" I say.

Pete hits some keys and shuts the lid.

"Nothing."

Gareth stands up. "What do you mean, nothing? You just said there was a signal."

"Too weak."

"Give it to me." Gareth moves toward Pete.

"You can take it if you want." Pete looks up at him with his pale green eyes. "And spend the next ten minutes wearing out the battery. Or we can wait till the dust settles down there" — he points through the trees at the café — "and go to the source. If you weren't online at the garage, the Cheery Chomper is the only place the Wi-Fi could be coming from. But with so little juice, we only get one shot."

"Let's vote," I say. "All those who want to wait." I raise my hand.

Pete smiles wanly and raises his.

"Yeah." Alice is reluctant, but with us.

"All hail democracy. You're outvoted, mister," Smitty says. "We watch" — he snatches the binoculars from Alice — "we wait till the smoke clears, then we're down there."

Gareth laughs. "You stupid kids know nothing. That fire will be burning bright all night. It's petroleum, not some garden bonfire."

I look at the flames glowing orange at the bottom of the hill.

"Then that's as good a signal as any. Someone will come."

6

It takes us until the last of the dying light to shore up the glassless back window.

Pete produces duct tape he carries in his backpack. (I *know*. It's probably a geek thing, like ironed jeans and a Comic Con tee.) Smitty braves the outside to open the main luggage hold. He cuts the tops off the suitcases with an evil-looking penknife and Frisbees them out into the snow, where I run around collecting them like some demented Mario character. Then there is the tricky part of attaching them to the back window. Not to mention the fact that the driver is still unconscious on the backseat. It's easier to work around him than move him again, but the downside is he gets the occasional thing dropped on him. He doesn't seem to notice. We find some cord in an overhead locker and there are curtain hooks on either side of the window, but really the suitcase tops are held up by tape. It's more of a windbreak than a barricade, but it's the best we can do.

We form a human chain to retrieve anything from the hold that might be suitable for the night, for survival, for whatever may come next. I say "we" — Alice is on lookout with the binoculars, since she refuses to get off the bus, while Gareth has found a first-aid kit and is sitting in the driver's seat, fiddling with various imagined wounds. Regardless, rows 20 and 21 are soon crammed with skis, poles, and clothing, and Smitty has replaced his precious snowboard—the one that was locking the door—with an alternative belonging to one of our unfortunate ex-classmates.

As darkness falls, the gas station alarm is still screeching, the fire is still burning, and a new argument is a-brewing. About lighting. Alice wants it on, Pete and Smitty think not. I agree that it could make us an easy target, but I have to grudgingly concede with Alice that it will also make us easier to rescue. Because the rescuing part is absolutely going to happen. But if it doesn't . . . what if we have to drive the bus down the hill again and the battery is dead because we kept the lights on? And we might need to turn the heat on. The work and adrenaline has made us hot, but now that night has come, it's going to get cold—maybe unbearably cold. We're going be creating our own version of one of those TV shock docs that are called cuddly things like *I Shouldn't Have Survived the Night* or *I Ate My Best Friend to Live*.

Speaking of which . . .

"Do we have any food?" Gareth finally stops playing with himself long enough to stalk the aisle.

"No," Smitty says. "Pity you didn't think to grab something from the shop while you were swinging that bat around, Gareth."

"I have a sandwich I can share," I interject before they can beat each other up. "And if you look in the locker where Ms. Fawcett was sitting, there are some chips—er, crisps—and sodas. I think she was planning on handing them out later anyway."

"Oh, well, if she was planning on doing that, it must be OK to take them." Smitty shoots me a look.

I feel myself redden. What a dumb thing to say. Like any of that matters anymore.

Alice clambers up onto Ms. Fawcett's seat and tosses bags of ~~chips~~ *crisps* and cans of soda around the bus. But not at me. "Guess you'll be OK with your PB and J," she smirks.

Wot-ever. I'll save the sandwich for later, preferably when Alice is at the leg-gnawing stage, then I'll eat it in front of her, slowly and deliberately and with sound effects.

They eat all of the chips. Alice finds a packet of Scotch eggs in someone's bag — hard-boiled eggs cased in sausage meat and then deep-fried: now *that's* a snack you don't find in the average American lunch box. And then there's nothing more to do except put on as many clothes as we can fit into, and wait: for the troops, sleep, or asphyxiation from Pete's toxic egg farts, whichever comes first.

Time to change from my ripped-up jeans into comfortable leggings, and I finally get to tackle my leg. Armed with the first-aid kit and some antibacterial wipes from Ms. Fawcett's bottomless backpack, I peel back the denim on my right leg tentatively. Blood has already clotted through the material, which is stuck to my skin. I grit my teeth but keep peeling, and the blood runs anew. I feel chunks rising in my throat with the pain . . . and I take a look. There's a big scrape, and a gash that's small but kind of deep. I can see something startlingly white in there. It takes me a moment to realize it's bone. Gah.

"That needs stitches," Smitty says matter-of-factly as he appears over my shoulder, making me jump. I stop myself from pulling the bloody jeans back up again. It's not like I have anything to be ashamed of.

"Don't get any ideas," I say. "There are some butterfly bandages in this box." I rifle in the first-aid kit. "They'll do the trick."

"Shame." Smitty sits on the dashboard and slurps on a soda. "I'm a dab hand at needlework."

Yeah, like I'd let that happen. "So, you OK?" I casually switch the focus to him as I take out some antibacterial ointment and put a big glob of it on the hole in my leg.

"Is this the part where we do competitive injuries?" He laughs, and the sound warms me up a little. "You win. I've got nothing except a sugar high."

"I think Pete beats us all with his busted head." I glance down the aisle in his direction.

"No kidding." Smitty grins at me. "Petey-poo! Come and see the naughty nurse!"

Pete takes some persuading, but he eventually sits on the top step, and Smitty and I look at his head. White-blond is the best hair color if you're aiming for maximum horror effect with a head wound. The blood has pinkened thick sections of his hair, and there's angry-looking swelling around the place where the metal was sticking into his skull, although the wound is already scabbing. I leave it alone, and clean the surrounding scalp as best as I can with a wipe. He's uncomplaining, stoical even. A far cry from the wobbling mess I found in the toilet stall. He's probably still pumping adrenaline right now. Or maybe it's all the chemicals in his inhaler. Hope I'm not around when he crashes and burns.

"So, before . . . how did you end up in the bathroom?" I say conversationally as I fasten a pad of cotton around his head with a polka-dot bandanna that I think used to belong to one of Alice's cronies. It's mint-green and white, and it makes him look like a Lost Boy. The Peter Pan ones, not the fugly eighties vamps.

"I ran." He breathes in deeply and his chest rattles. He delves into a pocket and takes a hit off his inhaler.

"You were in the Cheery Chomper when it all . . . went down?"

There's a brief smile, wry and sharp and beyond his years. "Yes. In the gift shop, out of sight. Browsing the magazines."

I smile back encouragingly and he continues.

"Yes, I suppose you could say I was in a world of my own." His eyes glaze over. "Intellikit has just brought out a new computer chip—it's beyond clever. I was reading an article in *PCWorld*—"

"Get out of town, that's intense," Smitty mocks. "Why didn't you tell us this before?"

"Don't worry, I'm not going to bore you with it." Pete raises an eyebrow. "But suffice to say, absorbed as I was in the magazine, I wasn't entirely present."

"Everybody else was eating in the café?" I ask.

"Just a few feet away." He nods slowly. "Baying like dogs for their burgers. I shut them out; I always do."

"Yeah, me too." I try to bond, but he gives me a strange look, and so does Smitty. "So what happened?" I ask.

"Mr. Taylor came in." Pete frowns. "Asked me if Smitty was allergic to nuts. Why he wanted to know, I couldn't tell you."

Smitty chuckles.

"Then what?" I urge.

"That's when he collapsed."

"What?" I say. "Mr. Taylor?"

"Yup. One minute he's dithering by the cold drinks, next he's keeled over on the floor."

"What did you do?"

Pete looks at me, surprised. "Nothing. I waited for someone to notice, but the woman behind the register was gone and nobody else appeared. It was only then that I realized the baying had stopped." He cracks his knuckles. "It was quiet. Apart from a hissing noise: the deep fryers, I think, or maybe water running in the kitchen." His face gets a dreamy look. "It was rather lovely, actually."

"Oh, idyllic." Smitty swoons.

"Then what?" I lean forward.

"Then I walked out into the café." He blinks. "And there they all were, lying across the tables. Completely still. Like Mr. Taylor." He swallows, and I watch the white lump in his throat move up and down, barely covered by his weird, translucent skin. "Like everyone had fallen asleep."

"It must have been terrifying," I say.

"No!" His eyes flash and the corners of his mouth turn up in a slow smile. "It was wonderful! They were lying there, helpless. Imagine it . . ." He leans close. "I could do anything! They couldn't stop me!"

"You are a real head case, Petey," Smitty sighs.

"Um, right," I say to Pete. "So what did you do?"

"Nothing. It was only wonderful for a moment, then it *was* horrible." He shudders. "They started waking up. Mr. Taylor first — I was standing there, watching the others, and he appeared behind me. He grabbed my shoulder. I turned around, and there he was. His face was grotesque, distorted — he was making the most unearthly sound. He caught me and pulled me toward him. His mouth was open — he was trying to bite me!"

"Hardcore." I shake my head. "What did you do?"

"I still had *PCWorld* in my hand. I rolled it up and shoved it in his mouth, then I ran."

"Ha-ha!" Smitty laughs. "You've got some moves, Petey-poo."

"You left the café?" I say.

Pete nods. "Ran to the gas station. It was locked, so I went around the back and found the toilets."

Something's not right. I look down the aisle. Alice is lying across two of the seats halfway up the bus, covered in about five ski jackets. "Did you see Alice before you left?" I whisper.

"No," Pete replies.

"She says when she came out of the café bathrooms, only Mr. Taylor was standing. And when we looked through the binoculars, we could still see everyone lying on the tables."

"Well?"

"You said, 'they' started waking up." Smitty says, catching my drift. "Who else woke up before you left?"

Pete shifts uncomfortably. "I don't know. I didn't see, exactly. I just heard a noise — a groaning — coming from a direction that wasn't Mr. Taylor." He wrinkles his face. "Then there was a crash — like a door slamming. I didn't stick around to find out who or where or why."

"Could it have been Alice you heard — coming out of the bathrooms?" I ask.

"Possibly, if she banged the door. But I don't think it was her groaning, unless her voice dropped a few octaves."

It doesn't make sense. Alice said that everyone was passed out on the tables or on the floor. Maybe Pete was mistaken. Or maybe there was someone Alice missed, who came to life, then collapsed again? Or they'd left the building and we simply hadn't seen them yet?

"Thanks for the bandage, anyway." Pete gives me a tight smile, gets up, and walks back down the aisle.

Smitty waits a moment. "Believe him?"

I think about it. "Believe Alice?"

He shrugs. "Either way, we're stuck in a bus with a bunch of nutcases. That's school trips for you."

We take turns sleeping. I'm on first watch, too wired to rest. It's too cold to leave the hatch open, so I don an extra fleece and ski jacket and brazen it out on the roof for an hour. The snow is light and my leg is too cold to hurt. The flames from the gas station have died down to a glow, but the acrid tang of the smoke remains. The alarm that rang out so shrill and clear has been reduced to a broken-down and erratic buzz, like a cricket pathetically chirping after summer is long gone.

Somebody will come. Eventually. When the bus doesn't return to school and we can't be reached on the phone, the parents will start having *fits*. There'll be a search party, news reports — dammit, we'll be D-List celebs by the time this is through. We just might need to make it through the night first, though. I scan the dark corners of the parking lot for movement, feeling more like a target than a lookout, but all is still. Through the trees and down the hill to the left, the lights outside the Cheery Chomper have come on. They are probably on a timer.

Nobody remains.

7

My father is cleaning my face with a soft washcloth tucked into a pointed corner, and cold, cold water. Around my nose and eyes, it tickles, and it wakes me. I blink the water away.

It's bright, shockingly so.

But there's no Dad, just half a cold face.

It was a dream. For a moment, I think it's all been a dream, until I raise a hand to my cheek and see the white fluttering down upon me — snow. It's as if each flake is bringing memories of the day before. It happened.

I am lying across the double seat at the front of the bus, next to the door.

And the door is open.

Panic claws at me and I sit up. Where is everyone? A black-booted foot sticking out into the aisle tells me that Smitty is lying on a seat near the back. The makeshift window barricade is in place. Someone is snoring lightly behind me.

But the door is open.

I bolt out of my seat and hit the lever to shut the doors. They oblige, grudgingly. The snowboard that was holding them in place has been carefully moved inside, onto the steps. I quickly reinstate it. Someone has decided to go for a morning walk.

"Hey."

I spin around. Smitty is standing behind me, his face scrunched by sleep.

"What's going on?" He scratches his head.

"Who's missing?"

He frowns at me. "Malice and Pete are in Slumberland. That loser, Gareth? Who cares?"

"Gareth was supposed to be on watch." I return the frown. "He's gone, and he left the door open behind him."

Alice appears from behind a seat, her eyes half-closed.

"What happened?"

"Pete!" I shout.

"Eh?" He sits up suddenly, ruffled and confused.

"Where's the laptop, Pete?" I demand. "Please tell me you slept on it."

He smiles lazily. "I have it safe."

"Really? Because the responsible adult of the group has left us home alone," I say. "And I'm thinking he might not have gone empty-handed."

The smile disappears.

"It's in my bag." He duck-dives under his seat and retrieves a ratty black and orange backpack. It's unzipped and empty-looking. He checks inside anyway.

The laptop is gone.

Smitty lets out a battle cry and runs to the doors, flinging the snow-board aside. "Where has he gone? I'll kill him!" He launches himself into the snow and runs out into the parking lot, darting around the bus, as if Gareth might be hiding behind a corner, chuckling.

"Smitty!" I linger on the steps, unwilling to follow him into the snow. "Come in!"

I was sleeping right by the door. How did Gareth manage to make his escape without waking me?

Smitty climbs back onto the bus, fixes the snowboard back in place, and sinks down on the floor, defeated.

"He's gone? He's left us?" Alice is fully awake and getting up to speed.

"What does it matter?" Smitty spits. "He was useless. What matters is that he took with him our best chance to get help."

"Not necessarily." Pete stands up, and I'm treated to a whiff of pure morning breath. "He's probably taken the laptop to the café. That was the original plan. So we follow him."

I move back a little. "And if the café has Wi-Fi, it probably has a PC. It doesn't matter if we have the laptop or not."

Pete nods. "Or there's a chance we'll pick up the signal on Smitty's smart phone. There might even be a landline that works." He slides into the driver's seat. "Let's hope this thing will start on fumes."

"Wait!" I stop his hand from reaching for the ignition. "Can we make it down the hill? The snow's even deeper than yesterday."

Pete hesitates.

"So if we don't drive, we walk?" Alice says. "Count me out."

"But what if we can't get back up here?" I say. "What if there are more of those . . . people, the bus gets stuck, and we can't escape?"

"Yeah, you're right, it's going to be so much better if we're on foot," Alice snarls. "Anyway, someone has to stay here to take care of him." She points to the driver.

I feel a surge of guilt. We've pretty much ignored the driver since we finished mending the window. I approach him. He hasn't moved at all. I reach out to touch his hand and his skin feels waxy and cold.

Alice stares. "Is he . . . ?"

I move my palm over his face. There's a little warm air coming out of his nostrils. "No. He's still alive." But maybe not for much longer. Something about him has begun to smell, too, but I'm afraid to look at his other wrist and unwrap the makeshift bandage.

"Whatever we're doing, we should do it now," Smitty says. "I'll check out the road and clear a path." He grabs the binoculars and tosses them to me. "You see if we're likely to have company."

I stand on the roof with Pete and Alice. They followed me, and I didn't protest. More eyes. Mother Nature is playing ball; the snow has stopped falling and the sun is trying its best to break out from behind a lavender-gray cloud. The air is still, and there's now just a thin curl of black smoke from the gas station. A last desperate smoke signal. I try not to wonder too hard why nobody has come.

Smitty is riding his board down the road, pausing in places to scrape the ground.

Alice is trying the phones again. She's managed to acquire them all — even Smitty's prized smart phone — and she's holding them in her hands like a deck of cards, shuffling each one to the top, lifting it up, and checking for a signal. Judging by her pursed mouth, she is holding a bum hand.

There's a movement — I catch it out of the corner of my eye and spin around. A shuffle in the bushes. Steeling myself, I hold the binoculars up. A blackbird scuttles in the undergrowth, and flies out of the cover with a cascading shriek of alarm. Only a blackbird. What startled it? I grip the binoculars tighter. No movement in the bushes now; it was probably frightened by some snow falling from the tree, or another bird. I shiver. It has been years since I've heard a blackbird, and suddenly I'm sitting in a sandpit, at home — England Home — many years past. Dad is weeding nearby, whistling like the bird. It seems like a long, long time ago. He'd done no gardening in the States, and the blackbirds are different there. I feel a pang of missing him — raw and sudden. It's not like he's even going to be there when I get home. *If* I get home. I can't help but feel like this whole thing would never have happened if he was still with us. Certainly it never would have happened if my stupid mother's stupid job hadn't made us move back to this stupid country. Still, even if I want to blame my mother for Dad not being here, it might be a little extreme to blame all of this monstery stuff on her, too.

A *thump* vibrates the bus from within.

My heart jumps.

Alice gasps. "What was that?"

Pete rolls his eyes. "Must you scream at everything? Keep your knickers on. Something's just fallen off a seat."

"Are you mental?" Alice shouts. "I didn't scream!" She turns to me. "Did I scream?"

I shake my head automatically.

From below us, the noise comes again.

Pete drops to his knees. "The bus driver, then."

"He came around before, didn't he?" says Alice. "He does that, that's his thing. Wakes up, passes out, wakes up, passes out."

I crawl to the hatch.

"Slowly," Pete cautions.

I lift the hatch just a crack. We peep inside. From where I'm lying I can only see the front of the bus, and there's no one there. Or they're hiding behind a seat. I bob up and look toward the road. Smitty has climbed back up now. He's at the entrance to the parking lot. Soon he'll be at the bus door.

"I'm going to lift the hatch all the way open," I whisper to Pete and Alice. "We need to look in the back."

Alice clutches the neck of her jacket. Pete nods.

I carefully swing the lid of the hatch all the way over until it rests on the roof of the bus. We all shift around, three polar bears fishing in an ice hole, and peep in the other direction.

There is less light in the back of the bus — the improvised barricade on the back window blocks out the sun — and it takes a few seconds for my eyes to adjust, but I can see something near the backseat. A figure, facing away from us, bent over as if fastening shoelaces. Slowly, it straightens up, vertebra by vertebra. I recognize the regulation blue coat, the pale blue shirt collar, and thinning gray hair.

"It *is* the driver!" Alice shouts, her voice light with relief. "Thank god."

The driver's head turns around to face the direction of the noise. Turns around completely. Without the rest of his body following.

Then Alice really does scream.

The driver's visage rushes into view as if through a zoom lens. A face of purple and brown, like a bashed-up fruit. His jaw hangs slack, his head lolls, and there is some kind of green discharge oozing from his mouth. His eyes are milky, unfocused for a second, then his neck snaps up straight and his body turns to face the same direction. An arm is flung out toward us, and my mother's best cashmere scarf trails through the air in a bloody arc.

Alice screams again. I grab the hatch lid, shut it tight, and sit on it.

"Oi!"

There's a shout from the front of the bus. Smitty.

"What's going on? Let me in, will ya?"

I leap up. "Sit on that!" I command Pete and Alice, and skitter over to the end of the bus. Smitty is standing by the doors, hands on hips. "It's the driver!" I call down to him. "He's woken up and he's one of them!"

Smitty stares up at me as if I am speaking another language. A crash makes him look farther down the bus, and the expression on his face turns to sickening comprehension. No further explanation needed.

"We're stuck up here."

"How fast is he moving?"

"I don't know!" I shrug uselessly.

"Let's see."

Smitty runs along the side of the coach, slaps the window.

"Oi! Mister! Hell-o!"

"What are you doing?"

Smitty tracks back and slaps the next window down.

"That's right, this way!" he shouts. He moves to the next window and thumps again. "I'm here!"

"Stop it!" Alice slithers to the edge of the bus roof on her belly like a candy-colored salamander. "Don't make him angry!"

"I can outrun him, easy!" Smitty shouts. "I'll get him out and double back."

"Yes!" Alice cries. "Quickly!"

Smitty reaches the final window, then hits the button on the door. I realize what won't happen a second before it doesn't. Our snowboard locking system is doing its job too darn well. Smitty pushes the doors, trying to rattle the board free.

"It's no good!" he calls up. "Someone is going to have to open it from the inside."

"Are you out of your tiny mind?" Alice shouts. "You do it!"

"Like how?" Smitty says. "I can't get up there." He jumps and tries to catch one of the sideview mirrors to hoist himself up, but it's too high, even for his monkey skills.

"Then we should jump off!" Alice says. "Leave him locked up in there. Catch me!" She begins to swivel her legs around to dangle them over the edge. I grab her.

"No! Everything is inside the bus." I hold tight to Alice's squirming body. "We can't just leave and take our chances out there. There might be more of them in the café, and who knows how far we'll have to go before we're safe? You were the one who said we should stay inside."

"But *he's* inside!"

"Not for long." I let go and stand up, oh-so-decisively. "He's slow, like the others?" I shout down to Smitty.

He nods. "I'll keep him at the front until you're inside . . . then get him to come toward you while you dodge past."

"Easy." I swallow.

"Too right." He winks.

Pete is lying across the hatch like a starfish. He looks paler than ever. "You're going in?" he says.

"Keep the hatch open." My heart is hammering. "Promise me."

He grunts and moves aside. *Reassuring.*

I lift the hatch. "I'm ready!" I shout down to Smitty.

"He's still at the front," he calls back. "You're good to go."

I take a final breath of the cold, crisp air and lower myself into the bus.

8

I wriggle down behind a seat. The Undriver is at the front, swaying and slapping the windshield. Something is pissing him off. It's Smitty, jumping up and down on the other side of the glass like his own private whack-a-mole. I ease into the aisle and back down to row 20, where we stored the ski equipment. Carefully, I pull out a ski pole. It's not an ideal weapon, but it will have to do. I left my submachine gun back in the States. Ha-ha.

Smitty stops jumping and I can't see him anymore. Seems like the driver can't, either; he presses himself up to the glass, then stumbles back a step or two, contemplating his next move. I guess this is my cue.

"Hey!"

I bang my pole on the ground.

"Come get me!"

The head whips around again. That's a neat trick. Must be his signature monster move. It sure is effective. I resist the urge to pee my pants.

"That's right, mister! I'm back here!"

Oh, my Undead-taunting banter seriously needs work. I always wondered why the heroines in horror movies spend half their time making wisecracks when they fight their opponents. Now I know it's to distract themselves from thoughts of their imminent death. I edge toward the hatch, painfully aware that it's my only escape route. The driver begins to head my way. He's uncoordinated and shambling, but will he suddenly remember how to run? I hold the pole out in front of me and force myself to keep walking. Really it's just a test of how long I can keep my nerve as he staggers toward me. Maybe I should tell Pete to shut the hatch so that's not an option? I look up for a second. Alice and Pete stare down at me, faces pale, jaws almost as slack as the driver's. I cannot mess this up. I will look like a total loser. A dead loser. Or an Undead one.

Forget the hatch. I make myself walk past it. Now it's the doors or bust. I bang the pole again, take a step forward, one hand on a seat, ready to dart out of arm's reach.

The driver lurches closer, and believe me, there is no doubt in my mind that he is dead. There's nothing behind his eyes — no compassion, no anger, no fear. Any semblance of who he once was has gone, replaced by this stumbling, hungry-looking thing, reaching for me. And the *moaning*. It's a guttural groaning anchored so deep it sounds like he is trying to bring up oil. Does he have a wife? Kids? Anyone who would recognize him now? How would they feel if they could see him like this?

Get a grip. Concentrate. My dad always told me I have fast reactions — that's what makes me a good skier — and now I've got to test them to the max. The driver's nearly upon me. Just a couple of feet separate us.

Now!

I dodge into the seat on my left, throwing a leg over the seats in front, set to scramble past. But the driver isn't close enough to dodge; he simply sidesteps into the corresponding seat a row farther down, like a well-trained chess piece. *Oh, goody.* I dart back into the aisle, then across to the right-hand side, clambering forward over a row before he can react. For a second I think I've made it. Then he lunges at me.

Without thinking I thrust the ski pole into his chest. It sinks in surprisingly easily with a *clunk*, momentarily pinning him like an indignant beetle. He swipes it away, and his sudden strength is shocking. I let go of the pole and it falls out of reach. He lunges again, spit flying out of his mouth in cloudy, viscous globules. I flatten myself against the window, my back slipping on the pathetic little nylon curtain that serves no purpose whatsoever except to hinder attempted escapes from flesh-eating monsters. As I slide down the window like broken egg, I notice that the ski pole has wedged between my row of seats and the one in front, making a feeble barrier between the bus driver and me. He presses against it, frustrated as he reaches for me, his fingers a few inches from my face. If I die right here, right now, I will be *ashamed*. What a fail. Struck down and eaten by a *bus driver*, for crap's sake, in Scotland, on a lame school trip. Just as the pole starts to buckle and his fingers clasp my hair, I throw myself over into the seat in front — and roll into the aisle.

I embrace the floor for a millisecond, willing it to open up and engulf me. "Move!" Alice screams from above.

I look up. The driver is bearing down on me, teeth gnashing. Alice screams again. Distracted, he straightens and swipes up at the hatch with his good arm.

It is time to stand up. But as I make to move, something attaches itself to my jacket. My hands scrabble underneath me. My ski pass has caught on something in the floor. I can't move.

A slam from above means the hatch is closed. I am on my own. Hey, they held out longer than I'd figured.

Desperately, I tug at the plastic pass. A silver ring pops up from the rubber floor. I stare at it. I know what that is. I pull on the silver ring with all my might and a trapdoor lifts up, slamming into the driver's face as he dives down to reach me. A black hole opens up underneath and I slither into it headfirst.

A thankfully brief fall, and cushioned by something squashy. I'm in the luggage hold, on top of an open suitcase — its lid removed to make the back window barricade.

It's dark but there's a rectangle of light above me. The trapdoor was not hinged; it came off completely before it whacked the driver in the face, and it is only a matter of time before his befuddled brain realizes I am still within reach.

Scrambling over the suitcases, spilling their contents on to the floor, I make for the doors of the hold. Doors in a hold are not designed for escape from the inside. I bang on the side of the bus with my fist, praying that Smitty will realize and open them up.

Above me looms the driver, staring blankly into the hole. The noise attracted him. Damned if I do, damned if I don't.

"Hey!" I move farther down the bus, through souvenirs and dirty laundry, slapping the doors. "I'm in here! Get me out!"

A crash behind me tells me I'm no longer alone in the hold. Panic, rising up like cold water through my body, threatens to overwhelm me. Wedging my backside against a suitcase, I kick the door with both legs, then again, and again, and again. In the gloom, the driver begins to swim through the sea of suitcases in my direction.

I kick again.

Just as I'm convinced I'm never going to see daylight again, the door opens and light floods into the hold. I roll blindly toward the light and fall with a *crunch* into the snow.

Smitty stands there, looking down at me. But not for long. A moan erupts from within the hold. He goes to slam the door.

"Wait!" I scramble to my feet. "We need to get him out." I pull Smitty a few feet away from the hold, and the driver emerges. "Keep on your feet. He's not too fast, but he's stronger than you think."

"Oi, you soft git!" calls Smitty to the driver, who is finding his feet in the snow. "Pick on someone your own size."

The driver stumbles toward us.

"You distract him while I climb back in," I babble. Smitty looks confused. "The door is still barricaded. Shut the luggage hold after me and get ready to jump in through the front door."

Unbelievably, Smitty does as he is told. He leaps through the snow, arms circling above him like it's all an elaborate dance routine.

"Come to me! Come to me!" he sings, then bends over, gathers snow into a ball, and throws it into the driver's blackened face. The driver's moans are momentarily muffled, but he plows toward Smitty regardless. "Oops!" Smitty cries in mock concern. "Excuse me, mister, I don't know what came over me."

What a maniac. I struggle to keep pace with him as the driver staggers closer. Two lunatics and one monster, galloping through the snow, I don't think my mother quite envisaged this scenario when she signed the check for the school trip.

As the driver gets within a few feet of us, I dodge around him and run flat out to the bus. Throwing myself back into that dark confined space goes against every instinct, but I have to get on board and open the door. I can only hope that Smitty doesn't get too carried away with driver-taunting to remember to shut the hold after me.

Back in the aisle, I fix the trapdoor shut over the hole in the floor:

better safe than sorry. Then I run to the front door, swiftly remove the snowboard, and press the lever to open.

In the parking lot, Smitty's driver-baiting is getting more and more dangerous. He lunges at the driver, then quickly spins away before the driver can grab him.

"Smitty! Close the hold!" I shout, a fist of fear and frustration rising in my chest. He ignores me, obviously finding himself too funny for words.

If you want something done right . . . I rush back out into the snow and slam the doors to the hold shut. Attracted by the noise, the driver does his head-spinning trick — starting to get old now — and begins stumbling toward the bus.

"Smitty!" I shout. "Snap out of it!"

I bound back to the door to find Alice at the top of the steps, hand on the lever.

"I was waiting for you to come back," she says guiltily. "I wouldn't have shut them yet." She peers out at Smitty, who is still running rings around the driver. "That'll end in tears."

I turn, hands on hips, ready to shout at Smitty again, when something causes all the breath to leave my body. Smitty slips on the snow and skids, right into the legs of the driver, who topples over on top of him.

"Smitty!" I scream, momentarily fixed to the spot, unable to move or to tear my eyes away from the pile of writhing limbs making deadly snow angels on the ground. Before I know what I'm doing, I've grabbed the snowboard on the steps and I'm rushing toward the pileup.

Smitty's head and body are completely obscured by the driver, but his legs stick out beyond the driver's legs, kicking frantically as the driver tries to bite him. I raise the snowboard and smack it on the back of the driver's head. It doesn't even make him pause. Snowboards are not built to knock someone out. Right now, that is a major design flaw. I ram the end of the board into the driver's side, trying to shove him off Smitty, who gets a hand free. I ram again, and Smitty pushes, and suddenly we've rolled him to one side for a second. Just long enough for me to remember the dangerous part of the snowboard and how it can be used. I lift the board up high above my head and with a superhuman surge of fear and desperation, bring the metal edge down on the driver's exposed neck.

There it sticks, stuck in his throat, like an awkward question.

The driver stops moving, a look of dull surprise frozen on his face. Smitty scrambles to his feet, and the driver drops onto his back, the board still sticking halfway through his neck.

I crouch down, hands over my mouth.

"Awesome job, Roberta." Smitty stands up and brushes himself down. "Although I totally had him."

"My name's not Roberta," I whisper through my fingers, the cold of the snow seeping up from the seat of my leggings and into my core.

"Whatever you say." Smitty hunkers down next to me and smiles, his eyes twinkling in a way that might have made my cheeks warm if I hadn't been staring past him, at the thing, the thing that I killed. "Not bad going for a ski bunny."

I almost feel the movement before I see it. The driver's mouth opens, an arm shoots out, and fingers catch the edge of my jacket. I fling myself backward, a scream falling out of my mouth as I tumble into the snow, then quickly scramble up on my elbows, ready to kick, to claw, to fight . . .

In a single movement Smitty stands, raises his leg, and drops his big black boot down hard on the snowboard. There is a crack and a gurgle, and the driver's head is liberated from his body.

"Oh my god, what did you do?" Alice is behind us.

"That was incredible!" Pete enthuses. "Best use for a snowboard I've seen all week!"

"Nobody is going to believe this when I post it!" Alice is holding a phone up. She's been filming the whole thing.

I feel the sting of bile in the back of my throat as I tear my eyes away from the head. I half expect Smitty to pick it up by its hair, or kick it into the air and shout "Goal!" but surprisingly he stands somberly, almost in respect, gazing down at the driver and his head. Then the moment is gone.

He gently pulls me up, puts a strong arm around my shoulders, and together we walk toward the bus.

"We're going to need a new board for the door."

9

We leave the body in the snow. What else are we supposed to do?

Somehow Pete manages to drive the bus on fumes, out of the parking lot and down the road that leads past the gas station and to the café.

I feel empty. Should I be crying, or crazying it up? I killed the bus driver — or Smitty did. Or neither of us did, because he was already dead. This is way worse than Mr. Taylor. I killed a person I had been trying to heal a few hours before. I've heard of post-traumatic stress disorder — is that what I should be feeling? I sit, silent and strangely unafraid, as Pete teeters the bus down the hill, Smitty shouting directions, Alice watching for movement through the binoculars. I feel a catch in my throat, like some kind of weird, flipped-out pride. We're still alive.

The bus creeps past the gas station at a respectful distance. The black smoke has almost gone. I glance at the ground for blackened bodies, but there are none. Maybe they disintegrated in the explosion?

Likewise, the spot in the road where Mr. Taylor lay has been covered by fresh snow. I think I see a lump, but I can't be sure.

Good. It's easier not to see.

By the time we reach the café, I can feel the blood running through my veins again. This is no time for wallowing, or crying, or imagining, or asking why. That time will come later. This is the time for pulling together every ounce of strength and reserve and hope. I clench my fists until the white bones of my knuckles show through the skin.

Pete draws the bus to a halt outside the Cheery Chomper.

"Last stop, everybody off!" he calls. He's almost enjoying this. "End of the line."

"Don't *even*," says Alice quietly, but we're all ignoring him anyway.

The inside of the café is dimly lit — and there's an erratic flickering, like a strobe light. I can't see anyone, alive or dead or in-between.

► CARROT MAN VEGGIE JUICE! PUT SOME FIRE IN YOUR BELLY! ◄

The banner that was hanging above the entrance to the café has come undone at one end. It's flapping gently in the wind, beckoning us in.

"I think we can safely assume that everyone who was in there is now gone," Pete says. "Vaporized by Smitty at the garage, probably." But he stays at the wheel, and the engine is still running.

"Yeah?" Smitty says. "How about you test out that theory?"

Pete turns off the engine, but stays put.

We all stay put.

"We're not going to get anywhere chillin' on the bus." I try to convince myself, as much as anyone else. I peer into the café. There are Christmas lights twinkling by the counter. It's January 9; they should have been taken down. Isn't that bad luck? "We have to assume nobody's coming," I continue. "They would have come by now."

"Where's Gareth?" Alice asks suddenly. "If he was heading here with the laptop, how come we can't see him?"

"He's probably in another room, in the back," says Smitty. "I am going to kick his arse when I see him."

Alice turns, blinking. "And the arses of anything else hiding in the back, too?"

She has a point. Just because we can't see jack doesn't mean that Undead Jack and Undead Jill aren't lurking in there with all of their friends, ready to Cheerily Chomp on us. But the fact remains, we have to do *something*.

OK, I've seen the movies. Believe me, I have shouted at my TV with the best of 'em. *Don't go in that haunted house, you losers! Don't walk through that graveyard! Don't check out that noise in the basement! Stay on the nice, safe bus and don't go in the creepy café!* I know, *I know*. We are relatively safe here. We're mobile — up to a point. Ms. Fawcett has packed way too many sugary drinks than is wise for a group of teens. We have all of our limbs. There's even a bathroom. We should just sit tight, right?

What you don't realize until you're right there in it, is the itch to keep moving. Maybe it's hormones, or a death wish, or the lack of access to social networking sites, but *jeez* it's hard being cooped up on a bus. And we're curious. We're hardwired to go into that café and face potential death, no matter how you slice it. It is *on*. It's just a matter of how long it takes to build up the courage.

"I'm going in." Smitty moves to the doors. Not too long, then.

I sling my own backpack over one shoulder, then arm us with skis, poles, boards — because hey, it worked last time — the door is opened, and we all troop out. Pete thoughtfully shuts the door after us. There is a fresh layer of snow on the café steps, but it is lumpy with the footprints of our Undead classmates, and we advance up to the door awkwardly, walking like the first men on the moon. We look through the glass.

All clear. Smitty slowly opens the door . . . a little, then wider, then all the way.

As he steps in, there's a loud *beeb-beep*, the modern equivalent of the shopkeeper's tinkling bell above the door.

"Great." Smitty stops as if he's stepped on a land mine. "So much for the element of surprise."

I step past him. *Beeb-beep.* Then Alice and Pete follow in quick succession. *Beeb-beep. Beeb-beep.*

"Friggin' fantastic!" Smitty snarls. "Why don't you play a sodding tune on the thing!"

"Sorry." Alice isn't, particularly.

"I thought it was the door," I mutter.

Smitty points to the WELCOME beneath our feet. "Pressure mat."

"Oh," I mouth, as if I'm suddenly all about the quiet.

The door swings shut, Smitty holds up a hand, and we listen. There's an irregular buzzing noise that matches the flickering lights. And a strong smell of burnt oil. I guess the cooks forgot to switch the fryer off before they turned all dead and dribbly. To our left are the tables, with plates of half-eaten food and packets of opened sandwiches. There are coats draped over chairs, abandoned, their occupants no longer needing their warmth.

Beyond the eating area is a diner-style kitchen with ovens and a grill. This is the source of the flickering light.

To the right is a small shop selling snacks and magazines, and ahead of us a corridor leading to bathrooms and who knows what else. We wait for something to happen. Nothing does.

"On three," Smitty says. "One, two —"

"On three what?" Alice says.

He rolls his eyes. "We get off the mat. One, two, three."

As one, we tiptoe off the mat. *Beeb-beep.* Again. We wait to see what we've disturbed. Nothing comes.

"If Gareth was here—" I begin.

"He would have popped his cowardly head out the door to say hi?" Smitty finishes. "Not necessarily." He advances toward the dining area and kitchen, brandishing a snowboard. I follow, checking out the shop on the way.

The good—or bad—news is that there aren't many places to hide. I check the corners. You always have to check the corners of the room—it's like Danger Sitch 101. That's where the bad guys lurk. There's an old-school phone on the counter in the shop. I try it, but the line is dead. Not dead, exactly—I can hear a kind of static, like it's plugged in but there's no dial tone. I press the buttons a few times, and I hear them dialing down the line but connecting to nothing. It's as if I'm already on a call and the person on the other end is listening, but not saying anything. Too eerie for words . . . I give up on it—disappointed and almost relieved in equal measure—and glance around the room for other options.

Leaving Alice and Pete standing back-to-back in the middle of the café as if tied to a stake, I make myself walk through the tables, gripping my ski pole as I peer around a half partition into the booths beyond. No one.

Smitty whistles at me and points to the counter at the open-plan kitchen, making some elaborate SWAT team hand signals. I think he just made them up, but it's clear what he means. We need to check the kitchen. Looks clear enough, but it would be simply amateur not to check it. Smitty approaches from the aisle; I'm threading my way through tables. If something jumps out, he's got a free run back to the exit while I'll be hurdling bolted-down furniture. *Great.* We reach the counter, the fluorescent light fluttering on and off with a metallic ting. Smitty holds up a hand, three fingers held upright. OK, another countdown. The boy clearly likes his countdowns. *Three, two, one . . .*

I jump onto one of the plastic stools and scramble on top of the counter, ski pole aloft, my eyes darting — below, then to the corners of the kitchen, looking for a dark shadow, a nook, a cranny where evil lurks. The light strobes make everything into monsters.

Smitty giggles. He hasn't moved.

"All clear?" He's flat-out laughing now. My irritation makes me bold; I leap off the counter into the kitchen. It's empty. I stroll up to the counter door and swing it open.

"Want me to do all the work?" I saunter out past him, controlling my breath, not letting him see that I'm bothered.

"Hey, losers," Alice hisses. "What about up there?" She's pointing to the rooms down the corridor.

Before I think about it too much, I'm walking up stained blue carpet. I call to Smitty, "You take the men's, I'll take the ladies'."

"No, this time we go together." He's by my side. I hate that I'm grateful.

There's nobody in the bathrooms. After we've checked them, we wait while Alice does what a girl's gotta do. She absolutely refused to go on the bus. I know where she's coming from, but man, that's some bladder control.

A storage room beyond the bathrooms is empty. Well, empty of people, laptops, and monsters. The door is ajar, and the light is on — which I can't help feeling is strange — but there's nothing in there except boxes of cleaning supplies and toilet paper.

Back in the corridor, there's only one room left, and it's marked STAFF ONLY. Smitty tries the door, but it doesn't open.

"Da fuh —?" He kicks out at it halfheartedly. There's a keypad on the wall with a little red light. Seems like the Cheery Chomper might have something worth protecting other than 10-percent-off-your-next-visit coupons. "You!" Smitty points at Pete. "Do something."

"Me?" Pete stares at him. "What am I, R2-D2? Just because I'm the brains of this particular outfit, do you think I can circumnavigate a digital keypad locking system?" He holds a finger aloft and walks toward the keypad. "Excuse me while I access the security files through my wires." He sticks his finger on the keypad and jolts around a bit, eyes flashing. It's quite a performance.

"You should get an award for lame." Alice pushes past him. "Place like this, they'll keep it simple. Anything too complicated and the pondlife who work here wouldn't be able to remember it." She types 1234. For a second, I think she's onto something. But the little light stays red, and the door won't budge. She tries 0123. Same deal.

"We should just smash it," Smitty says.

"No!" I say. "What if it breaks and the door still won't open?"

He makes a face. "I mean, we should smash the *door*."

"And then what?" I counter. "This is a pretty good spot to hide. It's warmer than the bus, we've got food and running water and who knows what else behind that door. But if we smash the door down, it means we can't lock it again. We won't be secure."

"There's got to be a window in that room," says Alice. "Or maybe another door." She turns to me. "Go outside and look. When you get in, open the door for us."

"Yes, ma'am." I mock-salute. "Because *I'm* the expendable one?

Does anyone want to take a vote on who we should risk here?"

"Oh, give it a rest." She acts bored. "Take him with you." She thumbs at Smitty. "You know you'll end up going — why waste time?" She pouts. She has lip gloss on. When the hell did she think to freshen up her makeup? There's shimmery eye shadow and long black lashes, too. She's one crazy chick. Mascary.

I clamp my ski pole to my side. It's oh-so-tempting to make an Alice kebab right now, but then I would be guilty of time-wasting. Smitty, as is his habit, is already halfway out the door. I tut pathetically at Alice, wishing once more for the retort that rarely comes, and follow Smitty back into the snow like the lunatic I am.

After the warmth of the café, the cold hits my face like a splash of ice water; the wind has picked up and the snow swirls around the entranceway. I cast a quick look around the parking lot. Smitty doesn't pause much to check for movement, but ducks around the corner of the building, following a path to the rear. I start to follow, but something jars in the corner of my eye, and I turn back. I look at our bus.

The door is open.

10

I back into the wall. Pete shut the door; I know he did, I saw him. I saw him because I was going to shut it myself, but he beat me to it.

I stare at the bus, looking for movement. Everything *seems* still. My eyes drop to the snow in front of the bus door—can I see footprints? The snow is too messed up to be able to make anything out. But the fact remains, the door is open and that means someone opened it. Gareth? No—can't be, he would have closed it behind him, surely? Someone come to rescue us? Then why can't I see them? They would have appeared by now. I look over my shoulder back into the café. Alice is in the shop, nom-nomming a candy bar; Pete is nowhere to be seen. He's probably still trying to bypass the keypad lock, no matter what he says. Anyway, they're useless to me. I turn the other way, and nearly jump out of my boots.

"Hello!" Smitty is waving a hand in my face. "What are you doing here? There's a door around the back and I think I can get us in—" He stops when he sees my expression. "What's wrong?"

I point to the bus and he whips around. His face drops.

"We closed the door, didn't we?"

"Pete did," I say.

Smitty sinks back against the wall with me. "Anyone on board?"

I shake my head. "Not that I've seen. But maybe they don't want to be seen."

"Balls." He sighs. "We have to check it out, don't we?"

"Maybe send Alice?"

He chuckles quietly. "Yeah, that'll happen."

"Well," I say, "with all the abuse that door's been through in the last twenty-four hours . . . maybe it malfunctioned or something? Maybe Pete didn't hit the button hard enough, or maybe something got caught in the door and it swung open and we just didn't notice . . ."

We look at the bus a little longer.

"Come on, then." Smitty leads the way to the bus. He climbs up the steps and I follow, with legs of granite and a dragging sense of dread in my gut. The seats greet us silently, our home away from home, familiar and sickening at the same time. We stop at the first row; it's impossible to see if we're on our own, but there are no obvious monsters swinging from the overhead lockers. Yeah, that much we knew already. Smitty turns to me, shrugs, and before I know it, he's running — screaming — down the aisle at full speed, at a volume that makes me shrink in my jacket. He reaches the backseat, crashes against it, and ricochets off and up toward me again, still screaming. *What the hell?* When he reaches me, he swings around, hands outstretched like a crazed magician revealing the empty hat.

"Ta-da!"

"What are you doing?" I gasp, eyes behind him, looking for the monsters that he's unearthed.

"Don't you think this creeping around is getting old?" His eyes flash, like he's totally amped. "Flush 'em out, knock 'em down!"

The bathroom door flies open with a bang; Smitty hits the floor like a six-year-old playing ring-around-the-rosie.

The bathroom is empty. He recovers, but it's too late to save face. I laugh a little too hysterically, sinking into a crouch on the floor. He looks aghast, but then he laughs, too, the pair of us rocking back and forth on the floor like we've been hitting the crazy juice.

It feels so good. But I stop just before the bubbly mania segues into the crying type, because it might.

"There's nobody here." I stand up and skip past him. "Must have been a problem with the door. We should make sure it stays shut."

We barricade the door with a couple of skis wedged against the curb, and return to our original quest — the back door of the Cheery Chomper.

"Reassuring to know that all this time we've been gone, Malice and Petey haven't sent out the search party," Smitty says.

I pull up my hood, mmm *yes*, and we plow through the snow to the rear of the building. There's a single-paned window, with blinds down, and a plain door with a normal lock. No digipad here. Smitty bends down to the lock.

"Gimme your plastic," he says.

"Pardon me?"

He looks up, snaps his fingers. "The AmEx will do, but you should know that generally it's not so widely accepted here in the UK."

I redden. How does he know I have a credit card?

"OK, it's freezing and we don't have time to get all grumpy — remember when we had our boot fittings back on the first day?" He makes a squirly mouth. "I went through your stuff. Sorry. I didn't take anything."

Blood rushes to my head with rage. "You did *what*?"

"Nothing personal." Smitty shrugs. "We're all cooped up in that stupid ski lodge, no cash, what's a boy to do?" He thinks he's being so cute. "I was going to borrow a tenner for beer, but unluckily for me you didn't have any dosh. Hey, it's all irrelevant now."

"Like hell it is." I glare at him.

"I didn't even know you then," he sighs. "Anyway, hand over the card."

I will do no such thing. Fury and violation whip up around me like the whirling snow and stick me to the spot. Smitty stands up and stares at me, his face passive, the blue-gray eyes almost sorrowful.

"I'm a doof." He lays a hand on my arm. My first impulse is to throw it off, but I search his face and, incredibly, he's genuine. "I should never have gone through your pockets." There's no trace of sarcasm, and I'm looking really hard. Then he allows a small smile to creep onto his lips. "I just thought you were a Yank, so you were bound to be loaded."

Ugh! My first impulse was right. I pull my arm away from his reach. "I'm not a 'Yank'!" I shout, as if this is the issue. I stomp toward the door, unzip my jacket, and reach inside for my red Chinese silk purse. My dad brought it back from one of his work trips overseas. It houses a credit card, Band-Aids, lip balm, a tampon, and a small roll of emergency quarters. Not that a quarter would do me any good in this cold, damp, stupid country. As my face burns and anger continues to bubble inside my chest, I slot the card between the door and the wall, and wiggle it.

"You need to —"

"Back off!" I roar. He thinks I'm some dumb American? He thinks he can bat those long lashes and I'll simper and forgive him? I wedge the corner of the card into the place where the latch is snug in its slot, and rattle the doorknob.

"How come you speak like one, then?" Smitty asks.

I ignore him and concentrate on my task.

"A Yank," he says helpfully. "You sound like one, or almost. Not that I have anything against Yanks, you understand."

"Really?" I look up. "That's great to know, thank you so much." I get back to the lock. "If you must know, I'm British. I was born here and I grew up here. We moved to America when I was nine because of my mum's stupid job. We moved back here last month. And *blimey*, it's just been so *bloody brilliant* to be back."

Smitty kicks the snow. "Things have changed since you were last here, yeah?"

"Not at all." I tilt the card a little. "It's all exactly how I remember it. Miserable weather, smart-ass boys." I feel something shift in the lock. *Yes!* One more wiggle of the card and the bolt springs back into place, the handle turns, and Houston, we have liftoff . . .

"You did it!" Smitty can't believe it, and frankly, neither can I.

"Just a little trick I picked up in the 'hood," I mutter, and pull the door open.

We bundle in way too quickly, given that we don't know what's waiting for us, but it's too cold to hang outside.

The small room is greenish-gray, like a hospital. There's a dirty, paisley-patterned couch, and a chaotic mess of a desk. The room smells musty, as if it's been shut up for days, and there's a layer of dust on everything. Boxes — filled with large, blue bottles of disinfectant — are piled high on either side of the room. It's immediately obvious that we're here alone. If anyone is hiding behind the couch, they're anorexic. I check anyway, then close the door to the outside. The latch snaps into place; we're safe. Well, unless there are any dribbling fiends wielding credit cards to jimmy the lock.

We look for the obvious — a phone that works, a computer, a stash of weapons — and come up short. It's discouraging in the extreme: kind of like waking up Christmas morning and finding the presents under the tree are the same as what you got last year. And broken.

"Votes for leaving Malice and Petey in there?" Smitty stands by the door to the café.

I don't smile. He's not off the hook with me yet. Not by a mile.

"Sadly, the food's that way, too." Smitty unlatches the door. Pete is still bending over the keypad. I bet he's been at it all this time.

"Gareth?" he says. "Laptop?"

"Nope and nope," I say. "No PC, either. I guess we traveled back in time to before they invented proper offices."

"Hmm," Pete says. "The laptop would have been nice, but the wireless has gone AWOL anyway. I tried to pick it up on Smitty's smart phone when we got here. Now Alice is climbing on tables, trying to get a signal." He waves a hand in the direction of the seating area. "Nothing. Is there a landline?"

"Like everything else around here, dead." Smitty holds a white plastic receiver in his hand. "Couldn't they give us a single break?"

Pete sits down, paler than pale, on the grubby couch. "I think *they* meant to make it as hard as possible."

"What do you mean?" I say.

He scratches his head, and I wince when I see he's scrubbed off a bit of fresh scab. "The people who have done this. They've disabled all the usual ways of escape, made it virtually impossible to contact the outside world."

"Eh?" Smitty leans against the desk. "Who's *they*?"

Pete shrugs. "The government. The military. The New World Order. Whoever orchestrated this and is using us like rats in a lab."

I stare at him, openmouthed. When he doesn't elaborate, I look at Smitty, but he's wearing the same expression as me. I turn back to Pete. "Are you kidding me? You think that this is all on purpose? What's happened, with everyone . . . getting ill?"

"You mean everyone dying and coming back to life," Smitty corrects me.

"OK, so we're going to talk about this now?" I realize I'm still holding my ski pole, and fling it to the ground. "We don't know it's true that they died. For all we know, this is some whacked-out Scottish Flu." I'm saying it, but I'm not entirely buying it.

"Yeah, or rabies." Smitty *drips* sarcasm. "Or they were off their trolleys on shrooms or speed."

"Face facts!" Pete shouts. "We saw what happened with that driver. He got infected, he died, he came back to life. Just like the others."

"We don't know that for sure—"

"We do." He cuts me short. "Anyway, whatever you choose to believe, you can't deny that we're captive here. And the powers-that-be are watching every move we make, waiting to see what we do next."

Smitty smiles at me. "The Great White Dope cracked his skull. We have to remember that." He turns to Pete. "*Watching* us?"

Pete nods. "Don't look now, but there's a closed-circuit TV camera on the wall behind you."

Smitty and I struggle with the urge to turn around.

Pete reads us and smiles. "In the café, too. And the shop. I checked. No microphones, so I think it's pictures only, not sound. Of course, I haven't had time to do an adequate sweep, but clearly we could look all day and not find a bug if they didn't want it found—"

"This is crazy!" It's my turn to butt in. "Of course there are cameras;

they're everywhere these days! But it doesn't mean that they've all been planted to spy on us in the event of a zombie apocalypse!"

That gets their attention. "OK, I said it." I flop on the couch, exhausted. "I said the word. Is everyone satisfied now?"

"Ha!" Pete says. "So you'll accept that we're dealing with zombies, but you find the idea that we're being watched too incredible to consider?"

Smitty shakes his head and laughs. "You are *ridonkulous*, Frosty. Like anyone would be interested in watching us."

Alice runs into the room, her face flushed. "There's something *très* bizarre going on outside!"

Smitty raises an eyebrow. "Have you been drinking corn syrup again, Malice?" He pushes past her, out of the room. "You're seeing things."

"The bus door, you idiot!" Alice shouts after him. "Somebody's barricaded it!"

"We did that," I explain. "We thought . . ." Something stops me from telling her the whole truth. "We decided it would be better if we wedged the door shut. Just in case it blows open in the wind."

"Yuh-huh?" Alice's eyebrows are practically in her hairline. "Sure you're not keeping one of those things in there as a pet?"

"I'm sure," I say. "After all, we've already got Smitty."

"Heard that." A voice comes from outside of the room somewhere.

"Meant you to," I reply.

Alice rolls her eyes. "You two are so made for each other." She flounces out of the room. "Weirdos."

"Weirdo yourself," I say, flustered, and busy myself with my backpack on the floor, cheeks burning. Pete is shuffling through the mess on the desk. He dumps a load of papers on the floor next to me.

"What are you looking for?" I say.

"Keys." He rifles through a drawer. "Storage cabinet over there."

I turn around. Behind a particularly large stack of boxes is indeed a storage cabinet. "What do you think is in there?"

"Well, I don't yet possess the ability to see through solid matter, so I don't know," Pete says. "But I'm guessing that, as this room is completely devoid of any kind of hardware, it might all be hiding inside."

Hardware? "What, like a laptop?" I say.

"Yep." He empties a pen holder. "Or a wireless router, or a phone — a fax, even. Maybe they locked up anything that could have been of any use."

There he goes with that *they* again. I get up and start looking for keys. We could probably find something to break the lock with, but it would be so much easier to open the . . . *whoa* . . . I sit down abruptly on the floor, the room spinning. I feel faint. I make like I'm looking on the carpet so he won't notice something's wrong.

"So . . ." Alice climbs over the chair back into the room. "Smitty's planning on eating all of the food, in case you're interested."

I am. My stomach feels like it's folding in on itself. Nothing like adrenaline and near-death experiences to kill your appetite, but even that will only work for so long. My head is suddenly buzzing with all of the things that need to be done, and the order we should do 'em in. If I'm honest, I need to chow down for a good twenty minutes and feed some brain cells.

"We need to get into that filing cabinet," Pete says.

"After we've eaten." I stand shakily and head for the door. "We need to barricade the front door and arm ourselves, we need to eat, then we should decide what to . . ."

Spangles of light erupt in the corners of my vision, then Blackness punches me in the face, and I fade . . .

11

Something is fluttering around my face. My eyes open, just a squint. It's a dove, a white dove, beating its beautiful wings and fanning my face with air. I shut my eyes again. Lovely.

Right up to the point where the world rushes in and I remember where the hell I am and what I'm doing here. My eyes snap open.

It's not a dove. It's Smitty, wafting some paper napkins in my face. I'm lying on the grubby couch and he's kneeling above me, grinning, like he's trying to annoy me, not revive me. I wouldn't have thought it possible to nurse someone sarcastically, but Smitty pulls it off.

"Better?" he asks, clearly peeved that I'm not reacting to his fan action.

"I'm fine." My voice sounds wobbly even to me. I shift my head. Alice is sitting on the desk, chewing her cud, and looking me over with a malevolent eye. Pete is fiddling with the lock on the filing cabinet, but casting me weird glances. What's with them? I shift my weight and sit up. It's a little quick; black shadows close in from the corners of my vision and threaten to make me pass out again. *No*, I tell the shadows. To faint once is embarrassing; to do it twice would be beyond mortifying.

"Are you sure you're fine?" Alice asks.

"You look really pale," adds Pete. *Yeah. Pot, kettle, white, Pete.*

"Totally fine," I repeat, swinging my legs around onto the floor. My embarrassment is undiminished, but I'm touched that they care. Who knew?

"So you don't feel like you're going to die and then come back to life again?" Alice cuts to the chase.

Aha. So that's where this is going.

I jump to my feet. "Of course not!" The room is undulating slightly, but I choose to ignore it. "I just fainted because I'm hungry. It's no biggie."

"You sure that driver didn't bite you when you were on the bus?" Alice demands.

Holy crap. Her hand — tucked ever-so-casually behind her on the desk — is holding a knife. A huge, gleaming carving knife, with a black handle.

"Bite me? No, he didn't bite me!" I shout at her. "What the hell are you doing with that?" I point at the knife.

She brings it out in front of her.

"Son of a biscuit." Smitty scrambles to his feet. "Malice has got a blade."

"So?" Alice says. "You said we should arm ourselves."

"Not against each other!" I cry.

"Uh-oh," Pete says helpfully from the corner.

"Put the knife down," Smitty says.

"No!" Alice backs toward the chair. "I can do what I want."

"Not if you're going to slice and dice your friends, you can't," Smitty says.

Alice tosses her head. "She's no friend of mine. None of you are. What, just because we're flung together in this nightmare we're suddenly supposed to be best buds? If so, then kill me now."

"That can be arranged, trust me." I take a step toward her. Smitty's by my side.

"Who has got the knife here, losers?" Alice jiggles it at us and climbs onto the chair in the doorway.

This is *ker-razy.* I struggle out of my coat and throw off my fleece. "Look at me!" I hold up my arms to her. "Check me out!" I pull up the sleeves of my long T-shirt. "Where are the bite marks, Alice? Huh?" I tug at my leggings on my good leg and show her my goose-bumped calf. "See? I'm clean."

Alice flinches. "You could have been bitten somewhere else."

"Where?" I lift my shirt up to reveal my stomach, then my back. Pete makes a kind of choking noise in the corner. "There," I say, with the new-found braveness of a flasher. "What else? What will make you happy?"

"Actually, you should take everything off, just to be sure," Smitty says.

I reach as if to slap him, and he dodges out of the way, laughing.

"All right." Alice comes down off her chair, knife still aloft. "But if you turn purple and start drooling"—she narrows her eyes and positively glowers—"I will *finish* you." She jabs at me with the knife, which slips and catches her hand as she drops it. "Ow!"

This finishes Smitty sure enough. He's rolling on the floor laughing his ass off. I pick the knife up and slap it down on the desk.

"I am way too hungry to cope with all this drama," I announce, and climb over the chair out of the room and away from them all, so they can't see me shaking.

We sit in the café at one of the tables nearest to the office. That's in case we have to run back in there. It feels safe, or safe-ish, in the office: a smaller hole to scurry into. Smitty has moved the couch in front of the door to the outside, and out here he's also managed to improvise a barricade for the main entrance. I take my hat off to him; it's not easy when most of the furniture is fixed to the floor. The snow is doing some kind of crazy tornado thing outside the windows: It actually looks like the flakes are falling *up*. I don't know if we'll need the barricades; if it keeps up like this, the Cheery Chomper will be igloo-ized by nightfall. That's not such an unattractive prospect.

I have wiped down a table with some disinfectant from the boxes in the office, and appointed myself head waitress. Thanks to my efforts, we are now sitting looking at a table full of prepackaged sandwiches. There is egg salad and celery, roast beef and onion, cheese and pickle, and tuna and sweet corn. Why sandwich makers in this country are quite so obsessed with two fillings—no more, no less—is beyond me, but there you go. I play with the plastic edge of my saran-wrapped cheesy delight.

Alice looks at me. "You first." She may have lost the knife, but she hasn't lost the attitude.

"We should cook up some burgers, I'm telling you." Smitty tosses his sandwich packet down on the table.

It's like Russian roulette between two slices of bread. Nobody wants to eat. We're starving—or, in Alice's case, hyped up on chocolate that she was pigging out on while we were busy doing all the hard work outside—but nobody wants to take the risk. It's Pete's fault. He dared to voice what all of us were thinking. Smitty was busy building barricades, I was hunter-gathering, Alice was doing whatever that girl does—and then Pete went and said it:

"What if the food's infected?"

"These sandwiches from the shop are sealed." I'd pointed to my cache on the table. "I figured we should avoid the stuff in the kitchen. We don't know what state it's in."

"What if it's the sandwiches that are the problem?" Smitty said. "At least if we cremate a few burgers, we'll kill anything in there."

And so the debate began. A quick examination of the tables of our unfortunate ex-classmates revealed that they had been eating a complete cross section of the Cheery Chomper's menu and the shop's refrigerator. So nothing could be ruled out. If we want to be safe, we eat nothing.

I need to eat something. Badly.

"Let's think about this logically," I say. "As far as we know, everyone who went into the café — except present company" — I point to Pete and Alice — "was affected. Mr. Taylor turned first, the others quite a lot later. What did Mr. Taylor eat?"

Alice frowns at me. "He didn't. He came in the door and went straight into the shop. I remember because the only free seat was at our table next to Shanika, and she was freaking out in case he came and sat beside her."

"It's true," Pete said. "He didn't eat anything from the shop, either."

"Well, then." I shrug. "Mr. T was the first to go zom, so it can't have been anything in the food." I pull a little corner of the plastic wrapping off my sandwich. "He was sick already. He had the flu. Maybe it made him prone to whatever infected him in the café? Maybe that's why he turned so fast?"

Smitty, sitting on the back of a chair, juggles three packets of sandwiches. The fillings squish up against the clear plastic and make me feel sick. "Driver dude didn't go anywhere near the café. What got him?"

I catch a turkey and stuffing on whole wheat. "The question is *who* got him. I think he was bitten — on his wrist, where we bandaged him. Maybe he was bitten by whoever bashed into the bus. That's how it spreads, isn't it?"

Pete raises an eyebrow. "Is it?"

"Yeah." I try to look nonchalant. "Traditionally."

Smitty drops into the seat and fixes me with a gray stare. "But that's not the starting point. What infected everyone in the first place?" He looks around. "Got to be something in here. And Mr. T had the fast track."

"Ooh!" Alice's face contorts with the effort of using her brain. "Mr. Taylor didn't eat anything, but he drank something. The juice that stupid vegetable was handing out."

I look at her as if she's finally come undone. Then it hits me. "Carrot Man."

Pete's eyes widen. "He was giving out free samples at the door!"

"Oh, you beauty!" Smitty makes a noise that is half laugh, half groan. "That is beyond sick!"

I feel the walls of the Cheery Chomper closing in on me. Could it be true? Something in the drink made everyone turn?

"Mr. Taylor drank an entire carton of that juice!" Alice thumps the table. "I heard him say he wanted the vitamin C!"

Pete gulps. "She's right. He was holding it when he came into the shop. He chugged the whole thing down and asked the lady behind the counter if she had somewhere to toss the empty carton."

"So if the juice was infected" — I bite my knuckle — "who else drank it?"

"Everyone!" Alice rises in her seat. "We walked in and the carrot was handing out these samples. God, he was so lame. Major LOLZ. Shanika had one drink, Em had two — she tried to give one to me, but I didn't want it — I mean, *très embarrassant*, a carrot man? I wasn't going to drink it. I was the only one, though."

"What, all the waiters and everyone?" Smitty says. "Every last person in this café except you, Malice?"

Alice glares at him and sharpens up her mouth for a retort, but Pete gets in first.

"She's telling the truth. I remember the carrot guy came in after everyone and was handing out the juice to all the staff. Even the cooks came out and grabbed some. They were all saying how delicious it was."

"But not you, Pete?" I ask.

He shrugs. "I have allergies."

I leap out of my chair and, ignoring a fresh onset of dizziness, march to the entrance. "So where's Carrot Man now?" I search for what I know I will not find—a small cart. "Where's all his stuff? Where's the juice?"

"If you were handing out zombie juice, would you stick around to see what happened?" Smitty says.

I return to the table. Pete strips back the plastic from his sandwich and tucks in.

"So that proves my theory," he says through a mouthful of egg. "This was deliberate, and they've covered up the source. My mother always told me not to accept anything from strangers."

I slowly sit and remove my sandwich from its wrapper. I bite into it cautiously. Smitty shows no fear and dives into his. Alice tears hers into little strips and eats them one by one, as if this will help. Suddenly Smitty grabs his throat and falls to the ground, choking and groaning. We ignore him, as we were all absolutely expecting him to do this. He picks himself up and rejoins us at the table, and we all munch in silence.

I eat a cheese 'n' pickle, a turkey 'n' stuffing, two packets of salt 'n' vinegar crisps, and an apricot muffin, washed down with a Diet Coke.

If we're wrong about the juice and I'm going to be infected, I'll do it on a full stomach.

Having eaten, we're back in the office, the door still propped open with a chair so the automatic latch doesn't close and lock from the outside. Everyone is groaning a little, but not because we're Undead, more that we are stuffed to the gills with what my mum would call "processed muck." Alice only ate half her sandwich, but then she disappeared into the shop and got busy with the candy bars again. I counted seven wrappers. Then she disappeared into the bathrooms. I hope she wasn't chucking them up. That's all we need on the team, a vomit queen. Maybe she just didn't want to take any chances with becoming infected, but I'm thinking that she's more worried about the size of her butt.

"In order to predict the future, we must learn from the past."

Pete is standing beside the locked filing cabinet. I sense a lecture coming on, and make myself comfortable. I think I preferred him when he was flipping out in the bathroom stall.

"What are you gabbing about now, genius?" Smitty says.

"I told you, we're being watched." Pete points to the cabinet. "Help me break that open. Fifty pence says we open it up and find surveillance equipment. Recorded footage of what happened here."

"Fifty *pence*?" Smitty moves toward the cupboard and snatches up a snowboard. "Are you in nursery school? Make it fifty pounds and I'm interested." He throws me a glance. "With exchange rates these days, that's worth more than fifty bucks, you know."

Pete's mouth twitches. "Done. If this really is the breakdown of society as we know it, currency will become useless. But whatever."

Smitty bashes the lock of the cupboard like he's bashing Pete's head. The lock falls off easily, the metal door swings open.

There are three shelves. The bottom one is full of boxed files. The top shelf holds a cash box and a large ball made of rubber bands. But it is the middle shelf that we are all looking at.

Six small TV screens and a large black box that looks like a DVR sit on the shelf. They are all switched on. Images of the café, shop, and entrance, two different views of the parking lot, and one of the office are displayed. And on the final screen we can see ourselves from above, huddled around the cabinet.

Pete turns to the camera in the corner of the room. He smiles and waves at us on the screen.

"I'll take that fifty quid now, Smitty," he says.

12

My life through a lens.

On screen, my hair looks shameful. Like I have the mange. I quell the urge to primp in front of the camera. Alice shows no such restraint, and she doesn't even need to primp.

"This proves nothing." Smitty is adamant. "Just because there are security cameras recording doesn't mean anyone's watching us. The tapes are for robberies, or whatever. Why else would that tosser Gareth have been guarding his cash register with a baseball bat?"

He's right, of course. It doesn't prove a thing—and what's more, if there were people spying on us, why on earth would they leave the TVs here for us to see? Even so, this is way high-tech for a roadside café. My skin is crawling.

"It's good for one thing, though." Smitty grins at Pete and Alice. "We get to check up on your stories."

"What do you mean?" Alice curls her lip.

Smitty points to the DVR. "Like Petey said: We've got it all recorded. What happened here, when and how."

A shudder runs through me. One thing to hear about it, another altogether to see it, up close and from multiple angles.

Pete fiddles with some buttons and manages to rewind the recordings to the beginning. Each screen has a time and date at the bottom. It seems they're on a 24-hour loop; a couple of hours later and we wouldn't have got to see anything. But lucky us, we're just in time.

I close the blind on the window so we can see more clearly, and we crowd in a semicircle, sitting on some of the boxes of disinfectant. My right shoulder is pressed against Smitty's leather-jacketed left shoulder, and as we lean toward the screens his hand brushes mine. He's warm. I can't help feeling grudgingly grateful for his presence. It must be shell-shock. Can't think of any other reason why I'd feel that way.

"Let the show begin."

Pete has managed to find a ruler and points it at the various screens to alert us to the action. It's kind of annoying, but I suppose it's his little reward for Being Right.

The TV screens show black-and-white footage, no sound.

"Not exactly full of customers, is it?" Smitty chews on his thumbnail.

"No one would come to this place unless they had to," Alice says.

The timestamp on the screens reads 1:43 P.M. About ten minutes before we arrived in the bus, by my estimate. There's a young couple paying their bill at a table by the door, a mother and toddler sitting with a teenage girl eating chips-not-fries, and two men wearing checkered shirts and jeans — builders or road workers, maybe. A couple of cooks are visible behind the kitchen counter, there's a waiter and waitress, and a woman behind the register in the shop.

I spot a random guy arriving with a cart, struggling with the main door.

"Bet that's Carrot Man before he costumed up," I say.

As one, we lean in to check him out. He seems average enough. He walks through the café, pushing the cart and dragging a large trash bag.

"What's in the bag?" Smitty says.

The Man Who Would Be Carrot disappears into the bathroom.

"Must be going to change clothes," I mutter.

"Thank god there are no cameras in there," Alice says.

"Oh, don't be coy, Malice." Smitty leans over me to her. "Bet you love it. Giant vegetable costumes do it for you, don't they?" He twinkles at her and laughs, and she squeals in protest—just the correct amount of righteous indignation, but I can tell she's not entirely hating it. I feel a stab of . . . what is that? *Jealousy?* I'm hit by a wave of nausea and self-loathing. What, I'm jealous of Smitty flirting pathetically with Malice? Really? Please.

Carrot Man emerges from the bathroom, fully carrotted up, with skinny legs sticking out of his furry orange costume.

"Be still your beating heart, Malice." Smitty's leaning over me to Alice again. She pushes him away before I can.

Carrot Man wheels his cart down the corridor through the café. As he passes the woman behind the register in the little shop, he offers her a sample. She laughs at him and takes a little cup.

"Who's that?" Alice points at a chubby, middle-aged man wearing a shirt and tie, entering the café as Carrot Man clumsily exits. He opens the door for him and makes a shivering motion, telling Carrot Man—if he didn't already know—that it's cold outside.

Carrot Man gives him a sample. He drinks it.

"That's a dead man walking, that's who," says Smitty.

"It's got to be Gareth's boss," I say. "He's wearing the same sort of name tag on his shirt."

The man walks into the shop and talks to the woman at the counter, leaning over, his shirt straining out of his pants in the back. She hasn't drunk her juice yet; it's sitting by the register. He's gesticulating toward the phone. She picks it up and listens, then shakes her head.

"The phone lines are down already!" Pete taps his ruler on the screen excitedly.

Meanwhile, the young couple finishes paying for their meal and leaves. Carrot Man gives them each a sample as they walk past. The woman knocks hers back in one gulp; the guy sips and makes a face, then throws the rest into the snow on the steps as he descends. Guess he didn't like it much; I can't blame him. They walk out into the parking lot, picking their way carefully across the icy pavement and into an awesome Mini Cooper with a British flag painted on the roof. *Shazaam . . .* That's the car that crashed into the back of our bus!

I shake my head as we watch them start up the car. "They nearly escaped. If they had left two minutes earlier, they would have totally missed out on the juice."

Back in the Cheery Chomper, Gareth's boss is heading out. He feels his back pocket and pulls out a phone.

"Won't work," predicts Smitty.

It clearly doesn't. But the man doesn't seem too surprised. He pulls out a pack of cigarettes, lights one, and hurries back toward the gas station, skidding in the snow. Before he gets to the pumps, he turns and disappears behind the trees.

"Where'd he go?" Smitty cranes his neck as if he can see around corners on the TV. "Oh, come on, at least show us when he turned!"

We watch, glued, but Gareth's boss has gone.

Back at the Cheery Chomper, Carrot Man is bobbing up and down in the cold. The little boy is wandering around the café; he can see Carrot

Man in the entranceway. Too wary to go right up to him, he never-theless is too interested to sit down with his mother and sister. He wanders a few feet closer. Carrot Man spots him and bends over and waves through the glass door. The little boy waves back. Carrot Man holds out a small offering of poison in a plastic cup. *Please don't,* I think. *Leave now, leave while you still can.* Carrot Man opens the door and takes a step toward him. The boy runs back to the table with his mother and sister. I breathe again.

"Hold up!" Pete shouts. "Here we come!"

In the far right of the first screen, our bus appears, passing the couple in the Mini Cooper with the painted roof as they make their way toward the exit. Our bus draws in to the curb at the bottom end of the parking lot. The doors fly open and my recently deceased class begins to unload, buoyant and happy and shivering in the cold air.

"Oh my god, that's me!" Alice cannot contain her glee. "Ugh, I look so fat!" Glee turns to disgust. "This screen is way out of proportion."

"No, that's what you actually look like, Malice," Smitty says.

Alice swears at him; he chuckles.

Meanwhile, the mother, daughter, and little boy prepare to leave. There's an awkwardness about the mother and daughter, as if they've had a disagreement. *Yeah, been there, done that.* I hope they're too miffed and distracted to chug some juice as they leave.

At the entrance, Carrot Man is swamped by our classmates, and although the little boy clearly wants to linger, I breathe a sigh of relief as his sister and mother ignore offers of juice and pull him firmly through the crowd and into an old-looking car in the corner of the parking lot. But after a second, the mother is out again and heading back to the Cheery Chomper, looking more pissed off than ever. Maybe she forgot something? I will her to hurry up and get it, and get the hell out again, but I lose her in the scrum of my classmates.

Most of them are in the café now, all holding little cups from Carrot Man, some in line for snacks, some sitting at tables. We see Pete hiding in the shop, and Mr. Taylor leaving us on the bus and persuading Carrot Man to give him a whole carton of juice as he enters the Cheery Chomper. Carrot Man follows him inside — clearly the cold has won out — and proceeds to shimmy around the tables and give juice to anyone who was lucky enough to miss out the first time. The waiters get their share, the cooks, everyone. Just like Pete said. We watch Alice head toward the bathrooms, just like she said. So far, their stories check out.

Outside, a car comes into view on the road. It's the Mini again.

"Look!" I point to it. "Why have they come back?"

We watch as the Mini gets closer and closer to our bus. And then it jerks to a stop a few feet behind us. The driver's door opens, a figure gets out. It's the guy. It's difficult to see his face from this far away, but it's clear he's panicked; he looks desperately from the bus to the Cheery Chomper, trying to make a decision. His girlfriend makes it for him; she's getting out of the passenger seat and she looks really pissed. Like staggering and dribbling kind of pissed. The man stumbles through the snow toward the bus, dragging his leg like he's injured, and she comes zombie-ing after. Just as he reaches the door, he pauses and she's on him, wrestling him to the ground. She bites.

"Augh!" the four of us yell in unison, like we couldn't see *that* was coming.

Smitty and I share a look, remembering the pool of red in the snow outside the door. Then the man springs up and rounds the front of the bus, pursued by his beloved.

"The hand on the windshield," I whisper. Smitty nods, silent. We watch the bus shudder as one or both of them get thrown into the side of it. Not kids messing around as we had guessed at the time, but an attack. An attack we could have prevented, had we known what was going on outside? But, of course, how could we?

The man has made it back to the car now. He flings himself into the driver's seat just as his girlfriend reaches the front . . . and just as our driver descends the steps of the bus.

"Monkeyfunster," Smitty says. "I think this is where our driver gets it."

Suddenly the screens go blank and the light above us flickers.

Alice squeals.

"What the — ?" Smitty doesn't finish his sentence. The power cuts out, plunging us into darkness. Alice gives another yelp, there's a *thud*, and Pete cries out, too. I grab at Smitty, and he at me, and for one horrible, desperately embarrassing second we fly into each other's arms like Shaggy and Scooby Don't. I immediately propel myself backward, fall over the box that I was sitting on, and land on something soft, fragrant, and screamy.

The lights come back on. I'm lying on top of Alice. Smitty is standing above us, with an expression on his face like he's just been slimed. Pete has managed to shimmy up the side of the cabinet and is sitting on top of it, shaking like a leaf. We all keep absolutely still, and wait to see what happens. Nothing does.

"Nobody panic," Smitty breathes. "The power goes out all the time in the country. Doesn't mean anything."

"You sure?" I ask.

"Yeah." Smitty smiles down at us. "Yowza. Seeing you two like that reminds me of the dream I had last night." He winks at me.

"Get the hell off me!" Alice pushes me with a strength that belies her skinny frame.

"With pleasure!" I shout, none too brilliantly, scrambling to my feet and avoiding Smitty's gaze. I turn to Pete, cheeks blazing. "So, a power cut, you think?"

"Clearly." He smiles at me and climbs down from his perch. Like he has a right to enjoy my embarrassment; he's the one who leapt onto a cabinet when the lights went out. I guess when you are used to being picked on daily, being discovered crouched and shivering on top of a cabinet—or a toilet—is nothing special.

He looks at the screens. "We're back on, but that's not what we were watching before. The recording has reset."

We all peer, and see ourselves peering. We're in real time again.

"Get it back," Smitty says to Pete. "We were just getting to the good part."

"Aw, shall I get you some popcorn?" Alice is brushing herself down with a vengeance, ready to spit bile at anyone who crosses her.

"Do you think that was the weather?" I ask no one in particular. I really, really want it to have been the weather. Why else would the power suddenly go down? "Should we take a look around?"

"Sure." Smitty's out the door before I can ask twice, and I'm glad that I can stop avoiding meeting his eyes. I think about his arms around me. *Shame Attack.* I think I actually grasped his butt with one of my hands. I stretch the offending hand out like I've touched acid, trying to shed the memory. I hope he doesn't think I did it on purpose. On one of the TV screens I watch him walk normally out the door and then crumple into a cringe, head in hands, as soon as he is out of sight. Except he's not.

I think it takes him a second to realize that we can still see him — and he cringes again. *What?* I can't help thinking angrily, *Was it so very disgusting that I even touched you, Smitty?*

"Maybe it was one of those monsters?"

Alice is talking to me again. I look at her blankly before I realize what she's saying. "You mean you think one of those things cut the power?"

Pete shakes his head. "That's improbable, from what we've seen of them so far. They have basic motor skills, and they seem to be attracted to things that were familiar to them in their former life. But it's quite a leap to suggest that they have the wherewithal to cut the power to the building."

"Yeah. What he said." My head pounds, and I sit carefully on a box. I'm not feeling too hot. But it's best not to mention it under the circs, especially given my previous fainting fit. Don't want anyone jumping to any conclusions. I rub my face with my hands. I must look like a wreck. Yeah, I know I do — I've seen myself on TV. "Anyway, we don't know for sure that there are any more of them out there."

Pete sucks in air through his teeth. "Ah, but we do, don't we? What about that couple? You didn't run into them when you rescued the driver, did you? Where did they go? Where are they now?"

I sigh. "We need to see the rest of the recording."

Pete nods. "Besides them, we can't be sure that everyone in the café followed the bus down to the garage and got vaporized by Smitty." He looks at the TV screens. "And for that matter, where has Gareth got to? I'd say it's highly probable there are more of them out there."

The wind rattles the window. I glance at the screens showing the parking lot. The snow is still whirling, thick and fast.

Alice shivers. "Hopefully they'll freeze to death." She turns to look at us. "Or Undeath. Whatever." She smiles. It's not entirely genuine, but it's a start. I want to return it, but I'm distracted by a movement on one of the TV screens behind her. The entrance of the café. A huge shape moves past the door. I nearly fall backward off my box again.

"What?" Alice says.

The shape has gone. I lean in close to the screen that shows the entrance to the Cheery Chomper. There's nothing there. Besides, Smitty is in the café now, on the other side of the glass — he'd have noticed something outside, wouldn't he?

"What is it?" Alice says.

"I thought I saw something."

Pete stares at me. "I didn't see anything. Which screen?"

I shake my head. "I'm spooked. Imagining stuff." It could have been anything. A plastic bag or a branch. The banner! Yes, that must be it — Carrot Man's banner that was flapping away over the entrance. It must have come loose and blown across the door.

"No bogeymen in sight." Smitty saunters in, coolness restored. "Barricades in place, perimeter maintained. Let's play the rest of the recording before the power cuts off again."

I look at him without, you know, really looking. "You think it's gonna?"

"Could, if this storm keeps up."

I stand. "Then we should prepare. Find some flashlights, or something." I look at my watch; it's three o'clock already, less than an hour before sunset. Time flies when you're having fun. I pick my backpack off the floor. "We should charge our phones, so when we do find somewhere with reception, we can make calls. Maybe we should pack some emergency supplies in case we have to leave here. We've got to start thinking ahead."

"We're leaving here?" Alice says. "And going out into that?" She points to the snowstorm on the TV. "Um, I think not."

"It may not be safe to stay," Pete says. "This is Ground Zero. And who knows what they'll hit us with next?"

"There isn't a *they*!" Smitty yells at him. "It's all in your head, Snowballs!"

"Whatever we think" — I try to calm things down — "we need to be prepared. Get some food together, our warmest clothes, a map. Just in case."

Smitty grits his teeth. "Fine. But we watch the rest of this recording first."

I don't know how much I actually *want* to watch the replay, but we're halfway through and if nothing else, I hate to walk out on a movie before it's done. I toss my backpack under the desk and sit myself back down next to Smitty, being ultra careful that no part of my body touches his. Pete resumes his position by the PLAY button. Alice rolls her eyes and makes a big deal out of pulling herself off the couch.

"All right," she says. "We'll watch. But let's at least get some daylight in here while we still have it, so if the power goes off again I'm not squashed by Nelly the Elephant fainting in the dark." She flicks me a look. I return it. She stands with her back to the window, reaches out a hand for the blind, and pulls it. The blind springs up. Daylight floods the room.

I see the dark shape behind her and my face stretches into a scream.

"What now?" Alice stares at me, pissed off.

Carrot Man is standing at the window.

13

I jump to my feet. There's screaming. I don't just hear it, I feel it; it slices through my ears and into my brain. Shrill beyond all measure. At first I think it's me screaming — my mouth is open and my throat is clenched, so it might be — then I realize it's Pete. He's seen what I see. Smitty, too. In fact, the only person who hasn't seen it is Alice.

She stands there facing us, pouting and still holding the cord. Then there's the flicker of confusion, and finally the terror of realization that we're not screaming at *her*.

It's behind you.

She doesn't turn to look, just propels herself forward instinctively. As she leaps, she drops the string of the blind, which clatters down over the window again. She slams into me — and Smitty, who is standing behind me — and we fall to the ground like human dominoes.

Pete is still screaming. Before I know how, I'm on my feet again and all four of us stand squashed together against the back wall — as far from the window and Carrot Man as possible. We all stare at the closed blind.

"What. Is. It," Alice rasps beside me.

Nobody answers her. We're all staring at the blind, which is swinging gently. At any moment glass could shatter and IT will be in the room with us.

"What—" she tries again, louder now.

"Carrot Man," Smitty whispers sharply from my other side. "Don't make a sound."

"Yeah, 'cause we were so quiet before." I can't help myself. Smitty gives a low snort, and I feel the thin wall gently shudder.

The blind stops swinging. I stare at the strips of white plastic with the tiniest creases of bright light between them, and wish for X-ray eyes.

"Think he's gone?" Pete wheezes.

"Want to go and check?" Smitty turns his head, raising his eyebrows invitingly. When Pete says nothing, Smitty winks at me. I feel his body begin to peel away from the wall.

"Don't!" I shoot out an arm to stop him, my fist balled tight so I can't accidentally grab a body part. "Don't you dare."

"Someone has to check." He stays in place on the wall regardless. I can feel him smiling at me provocatively, but refuse to meet his eyes.

"Wait a minute," Alice says beside me. "We don't know Carrot Man's bad, do we?"

"I think the fact that he was handing out the killer fruit juice is pretty conclusive," Pete gabbles.

"Vegetable juice, not fruit," I say, like this makes a diff. "Maybe he didn't know what was in it? Maybe he's freezing to death out there and needs our help?"

"If he didn't know what was in it, he probably drank it," Smitty says logically.

"Either way, he's hardly one of the good guys." Pete out-logics Smitty's logic.

"People!" Alice hisses. "I can't believe we're standing here even talking about this! We need to get out of here."

Pete steps away from the wall. "I think he's gone."

"Why?" Smitty takes a step, too.

Pete squints. "The light behind the blinds. Something changed."

I frown. "I didn't see it."

He nods his head. "See the light along the windowsill? A shadow moved along it." He takes another step toward the window.

"No." I ease myself off the wall, but stay rooted to the spot. "I was watching, too. I didn't see it."

"Don't touch that blind!" Alice begs, and as she does, the lights flicker again, then extinguish, plunging us into darkness once more.

Before we can react, glass smashes and the blind bulges into the room, light escaping around the sides. Out of the corner of my eye I see Smitty — lit momentarily by daylight — lunging for Alice's knife on the table as a huge killer root vegetable crashes onto the floor in front of the window.

"Come on!" I cry, seeing the shadow of my backpack under the desk, diving for it, and scrabbling to my feet again. In the dim half-light I can see that Alice and Pete are already through the office door into the café, and the knife-wielding Smitty is in a ninja squat a few feet from the writhing mound on the floor.

"Smitty!" I shout, not wanting to leave him. Then suddenly he's ahead of me, on the chair that we wedged in the doorway, his hand shooting out to grab mine, dragging me out of the room. We run blindly through the café toward the entrance. Alice is screaming and Pete is trying to pull down the barricade at the door. We pile into it, Smitty and me, frantically grabbing at the furniture and boxes we so carefully slotted together to make an impenetrable barrier. We never thought we might have to fight through it ourselves.

"Hurry!" Alice is screaming still, which is not exactly helping, apart from being a gauge of how much longer we have before Carrot Man gets here. Her shrieks suddenly multiply a gazillion times, and I know The Furry One has made an appearance at the office doorway.

"Just this last one!" Smitty yells, and Pete and I help him yank a large crate of water bottles away from the exit. As we do, the crate spills and bottles roll out onto the floor. I see Alice take a step backward, and can only watch as a bottle rolls under her foot with immaculate timing. Her legs fly up into the air, she falls back onto her head with a *thwack*, and she stays there. As I feel the blast of icy air that means Smitty has got the door open at last, I run to Alice and pull her by the arms to the exit.

The Carrot Man is here, and we have to go.

Smitty scoops Alice up and throws her over his shoulder with sudden and shocking Herculean strength, and we're out of the door. I glance back. Carrot Man's arms swing up in front of him. The eyeholes in his costume are cast into shadow. His green carrot leaf gloves are gone, and his hands are dripping with blood. He groans and takes a heavy step forward.

He's one of them.

Pete has managed to get the bus door open, and we scramble on board. Our sanctuary once more.

"Start it up!" yells Smitty, bounding up the steps with Alice's head bobbing over his shoulder.

"What do you think I'm doing?" Pete yells back. He's in the driver's seat, fumbling with the keys, and I thank all the angels that he remem-bered to pocket them when we made our exit. Who knows what we've left behind in the Cheery Chomper — water, food? No time to think about that now.

The engine starts with a sputter. Smitty hauls Alice unceremoniously down the aisle and dumps her in a seat, shouting at me, "Guard the door!"

Grrreat. Human shield time again. I race past Pete, who is wrestling the unresponsive steering wheel, and make my legs skibble down the steps. I fling myself against the frickin' door, arms and legs spread like I'm dancing a tango with it. Bang on cue, there's Carrot Man, the whole force of seven feet of orange plushy vegetable slamming itself against the doors with such a ferocity I want to weep. The sheer weight of him throws me off balance. The door shudders.

"Hurry!" I cry. *Please hurry, Pete, please hurry, Smitty, please hurry, the armed forces who are — please God — going to sweep down with weapons of mass destruction and save us . . .*

Carrot Man slams again. I press my shoulders and my arms and my butt and my legs across the door, bracing for the next impact, hoping the glass and metal and my spine and nerve will hold out.

"Why aren't we moving?!" I scream up at Pete. He looks like a kid sitting on a coin-operated car ride outside a supermarket, wildly spinning the steering wheel, jumping up and down in the seat, and going precisely nowhere.

"The snow's too deep, there's no traction!"

I feel the wheels turning underneath us as Pete stamps on the gas. "Smitty!" I yell as Carrot Man thumps into my back again. "I need help!"

"Here." Smitty appears at the top of the steps with a snowboard. He tosses it down to me and I catch it, swing around, and slot it across the doors. "And another." Smitty throws down a second board, and I fix it in place beneath the first one. It works. Carrot Man senses the door is not going to open, and he moves to the windshield and starts bashing on that instead. *Stupid orange meanie.* I wedge myself against a step and brace the bottom board with my feet.

Pete frantically thrusts the gear stick in a different direction and the wheels roar beneath me. But still we don't move.

"Cack." Smitty is still standing at the top of the steps but is staring out of one of the side windows. "Carrot Man's got company."

"What?!"

Smitty's face contorts into a horrible grin. "Heeeeere's Gareth!"

"No!" I run up the steps and look in the same direction. There, coming around the corner of the Cheery Chomper, is Gareth. Black pants, white shirt, tie, and name tag, and a grotesque gobbling face. And you know what? He's still holding the laptop . . . but it takes me a moment to realize he only has one proper arm. There's a stump coming out of the other shirt sleeve, a stump with a long, white piece of bone, as if something nibbled off the flesh like corn off the cob. I feel the sting of a sob clenching my throat.

"He never made it," I mutter.

"No," Smitty says quietly. "But he made some friends."

I look through the snow. Shuffling figures—four or five, possibly more—are coming this way.

"Pete!" Screaming, I turn to him. "Get us out of here!"

Something finally catches and the bus pulls forward slowly, gently nudging Carrot Man to one side.

"Hang on!" Pete shouts. "I won't be able to brake!"

There's a sharp smell of burning rubber, and I cling to my seat as Pete guides the bus through the snow. There's no real way to know if we're on the road or not, but as long as we keep going, there's no reason to care.

"Head for the exit!" shouts Smitty, pointing to the road that leads away from the Cheery Chomper and back into the wilds of the Scottish countryside. "It's our only chance!" His words hang in the air, strangely overdramatic, although if there was ever a time to shout something like that, it would be now. He moves to the back of the bus, looking out to see how quickly we're being chased. I follow.

I press my face against the window and stare out at Carrot Man leading the charge across the parking lot. Well, more of a shamble than a charge. The bus is moving slowly on the snow, but they won't catch us so long as we keep on truckin'.

Shit. Nothing in the tank.

I shake the thought away. The bus started, didn't it? Even if we only get a couple of miles, it will still be enough to outrun them. Glancing at the back of Pete's head, I can see he's as stressed as hell, shoulders up around his ears. But he's not hyperventilating, and he's wrangling the wheel like he knows what he's doing. He keeps this up, we're golden.

I stare out at Gareth and his new companions. "Who are the others?"

Smitty has found the binoculars. "Remember the couple in the Mini? And three blokes. At least, I think that one's a bloke . . . oh, no. There's a boob hanging out."

"Where did they come from? And where's Gareth been all this time? Do you think they got him when he went to the Cheery Chomper?" I rant. "Why didn't we see them before now?"

"Won't ever know," Smitty says. "Might have got some answers if we'd seen the end of that recording, but now —"

The bus screeches to a halt; I bang my face against the window. Pain and the indignation of a bashed-up nose sweep through me. Tears prick my eyes as my nose burns. I feel to see if it's still there, and my hand comes away covered in blood.

"What gives?!"

Shouting, Smitty runs up the aisle to Pete. I gather myself. *Don't cry, you're still in one piece.* At the front of the bus, they're yelling at each other. I hear a clatter, and the unmistakable hiss of the doors opening. I spring up from my seat and head for the front, nose trauma forgotten. Hot blood drips down my face and splashes on my coat. Pete stands alone by the steps. By the look on his face I know what's happened.

"Smitty's gone out?"

He nods.

"Why did you stop?"

"That." He points.

Through the windshield I see a big white lump across the road. At first I can't tell what it is, then I realize the lump has branches and roots. A tree has fallen across the road, blocking our way out. Smitty is furiously running around it like an ant, digging away at the edges with his board, leaning into the trunk with his shoulder, trying to push it, lever it, roll it. There's no way he'll succeed; ten people couldn't move a tree that size. You'd have to have chains and a tractor and a good thirty minutes to clear the road before the monsters came. None of which we have.

I shoot a glance back at our pursuers. We have a couple of minutes, tops.

I jump down the steps, Pete behind me. "It's no use!" I shout at Smitty. "Can we go around it?"

Pete picks his way through the snow to the root end of the trunk. The base of the tree on its side is almost the same height as he is. I know the answer before he gives it. The road is raised, with a ditch on either side, and the tree line is only a few feet from the road.

"No way." Pete bends low. "Besides, they put it here."

"What?" Smitty's face is red and steaming.

"Look, no hole where the roots were." He scuffs his boot on the snow. "This tree didn't fall; it was never growing here. It was moved, probably seconds after our bus arrived. Placed here to stop us from leaving. The couple in the Mini? This is why they came back: They couldn't get out."

For a moment I think Smitty is going to try his snowboard decapitation trick on Pete. Then he flings the board down and stomps back onto the bus.

"We need to go," I urge them. "Walk out on the main road, take our chances."

"Maybe not!" Smitty shouts from the bus.

"We'll get back on board!" Pete cries. "It's safe enough there!"

I dodge round the side of the bus. Carrot Man, Gareth, and the rest are almost on the exit road. In a minute, they'll be with us. "No way." I grab the snowboard from Pete's feet. "There are seven of them. Adults. They'll break through those doors and it'll be suppertime."

"What if we hide in the hold?" Pete's face is stricken. He's begging me, and I don't know if I want to hug him or slap him.

"For how long?" I shake my head. "We hit the highway, we keep moving. They can't outrun us."

"What about Alice?"

Damn. I forgot about Alice and her lack of consciousness.

"We'll work something out." I pull him toward the doors. "Come on! We have to gather our stuff, we don't have any time." As I reach the doors, the bus engine cranks up. Smitty's at the wheel. We leap out of the way back into the snow as the bus reverses, engine revving violently.

"No!" Pete and I cry, both knowing what's coming next.

Smitty pays no heed. He plows forward and rams the bus into the tree as hard as he can. The tree hardly moves. Smitty reverses the bus with its beaten-up fender again, and tries a second time. This time the tree shifts a little. Thinking he's on to something, Smitty reverses farther still and goes for third time lucky, hitting the tree with full force. The back of the bus skids and jackknifes, there's a shattering sound, and the windshield cracks and falls away. Smoke rises from the front of the bus.

Our sanctuary on wheels has finally met its match.

I jump on board. "We *have* to *leave*!" I shout at Smitty, who is still gripping the wheel. "I'll get your stuff, you get Alice!"

I throw our backpacks out into the snow and head to row 21 to fetch some gear. If we can somehow pull Alice along on a board, or use skis to carry her . . .

I glance outside; they're almost with us. We have seconds. I load up and begin back up the aisle. Smitty has moved Alice; we can make it.

The floor lifts up in front of me. Someone is coming out of the hatch. I stop in my tracks.

A small blond head pops out. A boy, not more than three years old, I'd guess. Then a second blond head. A girl, a couple of years older than me. For a second I wonder how I know them. Then it comes to me. The moody teenage girl in the café and her little brother. I raise a ski pole and brace myself to attack.

"Hi! Have we crashed?" The girl speaks with a lilting Scottish accent. "Are they here?"

"Bumped my head," the boy says.

I lower my ski pole.

The girl takes a good look at me and her face changes. "You're . . . you're not one of them, are you?"

I wipe at my face with my sleeve. "Just a nosebleed. And yes, they're here. We have to go. Now."

14

As I climb out of the bus with the two stowaways, Smitty's and Pete's faces are an absolute picture. It's a classic moment; I wish I had time to savor it. Pete actually does a double take, then kind of scuffles and falls into the ditch. The boy giggles, and his sister shushes him.

"Who the f—" Smitty starts.

"It's OK," I say. "They're not infected."

"You sure of that?" Smitty recovers quickly; he's fixing Alice's floppy feet to a snowboard.

Pete picks himself up off the ground, still staring. "You were hiding on the bus? Where did you come from?"

"I'm Lily," the girl says. "This is my brother, Cam. We were in the café, but then we went out—"

There's an ominous groan from the end of the bus. They're here.

"Great to meet you, stories later," Smitty grimaces, tightening the fastenings over Alice's feet. "We have to move. Malice is not home, but we can pull her along." He hauls her to her feet and flings one of her arms over his shoulder. "Muscle up, Pete, and take her other arm. She's heavier than she looks."

"Oh my god!" Lily screams as Gareth appears around the side of the bus.

I reach down and swipe up Cam, blood from my nose gushing onto his poor little face. Lily snatches him from me as he begins to wail, and they run through the snow to the other side of the tree trunk. Gareth looks really, really annoyed. Maybe he's got a nicotine crave on. That must really suck: being a zombie who can't get a smoke.

Two men appear behind him, staggering forward, drooling and groaning. One is wearing a torn, blood-spattered white shirt and checkered trousers, topped off with a little paper hat. The other guy looks like a builder; he's wearing the remains of denim overalls and a tool belt. Together they make me think of LEGO figures. "Here's LEGO Zombie Chef! Here's LEGO Zombie Builder! See their grasping hands and posable limbs!"

"Roberta, are you coming?"

Smitty's shouting shakes me into reality. I hitch on my backpack and hike another couple of bags over one shoulder, grab a snowboard, and scramble into the ditch and around the tree. Smitty and Pete are handling Alice-on-a-board just fine, but it's up to me to haul all of our bags. I throw the board down, stuff one foot in the bindings, and push off. I'm no natural boarder, but it's not like there's time to don boots and skis.

It's a chase scene in slo-mo, like one of those dreams where you try to run but can't. The snow is not too deep, but there's thick ice below it. We move as fast as we can — which is not very fast, just enough to keep the motley crew behind at a distance. Lily leads the way on foot with Cam on her back. The moaning behind us is louder — clearly *they* don't like finding an obstacle in their way, either — but I don't look around. *Keep going and they can't catch you.*

It's getting darker and it is mercilessly cold. At the back of my mind is a nagging realization that if we don't find shelter, the cold may well finish us off before the monsters do. I can see the junction leading out onto the main road. I push myself off and glide past the girl and her brother. *Please god, don't let me wipe out—Smitty will never let me forget it.* I reach the junction in no great style and try to remember which way we turned in — and did we pass through any villages before we got here? To the left is silent road and trees, to the right is the same, but leading up a steep hill. I'm stunned at my own lack of observation. I have absolutely no memory of what came before the Cheery Chomper. Luckily, I don't have to remember.

"Turn right!" the girl shouts. "We live up there."

"There's a town?" I ask as she reaches me, panting.

She shakes her head. "It's a wee village, really. But we'll be safe in our house, and there's a phone."

"How far?" Smitty and Pete have caught up.

The girl shrugs. "A couple of minutes in the car."

Smitty makes a face. "Lucky I brought my Ferrari."

She stares at him. "Maybe a mile or something?"

I can see Pete begin to wilt.

"That's nothing." I force a smile. "What, twenty minutes on foot? We can get there before it's totally dark."

"Dragging Alice?" Pete begins to shake. "Up that hill? With them behind us?"

I look behind me. They're still coming: the LEGO men, Booby Woman, the couple, and Gareth. All bar Carrot Man. Something tells me he's probably rolling around in a ditch.

"Look how slow they are, man!" Smitty says. "We keep going, they'll never catch us."

So we start up the road. I focus on the brow of the hill. The horizon undulates ahead of me, the trees leaning in on each other over the road, the road appearing to move as if I'm on an endless white treadmill. I fix my gaze on it, willing it closer. And then it does move.

I stop. We all do.

Smitty looks up the hill and frowns.

"What's wrong?" Pete asks, nervously looking behind us.

Our pursuers haven't made it onto the main road.

Smitty raises a hand. "Listen."

We strain our ears. There is *something*. Something is off. It's almost as if the pressure's changed, like when you're on a plane and your ears pop and you start hearing things in a different key. It's a hum, so low and constant that we didn't notice it creeping in at first.

"A car!" Pete says, elated.

A truck, maybe. Or a tractor. Something grittier than a car. And it's coming toward us from the direction of the hilltop. My mind races as I imagine truckloads of soldiers coming into view. I've never been one for boys in uniform, but I might be rapidly changing my mind on that one.

"Stay frosty, people," says Smitty, but I can hear the hope in his voice.

"They're coming," Alice moans, her head lolling on Smitty's shoulder.

"Hey, Malice!" Smitty says to her, almost affectionately. "Way to time waking up! Bang on, old girl!" He kisses her head, and a shameful little part of me dies somewhere deep inside. "Lean yourself against Uncle Pete for a mo', 'kay?" He practically throws her onto Pete, and starts to stride up the hill. "Woo-hoo! Here we are!" he calls.

Then he stops. And at the same moment, I realize why.

The gray blur on the horizon sharpens into focus just as the noise does. No trucks, no tractors, no military men to whisk us away to safety, but hundreds of stumbling shapes, growling and groaning and grumbling.

An army of monsters.

Lily lets out a strangled half gasp.

"Scaredy Lily?" Cam mumbles into her shoulder.

"What do we do?" Pete whispers. His head whips from up the hill to down, where Gareth and his cutie coterie have started up the incline toward us, slow but relentless.

"Don't panic," I say, which must go down in history as the All Time Lamest Comment Ever. We instinctively back into the tree line, dragging Alice with us. Smitty is still transfixed by the hordes.

"We have to go back," I say. And once I've made the decision, Pete's throwing himself down the hill at speed, leaving me to prop up semi-conscious Alice. Lily follows with Cam. "Smitty!" I yell. He's still staring up the hill at the oncoming masses. "Some help here!"

He looks back at me, utterly crestfallen. My heart breaks a little; I feel it, too.

The Gareth Posse are now walking in a line, shoulder to shoulder, across the road. Must be some kind of hunting instinct. Lily falters and turns to shout up at me. "We can cut into the woods!" She points. "Find a way up the hill to get to the village!"

I shake my head. "We're faster on the road. And newsflash," I add cruelly, "your village is infected. There's no point heading there."

"But what about — ?" She thrusts out a hand to the six who are cutting our way off, her face desperate and crumpled.

"We can get past them!" I struggle down the hill, sliding Alice on the board, and yes, she is heavier than she looks. There's a dark red mat of hair at the back of her blond head. All things considered, it's amazing she's still standing. Then Smitty's there, taking Alice's other arm, his eyes wild and his breath heavy. I look at him and swallow hard. "Take my board. Whiz down the road and do your thing. We need you to distract them while we get Alice and the kid past."

He doesn't need telling twice. In fact, he's almost too fast, already nearly down at the bottom of the hill before I can catch my breath. He buzzes Gareth, making him fall over on the hard ground, before doubling back and taking out the legs of Booby Woman.

"Quick!" I tell the others. "Get down the hill as fast as you can."

Alice shrugs me off. It's as if she's drunk. She kicks her feet free, sits on the snowboard like it's a sled, and before I can stop her, lies back and pushes off. The board flies down the bank. But she can't control it, and as she leans and banks sharply left, she wipes out LEGO Zombie Chef.

"Go, Malice!" yells Smitty as he dodges past Gareth again. "Zombie Luge Bowling!"

It hasn't done much for her concussion, though. She falls off the board into some soft snow by the tree line. Pete, Lily and Cam, and I hurry down the hill on the other side — as LEGO Zombie Builder stumbles toward her.

But Smitty's on it. He pushes his board into action, and reaches her before LEGO Builder can. He pulls her up in front of him, and they ride his board in tandem, like some kind of weird ballet.

We're past them. I look back up the hill. The growling legions are still advancing, but they don't have snowboards, or brains, or even fully functioning legs. As they emerge out of the shadows, I can see young kids and grannies, and probably the mailman and the guy who came to fix the frozen pipes. How did they all turn? Did they get the evil Veggie Juice, or were they bitten? And how are there so many of them? Is this everywhere? Where will we be safe?

I run clumsily after the others. Alice is walking now, occasionally shooting out a hand to steady herself on Pete's arm. Now I know she must be concussed — there's no way she'd consciously touch him if she wasn't. Smitty is trailblazing to who knows where. The road ahead gives no clues.

Full-on dark now. If it wasn't for the snow and a sliver of moon, we'd be totally screwed. We could be heading from the frying pan into the fire, for all we know . . . but hey. Anywhere but here is fine with me, and if we stick to the road there's always the chance we'll meet some more live, non-monstery people — preferably with vehicles and big guns.

Soon we'll be out of the zoms' sight. I wonder if they can track us, or if they only chase what they can see or hear.

I catch up with the others. They're having a discussion about where we're headed.

"So, is it near?" Smitty is — typically — striding ahead, the board now tucked under his arm.

"I said I don't know," Lily says, exasperated.

"Actually you said you 'dinny ken'!" shouts Smitty. "And unless he's *Ken*" — he points to her brother — "I don't have a clue what you're on about."

"Me neither," I say. "What are we looking for?"

Lily turns to me, breathing heavily as she struggles to keep walking with Cam on her back. "There's a village — or a small town, I think — a few miles away. I don't know how far because we only moved here a few weeks ago."

"Great!" Smitty blusters. "The only survivors we find haven't got a clue where the hell they are, either!"

"Here!" Pete shouts at us from the side of the road. "This way!"

We rush over to where he's brushing snow off a brown signpost pointing left. On it is a little picture of what looks like a chess piece and the words 1 MILE.

"It's a castle!" he says, triumphant.

"So?" says Smitty.

"Fortification." Pete's eyes gleam.

Smitty frowns at him. "Wuh?"

"Thick stone walls. Big wooden doors with solid locks. Little windows. And weapons, Smitty, weapons."

"Where is it?" Smitty's decided.

"Wait!" I say. "What about sticking to the road in case there's someone looking for us? And what about this village or town that might be a couple of miles away?"

"*Might* be," says Pete. "Bobby, it's cold, it's dark, we've had kind of a big day —"

"They must have a phone!" says Lily, jumping ship. "And something to eat."

There's a *thump* a few feet behind us.

Alice has fallen headlong into the snow; she can go no farther.

"Castle it is, then," I say.

Smitty and Pete gather her up. The turnoff is a single car-width of virgin snow.

I pause. "What if they can see our footprints?"

"More likely smell that trail of blood you're leaving," Smitty says.

My hand goes up to my nose. It's started dripping again. "They're not sharks, Smitty," I say snippily. "For all we know, it's your rancid feet they're attracted to."

We tramp down the lane in silence, Smitty and Pete sliding Alice on Smitty's board this time, me feeling like a packhorse with all of our bags. The trees block out the sky in places. I feel like we're trespassing, and that any minute now something is going to jump out of the darkness.

It doesn't.

Every one of us keeps stealing a glance behind, hoping not to see we're being followed. After a couple of times, it becomes a joke — let's see who can hold out the longest without checking. But fate is kind, and it seems like we might have given them the slip. The adrenaline of the chase has gone now. I'm cold and exhausted.

Finally the lane bends sharply, revealing a black mass against a glittering background. A castle and a frozen loch.

And there's a light on.

15

"There's a light," sings Smitty, "over at the Frankenstein place . . ."

We're standing at the castle gates. Most of us are standing, anyway. Alice has collapsed onto her knees, and we're too tired to pick her up. Smitty is the only one left with any energy: Manic, with a side of Musical Theater. He has been singing all the way down the lane since we spied the castle; at first it was kind of funny and creepy, now it's just plain annoying. The wind is picking up and my un-gloved fingers are threatening to drop off. The straps of all the bags are cutting through my shoulders like the thinnest of ribbons. I clamp my hands under my armpits and look up at what has stopped us.

The gates are high, with a heap of heavy chain wrapped around them like a snake, and a big ol' padlock. Whoever is in the castle is not at home for visitors. The light that led us here is from a ground-floor window next to a huge, dark doorway that I can barely see. One light on, and one only.

I look around for some kind of entry phone on the gates, but this is Scotland, not Beverly Hills. At the risk of losing my skin, I shake the gates of freezing metal, but they barely move. They're made of elaborate wrought iron with no easy foot- or handholds, and are attached to an equally high brick wall, which Smitty has already tried to bounce over, Tigger-stylee.

"Do you think we can get in around the back?" I ask.

"Wouldn't that defeat the point of having high walls?" Pete snaps.

"Why don't we shout?" Lily says. "Whoever is in there will come and let us in."

"No shouting!" Pete almost breaks his own rule, nervously glancing behind us. "For all we know, the hordes are close by."

"Why . . . don't we go in through the gates?" Alice slurs. She has dragged herself up and is leaning against one of them. She fiddles with the padlock and slowly unwinds the thick chain, which slithers to the ground with a muffled *thud*.

"How the hell . . . ?" Pete stutters.

"Malice?" Smitty says. "Did you pick the lock with a nail file?"

Alice makes a snarky face. "The padlock wasn't closed, you wanger." She holds it up in her hand.

We stare in silence. It has come to this. It takes the girl with the concussion to see what's right in front of our noses.

"I dunno," she mumbles. "Sometimes you losers like making things more complicated for yourselves."

Smitty lets out a peal of laughter and claps Alice on the back as he pulls the gates open.

Everyone is buoyed by our success, and once we've rewrapped the chain around the gate behind us, we hurry with newly strong legs over the expanse of snow that separates us from the castle door.

The dark hulk of the castle crouches above us, the light from the single window casting an orange glow at our feet. We climb a few shallow steps up to the door. The window is too high to see in; there's no curtain, but the glass is latticed with thin strips of lead. Not exactly prison bars, but way better than we could have hoped for. If we get in, there ain't no way any Undead are gonna follow without some kind of missile launchers, and I haven't seen them pull that particular trick just yet.

Smitty tries the huge, round handle. It's obviously just for show.

"Maybe we should ring the bell first?" I point to a discreet metal buzzer to the side of the door. "We don't want to scare whoever's in there."

Alice is already leaning on it. We wait, straining to hear approaching steps. Smitty presses his ear to the door.

"This is where the mad axman who lives here slices me through the face from the other side of the door." He grins at me.

"Don't," I say. Seriously, it could absolutely happen today.

Smitty tries banging on the door instead. Alice sinks to the ground again, little Cam starts to whine in his sister's arms, and Pete casts more freaked-out looks in the direction of the lane. But nobody comes to the door.

"So we go in the back." Smitty is already walking away.

"No!" Lily calls out. She puts Cam down and gets a plastic bag out of her pocket, lays it on the snow-covered step, and sits. "We've gone far enough. You go round the back. When you find a way, come and let us in, aye?"

Smitty is fine with that. Alice and Pete are more than fine. I hover between the two camps: part of me wanting to stay put, the other not wanting Smitty to go alone. But my pause for thought is enough to ensure he slips off into the darkness without me. *I'll wait five minutes,* I think, *then I'll go after him.*

The wind has dropped. As I sit on the step between Alice and Lily, something tickles me on the nose. I look up; it's snowing again. Just a few flakes.

"No," moans Alice. "Like we need some more of that stuff."

Cam begins to cry and squirm on Lily's lap. "Hey now, laddie," she says to him softly. "Any minute now we'll be cozy inside with a canny roaring fire to sit beside." He clings to her and she breathes onto his blond head. "We can make toast," she continues. "You'd like that, wouldn't you? Make some toast on the fire like we did at Christmas?" she says. The boy nods. "Who knows? They might have marshmallows in there, an' all."

I'm kind of dubious about her giving it the big buildup, but for now it seems to be working. Cam's excited by the marshmallows idea. He squirms out of his sister's lap and stands at the bottom of the steps, grinning.

"So, show me how you're going to toast marshmallows like a big boy, then?" Lily says.

He holds out his hand like he's got a fork, bending his knees and leaning toward us like we're the fire. It's too cute for words. Everyone laughs, even Pete.

"Watch out!" Lily says, her fingers wiggling like they're flames. "The fire's getting higher!" Her hands move toward him. "Don't get burnt!"

With a squeal of delight he snatches away the imaginary fork before her fingers can get too close. I raise my hands, too; the fire just got bigger. He does the same trick on me, and I leave it until a little longer before the flames rise, to make the joke better. He takes a couple of steps backward into the snow, which is almost waist deep on him. Then it's Alice's turn, and when she reaches for him, he retreats farther still, picking his way through our footprints, through the falling snow, his little legs working hard.

"Careful now!" Lily warns, but there's no real worry in her voice. It's soft snow. He can't go far and he can't hurt himself if he falls.

As if to prove the point, he does exactly that as he tries to return to the steps. He's on his back, swimming in a sea of the white stuff, giggling his head off. We laugh, too, and I wonder at how Cam can be running for his life one moment, then playing without a care the next.

"He's a sweetie." I turn to Lily. "Have you got any more brothers and sisters?"

"Just him." She smiles at me. "He's a right pain at times. You obviously don't have a younger brother, or you'd know."

"No, it's just me," I say.

Her face hardens. "Yeah, it's just us two now. Mam was in the café . . ."

"I know," I say. "I'm really sorry."

"Since we moved here she used to take him there every Saturday because he liked the milk shakes," she says quietly. "That's what we were doing there." She shakes her head. "She said it could be our new family tradition."

"So where had you been hiding all this time?" I ask gently. "You and Cam were in the car, weren't you? And your mum went back in. What happened?"

Lily exhales loudly, staring out into the dark, and I see her eyes water.

"We argued. Last thing I told her was that she was stupid to bring us here."

"So what happened?"

"She'd left her scarf in the café. Dad gave it to her last Christmas. I told her she should just leave it — like Dad left us — but she went back."

"I'm sorry," I say again. "And then?"

Lily pauses, checking to see if her brother is listening. But he's still playing in the snow, building a little nest around himself.

"Cam was crying. I turned up the radio really loud, shut my eyes, waited. When she didn't come back, I thought she was making a point. Wanted us to come after her or something. The car heater was on; I must have dozed off. The next thing I knew, the garage was exploding, and your bus was disappearing up the hill."

"Did you stay in the car all night?" Alice is incredulous.

"No," Lily says. "We went into the café, looked for Mam. Then we met one of those . . . things, and hid in a cupboard for the night. It was scratching at the door for hours, then it just gave up and went away. In the morning we went back to the car and tried to start it, but it wouldn't. I saw you come back in the bus. Thought if we hid on it, you would drive us out of there."

"And you left the bus door open," I say. "Smitty and I thought it was the zoms."

"We were in the hold all along." Lily almost smiles. "Didn't want to come out, in case you chucked us off again."

"You were brave." I try to sound reassuring. "You took care of Cam."

Lily shakes her head. "Should never have been at the café in the first place. Crap milk shakes in a crap café."

"Your village was totally infected, by the looks of things," Pete interjects. "If it makes you feel any better, you probably all would have bought it if you'd stayed at home."

"Pete!" I gasp.

"Shut up!" Lily scrambles to her feet, incensed. "Cam!" she calls. "Come here, now!" She turns to Pete. "You should watch your tongue, or I'll slap your stupid face!" she spits. "Don't you ever be saying things like that again around me or my brother, do you hear me?" She glances in the direction of the little boy again. "Come here, Cam! Now!"

"Doggy," says Cam, from the snow.

"I'm sorry." Pete is on his feet, too. "I was just trying to be realistic. I thought it would help."

"Well, it doesn't," Lily says. "Cam! Here, now!"

"Doggy," says Cam again. "Here, Doggy-Doggy!"

We all turn to look.

Cam is sitting in his nest of snow. And a few feet away is a large, black, snarling dog.

16

Lily half gasps, half yelps, and I instinctively shoot out an arm to stop her from dashing to Cam. He holds out a stubby hand and wiggles his fingers, as if offering to tickle Doggy under the chinny chin chin.

"Cam!" Lily shouts. "Keep still!"

Drool is running from the dog's chops.

"Shit," says Pete. "Is it infected?"

"Even if it's not, it's angry." I look for our stuff. Two boards lie at the base of the steps, but if I make move for one of them, the dog might attack.

"Do something!" Alice is cowering behind me.

Looks like Cam is beginning to feel cold and wet in his snow-nest, and maybe he's sensing the dog isn't too keen on becoming best friends. He begins to grizzle and twist around, looking back to us and holding up his arms to Lily, asking to be picked up. The dog doesn't like this, and begins to bark. As Cam flops onto all fours, the dog pounces toward him, stopping just short of Cam's nest.

"Hey, Rover!"

Before I know what I'm doing, I've leapt down the steps into the snow and am striding away from the castle as fast as I can. I clap my hands. "Here, boy!"

The dog backs off Cam and skitters around in a tight circle as if chasing its tail. It *is* acting kind of crazy. And lucky for me, I have its full attention now. It flattens its ears and runs a larger circle around me. Out of the corner of my eye I see Lily scoop up Cam, and Pete and Alice go for the boards. They flatten themselves against the door and start banging on it, calling for Smitty. The dog keeps running around me, as if it's herding up a flock of sheep. The snarling has stopped, but the crazy hasn't. I don't notice anyone stepping up to create a diversion so that *I* can get away. Now it's just me and the Hound of the Baskervilles.

There's a creaking sound from the direction of the castle. I see the door open and Pete, Alice, Lily, and Cam practically fall inside. Smitty appears in the doorway, confusion writ large on his face.

"What are you doing?" He stares at me, then spots the dog. "Oh, hello again, old chap! That's where you got to." He bends down and claps his hands. The dog stops running, pricks up its ears, and wags its tail. Without so much as a glance at me, it trots inside, barely pausing for a pat on the head from Smitty.

"Problem?" Smitty smiles at me.

"Not at all." I hurry toward him. "Except that dog wants to munch on Cam." I quickly move past him and into the castle. Alice, Lily, and Cam are hiding behind the door. Pete stands in the middle of a large, dark hall.

"The dog went in there." Pete points to the room where the light had been coming from. He gives a lopsided and proud smile. "I shut the door."

"Thank God." Lily shudders. "He was going to attack."

"Nah . . . soft old mutt like that?" Smitty says. "Probably just doesn't like little kids. Lots of dogs don't, and who can blame them, frankly? Anyway, his bed's in there, he probably just wants some shut-eye." He feels around on the wall. "Must be a light switch here somewhere."

"You took your time," I mutter. "Couldn't resist checking out the entire castle before you bothered to see if we were freezing to death — or worse?"

Smitty pouts at me, his eyes twinkling in spite of the gloom. "Only the ground floor. For everybody's safety."

If someone was going to appear, they would have appeared by now, I figure. We've made enough noise.

"How did you get in?" Pete asks Smitty.

"By cunning and ingenuity," he says. "And the back door. It wasn't locked, either. People who live in the country do the craziest things."

"Got it." Alice hits the lights, and we all gasp.

We're standing on a polished dark wood floor and the light is coming from a trio of crystal chandeliers that hang from the high ceiling. In front of us is a sweeping staircase, and on the walls hang faded tapestries of birds and dogs and horses. There are bookshelves and dressers and sideboards. Little statues and big statues. One of those old-fashioned bikes with one big wheel and one little one. And a huge globe of the world, the countries painted in yellows and greens, the sea a deep and stormy purple. Cam runs to it and pushes it, giggling. The colors blend into one as it spins.

"Careful," Lily says quietly.

It's like a movie set. You could have the best parties here.

"Oh my Goth," Alice says, pointing. "It's a coffin."

We move toward it. It's tall and black, standing on its end against the wall underneath the staircase. There's a glass square on the lid.

"A window!" says Alice. "That's sick." She turns and looks at us in shock. "Do vampires live here?" she whispers.

Smitty giggles. "Wouldn't you love that? Some pale-faced, doe-eyed pretty boy to suck on your neck?" He takes a peep into the window. "Edward's not home. Sorry, Malice."

She sticks her tongue out at him. He smiles back.

"Anyway, it's not a coffin, it's an iron maiden," he says.

"Yeah, right," Alice says.

"Actually, he is right," says Pete. "It's pretty cool to see a real one."

"Weren't you listening in History, Malice?" Smitty says. "It's full of spikes. They used to put you in there and close the lid if you'd been a naughty girl."

"Of course I remember," Alice says. "But who owns one of those things anyway? And why would you name it after some crumbly old rock band?"

Smitty is ROFL over this. I interrupt before he can rip her to pieces. The girl is concussed, after all.

"So, show us around," I tell him. "We need to secure this place before we can rest up for the night."

Smitty's in his element. He grabs a fencing sword, tries it for size, then tosses it to Pete. "This is more your style." He finds something that looks like a decorative ax. "Hmm. This'll do."

"Yeah," snarls Alice. "If you wanna look like some dwarf from The Lord of the Rings."

I think he's quite impressed Alice has even heard of The Lord of the Rings. Either way, his joy with the ax is undiminished. "Follow me!" he cries, and takes the door on the left-hand side of the hall. We follow.

"So the layout is symmetrical," he stage-whispers to Alice. "That means it's the same on either side of the staircase." She rolls her eyes. "Except for the tower that's at the back by the kitchen. Didn't check that, but it's locked and there's no key I could find." He flicks on the light and affects a posh Scottish accent. "This is the drawing room."

It's full-on McFancy: blue and green tartan wallpaper that feels like velvet, a deep carpet, and an assortment of uncomfortable-looking antique furniture. Next there's a dining room, with a long polished table and cabinets full of silver jugs and trinkets. Then Smitty's leading us through a kitchen with one of those big farmhouse ovens that look like they've come out of Noah's Ark.

"This is still warm!" Alice says, hovering her hands above the stove.

"They're always warm, those ovens," Lily says. Cam is in her arms again. After his burst of activity he's out for the count and snoring quietly. "It doesn't mean anything."

"What's this?" Alice lifts a shutter in the wall next to the oven and sticks her head in. "Urgh!" She clatters the shutter down again, and wipes imagined dust from her hands. "It's a secret passage!"

Smitty's straight in there, shutter open, his head up into the hole, looking around.

"Nuh-uh," he says. "It's one of those old-fashioned moving shelf things they used to send food upstairs."

"Dumbwaiter," I say.

"If you say so, Roberta," Smitty says. "I'm not *smart* enough to know."

Pete shouts from the other side of the room. "There's a pantry here. And two fridges full of food." He holds up a half-empty bottle of milk. "It's still fresh."

"Food! Gimme!" A day ago Alice would not have been seen dead rushing to get food, but that was a day ago. And once she goes for it, we all go.

The pantry is a large, cool room with shelves and shelves of goodies. Well, some goodies and then an awful lot of weird stuff in jars and tins that people from the War probably ate. Pickled pig's feet, goose fat, things suspended in jelly. But there are cookies and crisps-not-chips and reasonably fresh bread, and in the fridge, cheese and slices of cold meat and chocolate mousse with cream on top! We crowd together excitedly, cramming food in, not pausing to find plates or cutlery or somewhere to sit.

There are sodas in one of the fridges, and I make a grab for one.

"Pass me the juice," Alice says, pointing to a carton in the fridge. I pick it up and hold it out. She's about to take it when we both see the label.

▶ **CARROT MAN VEGGIE JUICE! PUT SOME FIRE IN YOUR BELLY!** ◀

Alice screams and I scream. I drop the carton like it's hot.

"What gives?" says Smitty. "Whoa . . ." He sees what gives.

We back off the carton like it's a ticking bomb . . . or a poisonous snake . . . or a carton of zombie juice.

"Is it open?"

"Is it leaking?"

"What's it doing here?"

"Get rid of it!"

"What's the problem?" Lily is staring at us like we're crazy. *Of course. She doesn't know.*

"You drink the juice, it makes you into one of them," I summarize.

We stare at the carton. It lies there, a little cartoon Carrot Man waving to us from the packaging.

"Bad juice." Cam shakes a finger at it.

"That's right, Cam," Lily says, pulling him closer to her. "We don't touch the bad juice."

"Somebody's going to have to!" Alice shouts.

It's Pete who finds the rubber gloves. He looks at home in them. We disappear into the kitchen while he wets a towel and wraps it around his face, finds three plastic bags, and triple-wraps the carton, tying the bags in a double knot. He carries his deadly package at arm's length through the kitchen, steps onto a chair, unlatches a leaded window. A blast of cold air blows in. Pete lobs the carton through the air and out into the snow. Then he unties the towel and unpeels the gloves, and chucks them out, too.

"That wasn't very environmentally friendly, was it?" says Smitty.

"What if an animal finds it?" I say. "We don't know how it could affect them."

"Ooh, killer bunnies and zombie hedgehogs," quips Smitty. "Can't wait."

"Killa bunneez!" says Cam, and claps his hands.

"Would you like me to go and get it back, then?" Pete says, deadpan. "Because I can absolutely do that if you would like. It didn't leak, by the way. And I don't think the seal was open. Whoever put it in that fridge hadn't sampled any yet."

"Let's just hope that wasn't the second carton." Lily gathers Cam up and heads for the door. "We need to get settled for the night. It's been a long day."

*   *   *

We explore the rest of the castle. Well, *explore* is not really the right word. *Explore* makes it sound fun. It also makes it sound like we do a thorough job, and we don't. We ignore the locked tower next to the kitchen. There is a big keyhole without a key. We're not going in, and if there's anything in there, it's not getting out. At least not tonight. We move the kitchen table in front of the door just to be sure.

Same with the basement, except this door has a key. Smitty opens it up and looks down the stairs. All is quiet. He relocks the door and we shuffle a large wooden chest in front of it to make ourselves feel better.

On the ground floor, as well as the rooms we've already checked out, there's a mudroom next to the kitchen, a library, a bathroom, and a room with a pool table. And then there's the room with the dog. It's also the room that looks the most comfortable. There are three bashed-up couches and a stone fireplace big enough for us all to stand in. It's obvious that this is where we should stay tonight, all together in one room. Smitty coaxes the dog into the kitchen with some slices of ham and moves the dog's bed beside the oven, where he'll be warm. As long as Smitty does the snack runs, we should be OK.

Lily stays in the living room with Cam and Alice, who has already bagged the plushest of the couches. Smitty, Pete, and I do recon upstairs.

Upstairs is spooky and dark, but it's just bedrooms. I count twelve. And two bathrooms. So we can totally have friends over, but we're still going to be fighting over who gets to shower first.

We check under the beds and in the wardrobes. The dark corners and behind the curtains. Your basic child's how-to in monster hunting. A few of the rooms have unmade beds, clothes on chairs, personal stuff on dressers. It's tempting to play detective and try to guess who lives (or lived) here, but not so tempting that it's going to keep us from our beds, er, couches, for too long. There'll be time for all that tomorrow.

After recon, we gather up some bedding and throw it over the banisters then run down, trying not to openly shudder at the relief of being downstairs again.

In the living room, Cam and Alice are already asleep, and Lily is raking the fire. She helps us with the bedding and tucks a blanket around her brother, then another around Alice. She's a nice girl. A couple of years older than us, but in some ways it makes no difference. I guess it's just what you go through that ages you. Lord knows the last thirty-six hours have been enough to turn us all into crumblies.

We move a chest of drawers against one door, a sideboard against the other, and check that the windows are latched. I pray I don't need to pee in the middle of the night. Outside is quiet; the snow is falling faster now, relentlessly. All good efforts made, we get ourselves comfortable while Lily builds a new fire, and lights it.

"The embers . . . ," she says. "When I was raking the fire, they were still warm."

"Someone was here recently?" I ask.

"No doubt," she says. "With our fire at home, we go to bed and the ash is still warm in the morning." She thinks about it. "Maybe ten or twelve hours later?"

"So that means someone lit a fire and left here this morning," Smitty says.

"They saw our smoke," I say. "The black smoke from the gas station. They probably set out to see what had happened."

"How? On foot?" Pete says. "We didn't see them. They obviously didn't make it."

"Where were you, Lily?" Smitty leans back into a beaten-up leather armchair. "When it all kicked off. You and Cam were in the café, we saw you on the security camera playback. We were outside on the bus, but we didn't see you run out. Next thing we know, you're playing stowaway."

"I told them already." She nods to me. "We were in the car at first, then hiding in the café, then back in the car." Lily pulls a blanket around her shoulders and shudders. "Don't want to talk about it just now."

"Why not?" Smitty appears relaxed, but I'm sensing he won't let this one go without a fight.

"Because I don't." She leans over toward him, her eyes wide and blue, a tendril of blond hair hanging artfully over her face. For the first time I realize how attractive she is. Not pep-squad pretty, like Alice, but grown-up good-looking, full-lipped and heavy-lidded. Kind of sultry. I think Smitty realizes it, too. He shrugs.

"I think you have a responsibility to tell us all of it in detail," starts Pete, and I'm glad he does because I want to know. But Smitty cuts him off.

"We can swap war stories tomorrow," he says. "Who knows how long we'll be here? We might need some entertainment."

Alice is making snuffling noises on the couch next to mine. Someone really should have checked her head before now. I chuckle to myself quietly. Alice has needed her head checked *way* before now. The warmth of the fire is so comforting, and I have a feather-filled duvet all to myself. Whichever way you slice it, we're oh-so-better-off here in a castle than on a bus. For the first time since what feels like forever, I allow my shoulders to lower, my jaw to unclench, and my hands to relax from the fists they've been making for the last two days. A wave of tired descends, like a wonderful soft blanket of dark.

"Should we take turns keeping guard?" Pete's voice sounds far away.

Let 'em work it out between 'em, for once. I surrender to the tired.

17

There's a dog barking, and I'm cold.

I open my eyes; daylight is streaming through the windows. The reason I'm cold is quickly clear. Cam has gathered all the bedding together and is making a giant bed in the middle of the floor. My duvet forms part of his cocoon. He wiggles around inside, then a shamble of blond hair and an eye peep over the top.

"'Lo," he says.

"Morning, Cam."

I sit up on the couch. Everyone's gone. The chest of drawers has been moved away from the door that leads to the kitchen. I leap to my feet and rush to the window. It's still snowing, the whiteness so fine it's almost like a fog. I can't see a thing. Somewhere, the dog is still barking.

"Where did everyone go, Cam?" I ask him, but he's pupating under the blankets again and doesn't answer. I reach for the handle of the rear door and turn it. "Back in a moment, OK?"

But the door refuses to budge. The handle is turning, but it won't open. Someone has barricaded me in.

"Yo!" I shout. "Can someone come let me out?"

Silence. Even the dog has shut up.

"Hey!" I try again, thumping the door with my fist. "We're stuck in here!"

Still silence. I head across the room to the other door. The sideboard is still in place, but after a few attempts I manage to ease it away from the door slightly.

"Smitty!" I shout through the gap. "Pete! Lily! Where are you! Cam and I are trapped in here!" There's no response. I try one last-ditch effort. "Alice!"

At the mention of his name, Cam has reappeared out of his big bed, for the first time looking a little more clued in to our situation. I calm my voice. "It's OK, buddy," I reassure him. "I'll get us out of here in a moment."

Crappy older sis I'd make. Cam does not believe me for one minute. His face collapses into a wail. He crawls toward me and a little stubby hand reaches pathetically up toward me.

"Need poo-poo," he cries.

Fantastic. Raise the stakes, why don't you? I force a smile.

"It's fine. I'll get us out in a jiffy." My mother's voice echoes back at me. Empty promises. Cam doesn't buy it, either. He waddles back to the floor-bed and buries his head in a blanket, like it's all too much to bear. Which it almost is.

But it's given me an idea. I leap off the sideboard and go to Cam. I stroke his head and he looks at me with suspicious wet eyes.

"I just need to borrow your blankie for a moment, Cam."

He shakes his little head and holds the blanket tighter.

"Come on, Cam. I need to take it, but I promise I'll give it right back. Why don't you have one of these fluffy ones instead? They're nicer than the stringy one anyway."

He won't be budged and I've got no choice but to pry the stringy blanket out of the hands of a three-year-old. He is incensed, and screams like I am cutting off said hands at the wrists with a hacksaw. The noise is so extreme I look around nervously, almost dreading that Lily will materialize and find me assaulting her little brother. But even with this cacophony, no one comes to my (or Cam's) rescue.

I win the blankie tug-of-war, and Cam throws himself on the floor, kicking and screaming. I'm evil, but I don't care. I wrap the blanket around one end of the sideboard and the other around my hands, then lean my whole body weight away from the huge piece of furniture and dig in my heels. Slowly it moves a little, then a little more, and then with a last heft, a little more still. It's just enough. I breathe in and squeeze through the door. I'm about to go, then I look back at Cam. Darn. Can't really leave him here when he can probably find a dozen ways to break himself. Plus there's that whole business of the "poo-poo."

I squeeze back, scoop him up, and manage to get the two of us back out again, somehow.

In the hall, I notice with huge relief that the front door is still shut and bolted. Good. So we haven't been overwhelmed in the night, at least not through that door.

Now to find everyone. The obvious place is the kitchen. I'm about to call out again, but something stops me. The hall is cold and shadowy, like a cathedral. It almost doesn't seem right to be hollering away in such a place. I didn't notice last night — probably because of the dark and the exhaustion and the post-traumatic stress disorder — but there is an immense stained-glass window above the sweep of the stairs. The weak sun manages to light the colored glass, casting rays of red and blue and green into the room. It's really pretty beautiful. On a proper sunny day it would be awesome. That's presuming the sun ever shines in Scotland.

"Poo-poo," says Cam in my arms, softly. He punctuates this with a short, sharp fart, in case I ever doubted his intentions. I fight back a giggle and move away before the smell can catch up with us.

I remember where the downstairs bathroom is, and we both do what we need to do. He's a little unclear of what's required after he's finished, and I realize in horror he expects me to lend a hand. Quite literally. I wrap a load of toilet paper around my hand and try not to visibly wince when I wipe away. Of all the stuff I've experienced over the past couple of days, I can't help thinking this is the grossest. Then I feel really bad about thinking the thought. But it's no good, it's thunk. We both wash our hands in gallons of freezing water and frothy oceans of liquid soap, and only then can I stop the grossness and the guilt.

Cam has a personality overhaul as a result of his über-poop. Now he's bubbly and full of generous vigor. He runs though each room en route to the kitchen, with me struggling to keep up. We arrive at the kitchen door and it's only the unwieldy handle that holds him back. I grasp him with one hand, and the handle with the other, and open the door slowly and carefully.

The smell hits me first. And then the frightening scene assaults my eyes.

Smitty, wearing an apron. Frying eggs and bacon.

"Wassup, Bob. Thought you were sleeping for England." He flutters the eyelashes at me. "Or Scotland." He shrugs. "Or the good ol' US of A, wherever you come from."

Pete and Alice are at the large kitchen table, eating. Lily is behind Smitty, making toast. Cam sees her and makes a run for it. Instantly, I hear a snarl and instinctively reach toward Cam and snatch him up, stepping back from the doorway. The door is slammed in our faces and Cam starts to cry. There's a scuffle from behind the door, I can hear Smitty's voice making coaxing noises, and after a minute or so Lily opens the door.

"Cammy!" she coos and takes him out of my arms. "Stupid crazy dog's gone now, hinny." She winks at me. "Want some dippy eggs?"

Cam nods and she leads us back into the kitchen. Pete and Alice are still wolfing down breakfast. Smitty is flipping bacon like nothing bad happened. I sidle up to him.

"Where's the dog?" I whisper.

"In the library with a plate of bacon," he replies. "He was being all friendly with us until Cam turned up." He lowers his voice and leans over the bacon. "He really doesn't like that kid."

"So why didn't you wake me?" I try to keep nonchalant, but my voice is shaking. "And why did you trap me in the living room?"

"Lily didn't want Cam wandering off," he says, cracking an egg. "And you were dead to the world." His mouth curls into a smile. "Besides, I thought you'd like breakfast in bed."

I flush as pink as the piggy in the pan.

"Sunny-side up?" He looks at me intently. When I don't respond, he slides the food onto a clean white plate and hands it to me. It smells so good. My hunger overtakes my embarrassment and anger, and I find myself turning away in silence and sitting down next to Pete at the table. The bacon and eggs taste amazing. I don't even really like to eat pigs; they're clever and cute and I'd actually like one for a pet, but on this occasion I find myself digging in and mopping up the grease with bread and butter and wishing for seconds.

"Wanna eat the plate, too?" Alice snarks from the other end of the table. *Ah.* Great to know her concussion hasn't had any long-lasting ill effects. I was going to offer to look at her head wound, but now I'll let her fester. Thinking of which, we should really all check our wounds today. Everything happened so fast yesterday there wasn't exactly time for that. I get a total recall of Pete's skull tuft and my white leg bone, and instantly feel sick.

"So, plan of action," says Pete importantly.

"Do we have one?" Smitty sits with his plate of food. I'm impressed that he's waited to serve himself last.

"I do." Pete forges ahead before anyone can stop him. "When I woke this morning, there was a break in the snow and I had a look outside. Through the windows, of course," he says quickly. "There's a telephone line. Definitely. One line in, appears undamaged."

"I thought you said there were no phones here?" Lily says.

"We didn't find any," says Pete. "But that doesn't mean there isn't a phone unplugged somewhere—in a drawer or a cabinet."

"Why would anyone do that?" says Alice.

"Numerous reasons, potentially," says Pete. "But all I'm saying is there's a line. And don't forget there are more rooms through that locked door." He points in the direction of the tower we couldn't get into last night. "And there's a stable block. Outbuildings, too. More to investigate."

"Don't forget the spooky basement!" Smitty spits through a mouth of egg.

"I've got all our phones," Alice says. "If we can get up into that tower, we might get a signal. Or find the landline."

I frown. "What do we do first?"

"Why don't I stay in here with Cam and clean up and have a look for the tower key?" Lily says in a cheerful voice. "It'll be like a fun game."

Yeah, what it's *like* is that she's pulling this whole domestic bliss thing so as not to freak Cam out. Or maybe it's so that *she* doesn't get freaked out. "You guys go off and check out the other stuff. We'll find the key" — she looks at Cam — "then maybe bake some cookies for later!"

"Oh, *très* marvelous," Alice says.

"Just don't use up too much food; we don't know how long we have to last here," Pete says.

"Oh, please," Alice says. "If I'm not out of here in twenty-four hours, I'll gladly starve to death." She pulls a grotesque grinning face at Cam. "Jokey-wokey!" Luckily Cam decides she's hysterical, and the two of them laugh, Alice rolling her eyes at the same time, the cow.

I rise out of my seat and go to the window. "What about the juice?"

It's still out there, for sure. The snow has almost covered it, but there's a blue plastic bag handle sticking out of the white.

"It'll be frozen solid." Smitty burps loudly. "So unless anyone fancies a toxic ice pop for breakfast, I think we're safe to leave it be." He jumps up and grabs me around the waist for a split second. "Race you to the basement!"

He does his best evil laugh and runs out of the kitchen.

Smitty has his dwarven ax, Pete his fencing sword. I saw Alice eyeing up a carving knife in the kitchen, but thank heavens she's chosen a golf club. I think it's a kid's one; it's kind of short. I could see Smitty bursting with the need to mess with her for choosing it, but I managed to shoot him evils just in time to stop him. Or maybe it was because I distracted him by picking the poker from the fire for my weapon. I think he's saving himself up for the countless comedic opportunities me having a poker could provide. Hey ho, something for us all to look forward to should we survive the morning.

"So bring on the spooky basement," says Smitty, savoring the words. "After which, we could find a creepy attic and a shadowy graveyard to wander through — then we'll have the full set of scary movie clichés."

We stand at the top of the stairs, looking down into the darkness. Smitty flicks the light on and it's a single bulb, swinging just above our heads, flickering and ominous. There's a shelf on the wall just to my left; among the bric-a-brac I spy a flashlight. I pick it up and switch it on. It works.

"Make sure the door stays open behind us," Alice whispers. "I don't want to get stuck down here."

"Yep, that would be textbook," says Smitty.

Pete props the door open with a box of nails from the shelf, and we slowly make our way downstairs.

18

The staircase is shorter than I thought it would be. I mean, for those first few steps it really felt like we were descending into the bowels of hell, or journeying to the center of the earth. I was kind of expecting skeletons and ancient wall paintings, burning torches or scarab beetles or something. But there is none of that: just a flight of stone steps and then we emerge into a basement that smells of mold with garden fertilizer mixed in.

A single room, about the size of the living room we'd slept in last night. Pete finds another light switch and, after a couple of false tries, a fluorescent strip clicks on overhead. We look around. The room is lined with shelves that contain everything and nothing. Plant pots and garden tools. Crates of books and piles of *Country Life* magazine. In the middle of the room are a couple of stools and a tarp-covered lawn mower. In one corner is a small wooden door with coal piled at the bottom. I stick my head around the door; inside there's a diagonal chute leading up to an inch of bright sunlight above. I force the door closed again. On the far wall hang sacks and dust cloths, aprons and netting.

"So this is it?" says Alice. "A whole load of rubbish? Nothing useful at all?" She sticks out a hip and puts a hand on it. "I suppose I should be used to this by now. I mean, I could have trusted you lot to find the one building in this whole area — no, country — that doesn't have a phone."

"Mmm, you know what, Malice?" Smitty is walking up to her, his ax swinging by his side. "We only came here because of you." He points his ax up at her head. "If you hadn't brained yourself back at the Cheery Chomper, we could have walked for miles and had our pick of tripped-out castles."

"That's not strictly true," Pete interrupts.

"How is that head, by the way?" Smitty smiles at Alice. "If it's still bothering you, we can take it clean off, if you like?" He raises his ax again.

"Get away from me, you bully!" Alice cries out, bringing her golf club up to knock away the ax.

"Bully?" Smitty laughs. "You wrote the manual, Malice."

"I've told you, don't call me that!" Alice roars, flinging herself at Smitty, golf club aloft.

He dodges out of the way before she can land a blow. But she's moving with too much force to stop in midair. Instead of slamming into Smitty, she's going to slam into the wall. I brace myself for the tears.

They never come. Alice doesn't hit the wall, she disappears. Completely. Into the wall where the sacks are hanging. There's a kind of muffled scream, then nothing.

Smitty, Pete, and I stand there looking at each other, and the wall, without words. I can't help but wish that we'd tried to throw Alice into a wall way before now if this is the result. We watch the place where she vanished, and wait.

But it's too good to be true. A few seconds later she's back, her head appearing between two of the big sacks, then a shoulder, an arm, and a leg. The most surprising thing is, she's smiling.

"Once again, I strike gold," she says. "Without me, you losers would be lost." She steps out from the wall and holds up her arm. In the place where her junior golf club had been is a large bottle of champagne. She waggles it at us. "But, finders keepers," she sings, disappearing back into the wall.

And we follow. It's not a wall, of course. Behind the hanging sacks there's a floor-length, stone-colored curtain, with a slit down the middle. Through the curtain is a whole new room. There's a lamp on the wall under which Alice is standing, champagne in hand. Behind her are racks upon racks of wine, dark and cobwebbed. The racks run around all four walls of the room, from floor to ceiling.

"The mother lode," whispers Smitty in awe. He pulls out a few bottles and examines the labels.

Pete sighs. "And here I was thinking you'd actually found something interesting."

"She did," I call from the far corner of the room. There's a gap between two of the racks, and in the gap is a door. I turn the handle and look through. A long corridor disappears into darkness. I aim the flashlight straight ahead and force myself to take a couple of steps forward into the black. The corridor is barely wider than the door, the stone walls dank and slippery on either side.

There's a noise of a shot and something whizzes past my ear, stopping me in my tracks.

I spin around, breath held. But it's only Alice; she's popped the cork on the bubbly. She shakes the bottle and shrieks as all of the champagne gushes into the air, soaking her and Smitty. Pete pushes past them, sighing.

"Another passage?" he asks. "Could be an escape tunnel. A lot of castles and manor houses have them. From the days when being attacked was a fact of life and people needed to make a quick getaway."

"The good old days in comparison." Smitty grabs for my flashlight, but I whip it away. "Touchy!" He grins at me. "Betcha there's a light around here anyway."

He feels the wall and finds something. There's a *click*, but no illumination. I point the flashlight forward resolutely and start walking, Smitty, Pete, and Alice following me Scooby-stylee again.

The corridor widens out a little after a few feet, then a little more. In the beam from my flashlight I can see something on the ground. It's Alice's cork, lying where one side of the wall seems to end, with nothing but darkness beyond.

I notice another switch on the wall. It works. Orange light reflects weakly off the slimy walls. I stare at the space ahead.

Jail cells — three of them — along one side of the corridor, with thick iron bars on the front.

"A castle has to have a dungeon, doesn't it?" says Smitty. He walks up to the first one and pulls the door toward him. He steps inside. "This must be where they keep the really good stuff."

I step up to the bars and look through. More racks, more bottles.

"Same here." Pete has already checked out the second cell. He moves on to the third, and stops.

"What is it?" I call to him.

"Nothing," he calls back.

I stride down to the cell.

"As in there's nothing in this one."

Nothing apart from a chair, a bucket, and a bundle of rags in the corner.

"Weird," I say.

"You called?" Smitty bounces up. "Hey, this must be the hangover room. Where you sit and throw up after you've drunk your body weight in Chateau Nerve du Plop, or whatever."

"You'd do well to bear that in mind," Pete says.

Alice has sloped up the corridor and is laughing with Smitty at the sight of the bucket through the bars. Suddenly those two are best buds.

"The corridor ends here." Pete is frowning.

"Are you sure?" I walk past the cell to where Pete is feeling the wall.

"Solid stone." He pats the wall. "No obvious switches or levers." He scrubs at the stone floor with his foot. "It's possible that if it was a tunnel, they bricked it up sometime in the last century. No need to escape anymore."

"That's probably a good thing," I say. "We don't want anyone creeping up on us while we're upstairs sleeping."

"Boo!" Smitty cries, creeping up behind me, because clearly that's the joke.

"Brilliant, Smitty," I say. I notice something sticking out of the lock of the last cell. A small, modern, metal key. Odd that it should look new. In fact, now that I look closer, this lock looks different from the others, like it's been replaced. I turn the key, open the door, and beckon Smitty in. "Would you like me to make a reservation for you while we're down here?"

"Only if you can be the Dungeon Mistress." He leans in, and I will myself not to blink. "Got your whip?"

"Ew! Perv alert!" shouts Alice, and pretends to retch.

As I flush scarlet in the orange light, Smitty dashes in toward the back of the cell, beyond the single chair to the bundle of rags. He turns to face us, pulling up his T-shirt to reveal his bare torso; his legs are akimbo and his arms shoot out to the sides. "Beat me for my sins, Mistress! Beat me!"

"Oh, gross!" Alice cries, propping herself up on the bars.

Smitty waggles his tongue at her, turns away from us, drops his pants, bends over, and moons. Before I know what I'm doing, I shine the flashlight on his behind. As if I needed a better look. Now I think I may have blinded the three of us for life.

"Sick!" screams Alice. "I seriously am going to puke my guts up!"

And then Smitty does just that. Pukes his guts up, with full ferocity and surround-sound echoing off the walls. Bacon and eggs in a waterfall of *ewwww*. I grab my mouth, feeling my own stomach clench in complaint. Alice squeals, and Pete just stands there, transfixed. Smitty pulls up his jeans and staggers toward us, a look of sheer horror on his face.

"What the hell is wrong with you?" I shout at him.

He's throwing out swearwords like a celebrity chef.

"That . . . !" He points to the back of the cell, at the bundle of rags.

"What is it?" I enter the cell gingerly.

"Look and see!" He splutters at me. I move toward the rags. "No! Don't look! You don't want to look!"

But it's too late. I've seen something poking out of the rags. It's a foot. A socked foot, with the bump of an ankle bone, and the tiniest amount of pink skin with black leg hairs, too. Now that I'm looking, I can see the shape of a leg and a hip of a person who is lying on their side . . . and the rise of the place where arms and shoulders are. And then it stops.

Where the head should be, there is nothing, just a bloodied stump.

This is not my first bloodied stump, nor is it Smitty's, but I understand why he felt the need to unload.

Maggots squirm in the well of flesh that used to be a throat.

I feel the blood rushing from my head, and the next thing I know I am running, back down the corridor into the wine cellar, through the slit in the curtain and into the basement. The others are close behind, Alice and Pete not requiring any immediate explanation beyond my fleeing feet.

As I near the top of the steps to the hall, the door opens. Lily stands in the light, with Cam in her arms.

She turns and shuts the door behind her, barring our escape.

"We have to get out!" I put my hand on her arm and try to force it off the door. "There's a dead body down there!"

"There is?" Alice cries from a few steps below. "Oh my god!" She scrambles up and tries to push Lily aside.

Lily bars the way. "Dead? Like one of those things?"

"Not anymore." Smitty pushes past me and Alice. "Headless and rotting, but if you're happy keeping him company, then be our guest." He goes for the door handle but Lily knocks his hand away.

She shakes her head. "We can't go out there."

"Why not?" Pete is panting and exasperated.

Lily fixes him with a steely glare. "Because whoever lives here just came home."

19

"There are three of them," Lily whispers.

We are sitting in the purgatory of the steps in between Maggotty Man Basement and The Strangers Who Came in from the Cold.

"Two men and a woman, I think. They must have come in the back way. Cam and I were in the downstairs bathroom, and I could hear their voices in the kitchen."

"Did you get a look at them?" I ask.

Lily shrugs. "I peeped through the gap in the door, but I couldn't exactly stay there." She nods to Cam, who is sitting next to her playing with the box of nails that had kept the door open. Normally not such a great thing for a three-year-old to be playing with, but normal kind of flew out the window recently. "They looked like students." Lily wrinkles her nose. "One of them has a beard."

"Sounds terrifying." Smitty stands up. "So give me a good reason why we shouldn't go up there and say hi? It's not like there's not enough room here to go around."

I nod. "Strength in numbers. And maybe they know what's going on, or how to get help."

Lily shakes her head vigorously. "They know someone's here, and they're really pissed off." She leans forward. "I could hear them checking the kitchen and the pantry to see what we'd eaten. And they were furious, really shouting about something. Then they started looking in the other rooms. I think they saw all our bedding, too. They sounded so angry."

Smitty sighs and sits back down on the step.

Pete stands up this time, like it's some kind of bizarro version of Musical Chairs.

"If what she says is true" — Pete's pale face is luminous in the dim light — "they'll be checking down here soon enough."

We all think about it. It's true. If they think we're hiding, it's probably the first place they'll look.

"Do you think they killed that guy in the cell?" I say.

There is silence. It's actually quite a terrifying thought. I don't know how I come up with these gems.

"Maybe he deserved it," Alice says eventually. "Maybe he'd turned and they locked him up and chopped his head off."

It's easier to hope that this version is true. The alternative could be that the dead guy was minding his own business living in his castle when a zombie apocalypse broke out and a bunch of ruthless students broke in and killed him so that they could make the place their own sanctuary. I mean, you'd think that, when faced with an Undead army, random human survivors would find a really good reason to get along, but that certainly hasn't happened in our own little test group. No, it's much easier to believe that the maggot-ridden corpse was a fiendish monster, locked up and dispatched by the reluctant but plucky students. Because otherwise, we could be headless and maggoty ourselves pretty soon, if they find us.

I remember holding the cold cell key in my hand. I look at Smitty. "Any chance you locked that cell before we ran up here?" I know as soon as I've asked him that it's a ridiculous question. He simply rolls his eyes.

"What?" Alice says. "The dead thing is not locked up?" She leaps to her feet. "How stupid could you be? It might be coming up here now!"

We all look down the steps.

"It had no head! That kills them!" But I don't sound so sure.

"This is the dumbest yet!" Alice is being way too loud. "We could be rescued, and we're sitting in a basement with a headless body?" She stomps up the steps. "I'll take my chances with the beardy-weirdy students, thank you very much!"

Pete is behind her, and I suppose we all assume he's going to grab her and bring her back, but he does no such thing.

"Pete!" I say, but his hand is on the doorknob already.

He turns to me. "Knowledge is power, Bobby."

With that, he and Alice are gone.

Smitty and Lily and I look at each other.

"What is that supposed to mean exactly?" Smitty says.

"Maybe they're right," Lily says. "Maybe we should give ourselves up. They might be able to help us."

I frown at her. "I thought you said they were really angry that someone had eaten their porridge and slept in their beds?"

She sighs. "Aye. The more I think about it, the more I think they were angry because they were looking for something. Something they'd lost."

"Like what?" Smitty says.

Lily makes a guilty face and reaches into her back pocket. "Like this?" She holds out a shiny silver thing. "It's the key to the tower. I found it when I was clearing the breakfast things away."

Smitty reaches for the key, but Lily reads his moves.

"No." She puts her hand behind her back. "I'm holding this for now."

"Fine." He smiles at her. "But do me a favor and don't tell anyone you have it, OK? Not even Alice and Pete. Until we know who these people are. And why they want that key so badly."

Lily nods coolly. "My thoughts exactly."

"So does that mean we're coming out of cover?" I look up at the door.

Smitty nods. "Might as well. Can't trust that Alice won't give us away if it suits her. You and me go up there, Bob. Lily and Cam should stay down here for now, until we know it's sound."

Lily's fine with that. Almost. She smiles thinly.

"Could you just go downstairs and lock up the headless body first, please?"

It's a reasonable request.

We go. I still have my poker, Smitty has his ax . . . but something makes me suspect that if decapitation didn't work, then we might be fighting a losing battle.

Around every corner I expect the body to leap out at us, maggots flying. But all is quiet. The wine is still in the racks — well, most of it is, anyway — the corridor is enduringly dank and dark but relatively harmless, and by the time we reach the final jail cell it's almost anticlimatic to see the bundled body still in exactly the same spot as we left it. And of course nobody locked the door. It's open, the key sticking out of the lock. I shut it firmly but quietly, and turn the key. Smitty reaches over, takes it from the lock, and pockets it. I look at him questioningly.

He shrugs. "You never know."

When we reach the steps, Cam has managed to empty the whole box of nails on the stairs and is lining them up nicely, head to point, like a long and skinny snake traversing an invisible maze. Lily is by the door, an ear to the wood.

"We're all locked up," I whisper to her. "Have you heard anything?"

She shakes her head. "It's really quiet."

"If everything's OK, we'll come get you," I say. "If you hear any trouble, hide in the coal chute."

Smitty adjusts his grip on the ax and puts a hand on the door.

"Ready?"

I try to think of something witty or inspirational or both, but come up short. I kind of snort and nod at the same time. Smitty gives me a raised eyebrow, and opens the door.

We're out into the hall.

I can't hear any voices. We pause for a moment, then tiptoe around to the front of the cascading staircase, where the light is filtering out of the stained-glass window, all heavenly and lovely and churchified.

Smitty has taken it upon himself to be on point, dashing ahead of me and stopping suddenly in shadows. He looks more than a little ridiculous. I mean, we're not Marines. He puts up a hand. I listen. There's a noise, a scratchy *click-clack* on the wooden floor.

The dog appears in front of us. After a moment's standoff he licks Smitty's hand and trots over to me. He sits, his long tail swishing and polishing the floor, head cocked as if expecting a treat.

"At least someone's happy to see us," I whisper.

"Woof!" says the dog.

"Sssh!" I say.

"Woof! Woof!" replies the dog.

"Great. Why don't we yell 'coo-ee' and get this over with?" Smitty says. We wait for a second, glued to the spot, expecting running feet and strangers to appear at any moment. But nobody does. Smitty pads toward the door to the living room, and the dog, deciding Smitty is way more fun than me, trots after him. I run after both of them.

Someone — presumably our new co-occupants — has moved the large sideboard well away from the door of the living room, and we enter without a struggle.

"Let's head for the kitchen," Smitty says, and I'm following him out of the living room and through the library when I hear the muffled voices. We pause and listen.

It sounds like Alice is holding court. That's promising; it's not as if they're hacking her and Pete to pieces or anything. Then again, they've only known them for a few seconds . . . give it time. I move my ear closer to the kitchen door and catch the words "stupid lame bus" and "brains hanging out"; she's giving them the full story and then some. Seems Alice has finally found an audience that is happy to listen to her for more than a few minutes without wanting to jump off the nearest cliff.

Smitty leans into the door beside me.

"Do we knock?" I whisper.

He considers it. "Probably. Surprises don't go down too well these days." He holds up a hand and I hold my breath as he raps lightly on the door. The talking inside stops. Smitty looks at me and in spite of the scary factor I feel a giggle well up inside me. We both raise our fists and knock lightly again.

There's a scraping of chairs and a scrambling noise. As one we take a step back from the door. Then the door opens and a head pokes out. Dark curly hair, sallow complexion, dark, dark eyes, and a beard. Early twenties, with kind of a soulful poet look. Under different circs, I might almost develop a crush.

The eyes register shock, but quickly harden. The door is left to swing open, and the kitchen opens up to us.

"I thought you said you were on your own," Beardy says snarkily.

Alice is sitting at the kitchen table with her back to us—at the head of the table, no less—with Pete to her right, his arms clamped to his sides. Alice turns to face us.

"Did I? I don't think so." She smiles at us, her face giving nothing away.

Wow, Malice didn't tell on us? Who saw that one coming?

"More school trip kiddies?" Beardy asks. I nod. "Get yourselves in here." He points his finger with his thumb cocked, like his hand is a gun. I walk into the kitchen—not too quickly, like I'm in control and am nonchalance personified. My 'tude has nothing on Smitty's, however. His lopsided swagger reeks FU, and he takes such a long time walking the few paces into the kitchen that I begin to think he might have had some kind of stroke.

At the other end of the kitchen is a frowning blond woman. She looks a little older than Beardy, maybe late twenties, and she's ice-cold and gorgeous, with arched eyebrows and a full pout. Like Beardy, she's dressed in cold weather gear but on top she has stripped down to a skin-tight black thermal T-shirt that shows some killer curves. Out of the corner of my eye I see Smitty taking her in and trying not to react.

Standing behind Pete is the other man. I say man, but only just. His skin is brown and his hair black, but really he could be a different flavor Pete, the way he hunches his shoulders nervously and cracks his knuckles. The resemblance is almost funny.

"So, who are you and what are you doing in our castle?" Smitty speaks.

"*Your* castle?" Beardy smiles. "And I suppose, big man that you are, you think you're king of the castle?"

Smitty slings himself onto the sideboard, where he sits, legs swinging, like he hasn't a care in the world. "Don't they say possession is nine-tenths of the law?"

Beardy laughs in that way that baddies do in movies, like they're not really that amused but they can't think of anything smart to say right at that second. "Clever boy. But unfortunately for you, we have *re*possessed."

"So you claim." Smitty stares at him. "Doesn't make it true." He taps his fingers on the counter. "Beheaded anyone recently? I did, just yesterday. At least we have something in common."

Beardy raises a black eyebrow. "You have been exploring the place, haven't you? Going through our dirty laundry, too?"

Smitty snorts. "I think I'm looking at the biggest skid mark right now."

"Look," I interject—because frankly this isn't going anywhere, "you were here first? Great. Tell us where the phone is."

"There isn't one," says Pete's older-brother-from-another-mother in the corner. "Don't you think we might have used it if there was?"

"That all depends if you'd figured out how to," says Smitty.

Beardy laughs again and shakes his head, like Smitty is really pissing him off and he doesn't want to show it.

"Do you know what's going on?" I turn to the blonde. "Where did you go last night? Is there anyone out there? Still alive, I mean? Have you got any kind of transportation? Is anyone coming to help us?"

"Full of questions, aren't you?" Beardy's smile is suddenly gone. "I think you'd better answer a few of ours first."

"Sounded like you already heard our story." I nod to Alice. "We're not here to cause you any trouble—we just want to stay safe, like you."

"You were hiding in the basement like Alice and Peter here?" Beardy strolls over to me and fixes me with his dark eyes. He raises the back of his hand and puts it up to my forehead, feeling my temperature. "How are you feeling, sweetheart? A little cold from being down there too long?" I shudder involuntarily. "You're not coming down with anything, are you?" Beardy studies my face and turns his hand around so his fingers trace my hairline from my forehead to my cheek. I want so badly to knock his hand away, but for some reason my arms stay stuck to my side.

"Get off her!" Smitty shouts, and launches himself off the sideboard with force, sending a drawer of cutlery spewing out onto the floor. He tackles Beardy to the floor, wrestling with him, trying to land a punch. I stagger back, too shocked to react. But Blondie is there in an instant.

"Get up and walk away, kid," she says firmly to Smitty, but Smitty is not giving this one up, and neither is Beardy. "I mean it," Blondie says.

The wrestling match is pretty evenly balanced, but finally Smitty frees a fist and goes for the right hook. There is a satisfying *crunch* and Beardy's head rolls to the side.

Blondie shouts, "Give it to me!" and Pete's evil twin throws her something long and thin. She holds it out in front of her and prods Smitty in the back, there's a sizzling sound, and he arches and cries out, springing back from Beardy. "Do not move or I'll shock you again," Blondie says as Smitty lies there, dazed.

"Don't!" I shout, and reach for the stick.

She turns on me, stick held between us. "Back down," she says quietly. "Or your boyfriend will suffer."

I open my mouth to correct her obvious mistake, but it seems a little churlish.

Beardy stands up, his hand to his jaw and his eyes blazing.

"Lock them up!" he shouts, with difficulty. "Lock 'em back in the wretched basement!"

Four of us and only three of them, but Smitty is being dragged by Beardy, and Blondie has the stick and is not afraid to use it. Alice and Pete troop past me out the kitchen door, Alice giving me the death stare, Pete protesting loudly and coming up with every logical reason why they shouldn't put us in the basement, or at least why they shouldn't put *him* there. I can tell by Blondie's fixed mouth and Beardy's barely concealed fury that we won't get anywhere, but I join in the protests all the way to the basement door, if only so that Lily and Cam can hear us coming.

"Please don't put us in here!" I fling myself against the door like a retro Hollywood heroine, slapping it with my hands in a way I hope is not totally obviously a warning to those within. Smitty has come to a little, and is playing his part by slowing his progress by grabbing random pieces of furniture leg and carpet, but he's impeded by the dog, who has reappeared and is attacking him with licks and snuffles.

Blondie unpeels me from the door with an iron grip I could have predicted, opens it, and pushes me — not roughly, but firmly — into the dark stairway. Alice and Pete follow, then there is a rush of legs and arms as Beardy half throws Smitty after us.

"How long are you going to keep us down here?" cries Alice.

"For as long as you need to stay!" shouts Beardy, and slams the door.

In the darkness, my ears are filled with Smitty's indignant pants, Pete's wheezing, and Alice's forced sobs. But my only thought is that it could be a lot worse.

I'm just glad they didn't try to lock us up with the last person they argued with.

20

"Grace *killed* Smitty with the cow prod." Alice, sitting on a plastic bin in the basement, has got her mojo back and is regaling Lily and Cam. They'd hidden in the coal chute, where I'd told them, and I felt a squeeze of pride when gutsy Cam emerged with a smudge on his nose and a big grin.

"She did not *kill* me, Malice," says Smitty, who is propped up on the tarp-covered lawnmower. "And it was not a cow prod. It was some kind of specialist army Taser."

"Bollocks," says Alice. "Cow prod. And she *slayed* you."

"Cow goes moo," says Cam.

"Blondie's called Grace?" I turn to Alice. "Didn't realize you two were on a first-name basis."

"We were doing just fine before *you* two came in and ruined everything." Alice glares at me. "You couldn't trust us to sort it out, could you?"

Smitty snarls at her. "No, Malice. We couldn't trust you not to spill your beans to the first person who asks, that's what."

"But I didn't, did I?" she spits back. And it's true, she didn't. I can't fault her on that. "Besides, Michael told us he wasn't going to hurt us. That's the very first thing he said."

"Who, Pube-Face?" Smitty grunts. "*Michael's* psychotic. I'm sure he couldn't wait to get his hands on you, Malice."

"There are three of them, aye?" Lily says.

"Yeah." Alice wrinkles her nose. "There's this small, weedy-looking bloke, too. I can't remember his name . . . I want to say, Shag?"

Smitty snorts.

"Shaq," Pete mutters. "Personally I think he's our best hope if we want to bond with them. He's the weak link, the vulnerable one."

"I'll keep that in mind if they ever let us out of here," I say.

"What will they do to us?" Lily says.

"Probably nothing," says Pete. "Smitty just muddied our collective prospects by beating up Michael unnecessarily."

"Unnecessarily? *Muddied?*" shouts Smitty. "What are you talking about, Pete? That psycho was trying to feel up Bobby. He's the one should be locked up."

"What else did you find out about them?" I ask Pete, willing myself not to blush at Smitty, Defender of my Honor.

"Not much." Pete chews the inside of one cheek. "I got the sense they've been here a while. But it's not like they own the place, either. Maybe they were on holiday here, or studying."

"Maybe they're part of some exclusive rehab program." Smitty forces a sardonic laugh. "Yeah, that's it. They were all detoxing in this castle, and there was some weird experimental cure with Veggie Juice, but it turns out that it turns people into zombies. As for those three, they were secretly working their way through the basement of booze and didn't take the cure. So they lived to tell the tale."

It's a stupid idea, but stupider ideas have been right. They are a strange group. I can't imagine them being friends or choosing to spend time with each other. And yet, there did seem to be some kind of power structure there. Beardy Michael acted like he was in charge, but Blondie — I mean, Grace — kind of had the last word on things.

"It's obvious they haven't found help or they wouldn't have come back," Pete continues. "But then again, they did seem really bothered about finding some key." He rubs his scabbed head. "Shaq was literally on his hands and knees looking for it when we walked in. And I think the others were blaming him for losing it."

Alice's face blanches, then she smiles. She's figured it out. "Oh my god. The *tower* key. That must be what they're looking for!" The smile drops from her face as suddenly as it came. "There must be something really important up there. Too bad we didn't find it first."

I glance at Lily and notice Smitty sneak a look, too, but she's avoiding eye contact by busying herself with Cam, who has decided to make yet another nest, this time in a cardboard box.

"I wonder why it's so important for them to get in the tower," Alice babbles on. "Do you think there's something in there that means we can get help?" Her mouth drops open. "Maybe they know they can get a mobile signal up there! That's what we thought when we first got to the castle!" She jumps to her feet. "We should offer to help them look. Imagine if a stupid key was the only thing standing between us and getting home safe!"

Lily looks up at her sharply.

Alice claps her hands. "With all of us looking, we're bound to find it! If they're alcoholics, they probably haven't got very good eyesight."

Smitty groans. "They're not really alcoholics, Malice . . ."

But Lily stands up. "She might be right about the tower. We could call for help."

"Then why didn't they try calling from the tower as soon as the trouble started?" I say.

Alice shrugs. "The key has been lost all this time? Or, no—they didn't have a phone between them—they probably weren't allowed to have them in *rehab*"—she looks amazed at her own powers of deduction—"and they went up to the Cheery Chomper to find one to use and now they can try!"

Fantastic. First we had Pete's government conspiracy theory, and now Alice is running with Smitty's stupid alco-zombies joke. There's a small chance she might be right about the tower, but that key's the only leverage we've got, and I don't want Lily to give it up before we know for sure. Plus, it begins to dawn on me that there must be a very good reason why that tower is locked in the first place. Either to keep people out . . . or to keep something in.

There's a noise from the steps. We all look up sharply. The little guy—Shaq—is standing there.

Damn. Lily and Cam. It would have been better to have kept both of them hidden . . . for more than one reason I can think of right now.

"'Lo!" Cam waves cheerily up at Shaq, who stares at him, horrified.

Smitty scrambles to his feet.

"What do you want?" he shouts up at Shaq. "Is Pube-Face itching for another round?"

Shaq raises his hand. "No!" He tentatively climbs down the first couple of steps. "They don't know I've come down here. Don't shout, OK?"

Alice gets up and sighs. "Do you want some wine? We won't tell."

Shaq continues down the stairs, face confused. "Er, no." He looks around at us, his eyes stopping on Lily. "How many more of you are there?"

"Everyone's here." I make sure I don't sound too convincing.

"Good, good . . ." His gaze flicks toward the curtain-wall. For all he knows, there might be an entire busload of teenagers behind it. He gestures to a wooden stool by the shelves. "Mind if I . . . sit down?"

"Sure, make yourself comfortable!" Smitty gestures extravagantly. "Might as well rest up before you decapitate another prisoner!"

Shaq sits cautiously, and pinches the skin between his eyes. "That was a . . . regrettable incident."

"Shall we go and look at him now?" Smitty's on a roll. "You can formally introduce us. I felt quite rude when I met him. I mean, I had no *idea* of his name. Maybe you don't know it, either. Did you cut off his head without asking?"

"Smitty!" Pete, who has been silent up until now, leans forward on his chair toward Shaq. "Tell us about it. Who was he?"

Shaq clears his throat. "Yes, we did kill him. Well, Michael did. You're right about that." He shifts in his seat and looks up at Smitty. "But you said you'd done it yourself. You know what it's like . . . when they *change*. He left us no choice."

"Who was he?" I repeat Pete's question.

Shaq's cool caramel eyes meet mine. "He was our professor. He was . . . my mentor. I . . ." He seems to collapse from inside, and his head falls forward into his hands. For a moment he stays like that. And then a moment longer. I don't know if he's crying, but clearly, some kind of meltdown is taking place. Alice giggles, embarrassed. Shaq shakes himself, and sits up again. The moment has passed.

"I'm sorry. It's horrible remembering. He was our professor. We were working on a . . . university project . . . and we'd been staying here for a few weeks, a kind of working vacation. Two days ago, one of those things turned up here at the castle and bit him. He passed out, then came to, and . . . Well, you know the rest." He shakes his head. "Michael did what he had to do . . ."

Smitty approaches Shaq and pats his shoulder, making him flinch. "I'm sorry, Shaq. That must be really tough." He crouches beside him and smiles. "But do you mind telling us what the merry frig you're doing down here talking to us?"

Lily gasps, and Pete sighs and glares at Smitty. But Shaq doesn't react. He looks down at Smitty and smiles back.

"I understand you're suspicious. But I just came down to see if you're OK, and, well — if I'm honest, yes — I need your help." He looks around at us to see if we're buying it. "Like I said, the others don't know I'm here. You see" — he wrings his hands — "I lost something. The key to the tower door in the kitchen. The others are really angry with me because all our stuff is in there. We need to get in. The others are paranoid that you've taken the key. That's why they've locked you down here." He smiles meekly at us. "So have you got it? Because if you do, just give it to me, and then I'll get you out of here. Immediately."

"Oh!" Alice flounces from her seat. "That key! We haven't got it, OK? If we did, we'd totally give it to you. Look" — she beams at him — "let us out anyway. We'll help you find it."

"What's in the tower that's so important?" Lily says quietly.

I look at her and try to make her meet my eyes.

"Just our things," Shaq says. "You know what it's like — you spend a little while without your stuff, you want it back."

"Phones? Laptops?" Pete says.

"Well, yes," Shaq answers. "Not that they work here. But there's an old transistor radio up there, and if I had someone to help me . . ."

He pinches above his nose again. "I might be able to rig something to contact the outside world . . ."

"I could absolutely do that." Pete puffs out his chest.

"Great!" Shaq nods. "But we need the key . . ."

Lily stands up — and as she does, Smitty blocks her way to Shaq.

"So yeah, we'll help you find the key if you let us out," he says loudly. "By the way, Shaq, what kind of study group?"

Shaq smiles. "Sorry, what?"

Smitty grins back. "What are you studying? Over Christmas? That's what I call dedication. What's your subject?"

Shaq licks his lips. "Shakespeare. We're studying Shakespeare, and we thought it would be great to read *Macbeth* in a real Scottish castle."

"Wow!" Smitty says. "Too right. We did *Macbeth* last year at school, didn't we, Alice? Great stuff." He leans in and stage-whispers to Shaq confidentially, "She made a very convincing third witch. And between you and me, Petey here was natural casting for Banquo's ghost. What a coincidence!" He beams around at us all.

"Yeah!" Shaq says.

"Kind of appropriate, *Macbeth*, isn't it?" Smitty says. "Spooky. And appropriate." He paces away from us, turns on his heel, opens his arms wide, and bellows, "'And graves have yawned, and yielded up their dead!'"

We all look at him as if he's lost his marbles.

Smitty winks at Shaq. "Macbeth was on the money with that one, wasn't he?"

Shaq nods. "Precisely! I couldn't have put it better myself."

"'Cry, "Havoc!" and let slip the dogs of war!'" Smitty the Thespian dances around the cellar. "Isn't that what he said?"

Shaq laughs. "That's right!"

Smitty laughs, too, dangerously friendly. He flings out a finger and points at Shaq. "My arse!" he spits. "Macbeth said no such thing! You need to sort out your Scottish kings from your Roman emperors!" He leaps onto Shaq and they crash to the ground, Shaq's stool spinning across the floor and narrowly missing Cam's box-nest. Cam screams and starts to cry, and Lily swears and scoops him up.

"Get the key out of his pocket!" Smitty yells from somewhere underneath Shaq.

"The key?" I say dumbly.

"To this basement!" Smitty rolls over and pins Shaq's arms behind him on the floor. "So we can get the hell out of here!"

Shaq twists on the floor, but Smitty has got him tight. I try to feel inside his pockets without actually *feeling* inside his pockets.

"You won't find it!" Shaq squeals at me. "I haven't got it on me. They locked me down here with you until I could get the tower key from you!"

"Right!" Smitty drags him to his feet. "So we'll lock you up with your 'Shakespearian mentor' down there and see if they'll let you out!" He turns to Pete. "Give me a hand!" The two of them drag Shaq through the wall-curtain.

Alice shakes her head. "Who knew?"

"What?"

She looks at me like I'm the one with the concussion now. "That Smitty could even read, let alone quote Shakespeare." She scuffs her shoe on the floor. "Too bad, though. Now they'll never let us out." She sighs, and follows the boys through the wall-curtain.

Lily is holding Cam, who is still sobbing. "This is getting to be too much." She holds a hand to Cam's forehead. "He's running a fever, too. We need to give them that tower key so they'll let us out and help us. And that radio Shaq talked about—"

"We can't trust them." My voice shakes. "Not yet . . . Please, Lily. He just told us a pack of lies. Who knows what they'll do to us if we give them the key? We have to hang tight for a while. Right now that key is the only power we have."

21

"Who are you really?"

I can't help asking. Shaq is sitting on the chair behind the bars, trying not to look at me, Smitty's puke, or the dead body beside him.

He doesn't reply. I don't really expect him to. I'm not even sure I want him to, if I'm honest. Why would he lie in the first place unless he had something to hide? But it passes the time while Smitty and the others are upstairs negotiating our release.

"What's in the tower you need so badly?" I try. "Wouldn't it be easier if you were just honest with us? What are we going to do, anyway? We're just dumb kids, after all."

He turns on the chair and looks at me.

"You're American, aren't you?"

I shrug. "No. Yes. Kinda."

His face goes dreamy. "I love America. I have family over there, in New Jersey. After all this is over I'm going to emigrate." He nods and smiles at me, as if he expects me to be thrilled, or applaud, or something. Or maybe start singing "The Star-Spangled Banner." When I don't, he continues, "Americans appreciate talent, you see. Not like here. In America, they give you the space and the money to do what you are destined to do. Here, everything is red tape, who your parents are, and where you went to school." He squints at me. "I bet you miss it, don't you? The Land of the Free?"

I look at him. "Don't try to bond with me."

There's a commotion at the other end of the corridor. I see Smitty coming toward me, but something's not right. When he emerges fully out of the shadows I can see he's being held by Michael—just like he'd held Shaq—with his hands behind his back.

Jeez. Smitty's stumbling, his eye is swollen, and there's blood running down his face. And Grace walks alongside, electric cow prod in hand. Behind traipse Pete, Alice, and Lily with a crying Cam in her arms, all like frightened lambs being led to the slaughter.

"Open that cell now!" shouts Michael.

I tighten my fist around the little key.

Grace steps forward. "Come along, now. Let's sort this out like civilized people."

I feel myself go hot. I nod toward Smitty. "You call that being civilized?"

Grace tries to look a little embarrassed. "He really left Michael no choice. But there'll be no more fighting"—she looks at Michael, then back at me—"because you'll let Shaq out, won't you?"

"Not unless you let us out, too." I hold her gaze steadily. She will not faze me with her perfect skin and silky voice. "We've done nothing to you. Why do you need to keep us down here anyway?"

"Unlock the door!" Michael yells, and throws Smitty to the floor, where he lies, moaning.

"No!" I face up to him, stupidly confident that he wouldn't dare hit a girl, a teenage girl.

But I didn't bargain on Grace. She steps up to Smitty and shocks him with the stick. He cries out and spasms on the floor like a fish out of water. She stares at me accusingly, as if I was the one who hurt him. She taps the bars with her stick.

"Where's this key?"

"It's in her hand!" Shaq shouts.

I step back against the wall, my fist clenched behind me, and Michael lunges for me.

"Stop!" Grace shouts at Michael. "There's really no need to scare her." She points the stick at Smitty, moves it slowly down his body until it hovers over his groin. Smitty's eyes widen.

"Don't give it to them, Bob!" he grunts.

Grace lowers the stick slowly and deliberately.

"Here!" I hold the key up, just in time to save Smitty, who shuts his eyes and gulps loudly.

Michael grabs the key and twists it into the lock, and suddenly Shaq is out, and Grace is pushing me into the cell, followed by Pete, Lily, and Cam. Michael drags Smitty in behind us.

Alice is still outside. Grace beckons her.

"No!" Alice wails. "I'm not going to be locked up there with that thing!" She backs off, but Michael seizes her and thrusts her toward the cell. At the door she manages to grab the bars and for a moment he can't move her. Then she suddenly lets go, swings around, and shoots a hand out through the door. She's in the cell now, and Michael slams the door shut on all of us, but I see what she managed to do. She has the key.

A second later, Michael realizes it, too. He opens the door and advances toward her, but Alice is too quick. Like a hungry hippo, she holds up the little key and swallows it in one gulp.

"There!" She opens her mouth and sticks her tongue out. "Now you can't lock us in!"

Go Alice.

Grace groans, turns on her heel, and strides off down the corridor, followed by Shaq.

"Michael! We don't have time for this!"

Michael kicks out at the chair, then at Smitty, and leaves us in the cell, slamming the door behind. It clanks in its place and — thankfully — swings open again. The last thing we need is for that latch to suddenly spring shut — the only solution currently being eaten away by Alice's stomach acid.

"Wait!" Lily calls to them. "Come back here! We've got the key!"

I cringe and close my eyes. *She's told them.*

But incredibly, they keep on walking. They think she means the cell key.

"*I've* got the key," Alice says. "And I'm not giving it up."

Lily half groans, half screams when she realizes why they haven't come back.

Smitty rolls onto his back, holds up an arm, and checks an imaginary watch.

"Give it a few hours, Malice," he splutters through thick and bloodied lips. "They'll be coming back to do a special toilet trip with you."

Alice looks at him and runs out of the cell. We don't need an invitation to follow her. The basement, with its tarps and boxes and coal chute, seems like five-star luxury compared to the cell.

Smitty refuses my help, even when I offer it begrudgingly, which is the only way I think he'll go for it. His face is a mess, but I think his pride is hurt more than anything. The others clear out faster than us;

I linger behind, pretending that my leg is giving me trouble.

"Nice catch, by the way." I lean against the cell bars and fiddle with my leggings.

"What?" He struggles to get up. I act like I don't notice.

"The *Macbeth* thing. Pretty cool that you knew those quotes. And he fell for it."

He shrugs, which in itself looks painful.

"No biggie. I knew he was lying."

He shuffles out into the corridor and I follow.

"What are they really from, those lines? You said Roman emperor. *Julius Caesar*?"

He rolls his eyes. "Dunno. Probably. I just knew them because they're in a Death Throes song."

Death Throes. In the half-light, I flush red. That badge he had on his jacket, the one we used to fasten the bus driver's arm bandage in place, way back when. Some British band I'm too uncool to know. But then, as I follow him up the corridor slowly, I see through it. He *did* know the lines were from *Julius Caesar*, otherwise how could he know they weren't in *Macbeth*? He just doesn't want to look like a geek in front of me.

When we reach the basement, Pete is disappearing up the steps, calling out that he's going to check that the door actually is locked. I sink onto a box. Alice has found another bottle of champagne. Smitty grabs it from her, untwists the wire cage, and pops the cork. He pours the foam over his sore face, then hands it back to Alice. Lily places Cam back into the box that has become his bed. He doesn't look well at all. Can't be easy coping with the apocalypse when you're three.

Pete descends the steps, his face telling us all we need to know.

"We're stuck, aren't we?" Lily stands up, her face solemn. "I'm going to do something about this. We can't stay down here forever. The time has come to—"

I jump to my feet. "OK!" I shout. "We need to know what's in that tower. If we can hear what they're talking about, we'll know why they're trying so hard to get into the tower, and"—I look at Lily—"if it turns out it will help to get in there, we will help them *find* the key," I say carefully.

Smitty looks up at me from his seat on the lawn mower. "And that works . . . how?"

"We get out of here!" I'm pacing now.

"Yay!" Alice says, acting her little socks off. "Oh, *pardonnez-moi*, I didn't see the sign for the Emergency Exit. Did I miss something? Or have you got your teleporter with you?"

I look up the steps. Can't go through the door. I briefly consider the jail cell corridor that ends all too suddenly and Pete's ideas of escape tunnels, but dismiss it. This is not *Nancy Drew*. We won't push the third brick up from the floor to activate a revolving stone door and reveal a smugglers' passage. Well, probably not . . .

And then it comes to me.

The coal chute. Has to lead somewhere. And if stuff can come down it, stuff can go up it, too. Stuff like me.

The small wooden door is partially open. Some coal must have tumbled down into the room when Lily and Cam hid in there, and it's keeping the door from shutting properly. I pull it wide and bend over to get into the bunker, but it's surprisingly spacious inside and I find I can stand up.

"Roberta, you're a genius!" shouts a voice from outside. It's Smitty, of course.

Then come the other voices.

"I'm not crawling up there, it's *filthy*." (Guess who.)

"Me and Cam will stay here." (Guess who.)

"The success of escape will depend on the gradient of the chute, of course." (And guess who.)

I climb onto the highest point of the pile of coal and look up into the chute itself. The opening begins at the top of the wall — which is about at my stooped shoulder height — a little high to crawl in easily, but not out of the question if I can find something to stand on. It's pretty dark, but there's a white horizontal line in the distance, as if the door at the other end is open a crack.

"Where's that flashlight?" I yell as I turn, and nearly jump out of my skin. Smitty is hunched behind me.

"Way ahead of you." He clicks the flashlight on and shines it up the chute. The length is about two-and-a-half Smittys, but wow, it's a tight squeeze. I move closer to get a better view and bang my bad shin on something.

"Ow. There's something sticking out of the wall."

Smitty shines the light down and we see three rusty rungs sticking out, one above the other. Steps. Someone must have wanted to climb up here before, maybe to clear a blockage. Maybe some poor kitchen boy or chimney sweep. Kid must have been pretty skinny to make it; then again, they were all malnourished and small back in Ye Olden Days.

I'm not malnourished — well, I could be now, but it's kind of recent. I am skinny, though. I put my foot on the first rung and prepare to push myself up.

"Nuh-uh, let me," Smitty says.

"You'll never fit," I counter.

"I will, and I'll pull you up after me."

"I don't need you to pull me." I glare at him in the darkness, and put my foot on the rung again.

"Too bad." He hands me the flashlight and curls a leg around my knee from behind, knocking me off balance. He pushes me lightly, and I fall back all too easily, my butt crunching onto the pile of coal.

"Hey!" I cry, but he's up the chute like a ferret up a drainpipe. At least for a few feet. And then he stops. He wriggles, his feet scuffing up coal dust as he tries to push himself farther. He manages to squirm onto his back and tries that way, his legs bending, trying to force himself up the chute. But it's no good. He's stuck.

"Problems?" I say.

I hear him sigh. "Turns out I'm way too muscular and broad-shouldered for this gig."

"I see. That's a shame." I'm not giving him an inch. And neither's the coal chute.

"In fact, I think I'm going to need some help getting out again."

"Wow." I mull that one over. "Smitty needs help? That must be . . . painful."

He's trying not to get irritated. "Not at all."

"What's going on in there?" Alice juts her head through the doorway. "Oh my god, there are probably humungous spiders in here." She sneezes. "I think I'm allergic. Hurry up and escape!"

She disappears, and I can hear her telling Pete and Lily how totally useless we are. I place the flashlight to one side, stand on the bottom rusty rung, and grab Smitty's ankles. I pull. At first he doesn't budge, but then I brace my other foot against the wall and heave with all my might. There's a scraping noise, a yell, and then he's free — tumbling through the chute and threatening to fall and squish me. I dodge and he lands like a cat on the coal heap, his leather jacket bunched around his shoulders.

"Yeah, thanks," he says. "I think." He takes off his jacket, picks up the flashlight, and examines it. It's majorly scratched up.

"Sorry," I say.

"Save it. It's the distressed look. Malice will probably say I'm bang on trend."

"You're kidding. Distressing was *so* pre-apocalypse."

He smiles, stretches an arm out to don the jacket again, and winces. It's a tiny intake of breath, before he can stop himself. He puts a hand on the back of his T-shirt and brings it out, the fingers wet and red.

"What have you done?" I snatch the flashlight and spin him around. He protests, but I lift the back of his T-shirt anyway. Long, vertical, bloody scrapes run from his waist up. "Oh god, Smitty," I whisper. "Your back's in ribbons. I'm so sorry." I search my pockets for something to staunch the blood, but I'm out of options. "I don't have anything to use on it," I panic. "You need to get it cleaned up." I rifle through my pockets a second time, fumbling and dropping the flashlight, which flickers and dies.

"Stop." He turns and holds my arms. "I'll be OK."

"But it was my fault!" I say, staring up at his barely lit face. "The scrapes could get infected—"

Smitty leans in and kisses me.

On the lips.

It's warm and firm and sweet and tastes of blood—and it's over before I can decide whether to kiss him back or punch his lights out.

"Get up the frickin' chute, Roberta."

Oh sweet Smart Retort Angel, where are you when I need you? I stare up at Smitty, not able to decide if I've just been seduced or insulted.

Speechless, and with shaking legs, I grab the flashlight off the floor and switch it on, turn to the wall, and shin up into that chute, half expecting Smitty to slap my behind. He doesn't, and I'm disgusted with myself that I'm almost a little disappointed. My mind burns.

He kissed me? On the lips! Like that's OK. It's not OK, it's totally wrong! Was he serious? Is he laughing at me? So why did I like it so much?

The thought makes me scrunch my face as I climb. Disgust fueling my ascent, I pull myself up that tunnel on my elbows, the flashlight in my hand flickering and clunking against stone until I'm nose to door with the exit. I slide my fingers under the gap and they meet cold snow. I slide the door up, wriggle through, and kick my way out into the frigid air.

I stagger to my feet, lean against the stone wall, and let my red cheeks cool. It's dazzlingly white outside, so incredibly quiet. The snow surprises me, like I'd almost forgotten it was ever there. I'm at the back of the castle, in a courtyard surrounded by stable buildings or outhouses. The tower surges up to my left, and beyond that must be the kitchen and the back door Smitty used on our first night here. *Last night,* I remind myself. Crazy. Feels like I've been here for weeks.

There's a muffled noise from below; Smitty is shouting something.

I shove the flashlight down the back of my leggings, bend down, and slide the door shut quietly.

I'm on my own now. Absolutely on my own.

22

I could run.

I don't have anything but the clothes on my back, but I could still run. I'd have at least five or six hours before sunset to get somewhere. How far could I get in six hours, on foot, in snow? Ten miles? Twelve? More? There are other villages, there'll be other places with phones, other survivors who aren't so psychotic or irritating, and who won't insist on kissing me.

Now would be the time to make a move. One person does not attract the same kind of Meat-Feast-Seeking Monsters as several loud teenagers burdened with injuries and a three-year-old boy. I can make it on my own.

I breathe. *Assess.*

There are tracks in the courtyard snow. Too wide for skis, too narrow for a car. They lead from an archway in the courtyard wall to an outbuilding with a stable door.

I creep up to it, half an eye on the windows behind me in case anyone is watching. They're not, as far as I can tell. I unbolt the top part of the door and peep in. All I need right now is a zombie Black Beauty.

Instead I see two Ski-Doos — one silvery blue, the other red with a small sled attached to the back.

I unbolt the bottom door and slip inside.

Oh gosh.

There are keys in the ignition of both Ski-Doos. Reckless? I guess if zombies attack, it doesn't help to be wondering where you put the keys.

Beside the sled are some boxes, like someone has unloaded them recently. I take a peek inside . . . disinfectant. I frown. Something familiar about this. In fact, the more I think about it, the more sure I am that these are the very same boxes we sat on in the office of the Cheery Chomper. I'm certain that's an Alice-sized butt dent in the top of one. So that's what they were doing while they were away from the castle? Getting disinfectant? Weird.

I fling a leg over Silvery Blue and feel the cool leather of the seat. I have driven one of these things before. Dad had a friend who loaned us a couple on a ski trip last winter in the US. Of course, I wasn't supposed to be driving it, just hanging on behind a parent. But Mum was back in the lodge on her BlackBerry as usual, so Dad and I rode all day, until our cheeks turned purple and my fingers had set in a clawlike grip.

I stroke the chassis of the Ski-Doo, the paintwork so smooth to the touch. I could get a long way on Silvery Blue. To a town, a police station. Given time and gas, maybe even home. I feel a pang as I think of home; the new house in the suburbs that is way too big for Mum and me, with its high ceilings, drafty fireplaces, and bad plumbing. We've lived there barely a month and nothing about it seems like home yet. No history, no familiarity, no birthdays or memories of a shared Christmas. Christmas this year had been at Grandma's with dry turkey and the Queen's speech and Mum crying quietly in her room when she thought I was downstairs.

Still, any version of home would be better than this.

I grip the handlebars of the Ski-Doo and wonder how much is in the tank.

I dither. It's a big move, leaving on my own.

If Dad was here now, he'd know what to do. He'd leap onto Big Red, fire up the engine, lead the way. He'd find our way home, kicking any monsters out of our path. I would be safe if Dad was here; he'd make it right.

I feel the hot tears rolling down my face, and brace myself on the bike as the crying comes so suddenly and overwhelmingly. Memories of his brave smile, his hand growing cold in the hospital bed, and the kind of helplessness and fear I thought I'd never have to go through again so soon. Shuddering, bending over onto my elbows, I let it all out. All the Dad stuff. And the snide looks and snarky words of the ski trip, and Mr. Taylor and his beaten-up monster face, and the driver and his head in the snow, and Smitty and how stupid I feel.

And then it passes, and Dad is gone again, and I realize I'm crying because I know I can't ride Silvery Blue off into the sunset. There are people relying on me, and for some jacked-up reason I can't let them down.

I climb off the Ski-Doo and leave the stable, closing the doors behind me. But not before I've pocketed the keys. Because, as Smitty said, you never know.

All right, back on task. Listen in on their plans and find out what the hell is going on.

I'm creeping past the tower, hugging the walls. I try to sneak a look in. But it's not going to happen. Where windows once were, there is modern brick.

As I edge around, I spot the place where Pete threw the Veggie Juice. It's just a white lump of snow now; I can't even see the blue plastic bag handles anymore. But I think it's still there, hibernating until the big thaw. Above it is the kitchen window, which is open a crack—Lily must have left it like that to clear the bacon smell, which probably wasn't too bright considering the zombie sitch, but I'm grateful for it now because I can hear Grace's low, calm voice punctuated by Michael's exclamations and Shaq's whining. They're all in the kitchen.

I can't stay out here too long. Even if I can get close enough to hear better, there's no cover. All it will take is for one of them to look out of the window, and I'll be busted. Not to speak of the dog, wherever he's lurking. I need to get inside again and find somewhere to hide.

I scoot past the window to the back door, willing it to be open. Turning the doorknob excruciatingly slowly, I send a silent prayer that no one will be waiting for me on the other side.

My prayers are answered. I'm in the mudroom, which holds nothing except a coatrack, boots, and a collection of walking sticks and umbrellas. The door to the kitchen is to my left, and there is another, narrower door to my right.

I creep up to the kitchen door. Grace is saying something about "adverse situations being expected." I shake my head and listen closer. *Really, Grace? Did you really expect the world to be overrun by the Undead when you woke up yesterday morning?* I jump as I hear Michael's baritone. He's standing right next to the door. He seems to have read my mind, too, because he's basically saying out loud what I just said to Grace in my head.

This will never do. Any moment now, they'll hear me standing here, or open the door and see me. What am I supposed to do, crouch beside the coats and make like a hunting jacket? I have to find another way to eavesdrop.

I pad toward the narrow door. It's stiff and gives a squeak as I start to open it. I freeze, hot blood running through my veins, my eyes on the kitchen door. But it doesn't move. They're too wrapped up in their own conversation.

I ease the door wide open. Steep stairs lead up. A servants' staircase. Of course. How else were they going to get breakfast trays full of delights for the masters and mistresses upstairs? It can't have been fun carrying things up and down there all day.

And then it hits me. A way to get into the kitchen that doesn't involve using doors. And it's quite possibly the *dumb*est idea I've had in the last three days.

Or ever.

I'm upstairs, and I've found it. The little hatch in the wall that corresponds to the one we found in the kitchen last night. The truth is, the servants didn't carry breakfast trays upstairs every morning. They put them on a shelf attached to a pulley and let the wonders of Victorian technology do the work for them.

A dumbwaiter. Basically, a little elevator shaft from the kitchen to upstairs.

A dumbwanker. Basically, a person who chooses to climb down the elevator shaft.

That'll be me, then.

I put my hands on the handle on the bottom of the hatch door and heave, and it slides up reluctantly. Eerie. A musty smell seeps out. Inside is a black space, just big enough for some foolish person to climb in. I lean in and look down, half expecting an ancient Scottish banshee to come rushing up to greet me. There should be a shelf, a little platform that I could ride down to the kitchen. But the shaft is completely empty, which, now that I think about it, is way better. The last thing I want to do is get trapped.

There are wooden bars on the shaft walls, a ready-made ladder. That's my way down. I feel for the flashlight stuffed down the back of my waistband. I'm a genius. Of course, I knew I'd be crawling up one dark tunnel only to be crawling down another. I shine the flashlight down the shaft. The dust clutches at the back of my throat and I step back, trying to stop myself from coughing.

Well? Think you can do this, Roberta? I hear him in my head. *Can you?*

Hell, yeah.

I stow the flashlight in my waistband again and climb in, testing the first wooden bar with one foot. It seems to be holding. I swing my other leg over and sit on the ledge, my hand reaching up for another bar. Good so far. Then before I can really believe it, I'm putting my full weight on the wooden struts and lowering myself down, already feeling for the next rail with my foot, moving hand over hand in a way that totally goes against the panic that's rising in my chest. It's almost like, if I keep moving, I won't fall. And if I don't keep moving, I'll chicken out and—

Shit!

A bar gives way, my right hand snatches air, and I swing around, losing one of my footholds. I shoot out the free hand and foot, bracing myself against the opposite wall like a cat in a chimney.

That was quite noisy.

I look down the shaft, absolutely expecting the hatch below to open. But it doesn't.

A salty bead of sweat runs into my eye. I blink it away and steady my breathing. *Keep going.*

I move again, slower this time, testing out the old wood before I trust it with my life. And then, suddenly, I can hear muffled voices. They're still in the kitchen, and they're still talking. Great. Now just don't say anything important before I get there . . .

And then I am there, at the hatch. There are three edges of light where the door doesn't quite meet the wall. I shine the flashlight down. The shaft continues a few feet below the hatch, and my grateful foot touches solid ground. The muted smell of bacon competes with dust and dead mouse. The hatch is at chest level; I bend down and put my ear to the door. If they do open the hatch, I'll look like a head on a platter.

". . . our primary objective should be to secure it."

It's Grace. Her voice is low but she's clear enough. What's she talking about? The castle? The dog?

"We have to contact someone!"

I jump. Once again, Beardy-Michael has exercised his remarkable talent for unknowingly standing right beside me. I hold my breath.

He continues. "We've got to be proactive. We can't just sit around on our arses waiting for the world to end!"

Too right, Michael, I think. But . . . huh? *World* to end? Is this everywhere? How does he know that?

"Useless!" It's Shaq. "It's useless contacting anyone until we've secured the product! Don't you listen, Michael? Don't you see the nonsense in our position? We've got nothing, nothing at the moment! Unless we can get in there" — there is an emphatic *thump* — "we can't possibly hope to have any leverage with these people!"

"Reality check, Shaq." Michael's voice gets quieter, and I can hear him walking across the kitchen. "Thanks to you, we *can't* get in there."

They're talking about the tower. *Bingo.*

"Hidden in plain sight!" Shaq's voice rises to a whine. "That's what you always said. No fancy keypad on the door to raise suspicion, key hung up in the pantry behind the door! I was only following the rules!"

"We have no guarantees they'll come here anyway." Grace's cool voice cuts through the hysteria. "They may well have had some counter-measures in place before they let this go nuclear."

There's silence in the kitchen.

I close my eyes. *Nuclear?* What the hell? The zombies are gonna be dropping bombs? That's it, this is not real. I'm dreaming. The last two days have just been a trauma-induced nightmare. Any minute now, I'll be naked onstage in front of the entire school and the boy I used to like in kindergarten will be trying to make me eat a huge bowl of creamed spinach. It cannot get any worse than this.

I open my eyes. Get a grip. *Nuclear* is an expression; she's not talking about bombs. But Shaq said *product*. What product? Some kind of anti-zombie protection? Or . . .

The pieces fall into place. I lean back against the wall, feeling like the biggest ignoramus in the world.

This has got nothing to do with zombies.

Product.

This is about drugs.

Product is what drug cooks call drugs, isn't it? Grace, Michael, and Shaq are drug dealers! Or manufacturers, to be precise. They are cook-ing up some weirdo pill in the tower. The boxes of disinfectant in the stable — they probably use that in their drug kitchen; it makes total sense.

And they need the product to have *leverage* with . . . someone who wants what they have. Some drug overlord? I imagine a guy with a big black mustache, a shiny suit, and several scantily clad women draped over him. Those sorts of people kill other people. They will not be put off by a mere zombie apocalypse. They will come here, and they will kill whoever they find. They won't care that we're only school kids and not drug cooks. They'll shoot us first and ask questions later. We need to get out of here, and fast. Take our chances with the Undead. At least they don't have automatic weapons.

"What of our moral obligation?" It's Grace.

"Don't make me laugh!" Michael laughs anyway. He's back at his post, right by the dumbwaiter hatch. "We didn't put the stuff out there! We created this, but we didn't put it on the street!"

"We gave it to them knowing full well what they might do," Grace says from the other side of the kitchen. "And we have the power to undo the damage."

"I'm more interested in staying alive," growls Michael. "Don't talk to me about morals. We did this for the best reasons."

"Yeah" — Shaq makes a choking sound — "and for a bucketful of money."

OK, that's it. I'm out of here. I straighten up and feel for the nearest rung. I'm going to climb out of this shaft, and we're all getting out of the drug kitchen. Now.

"Just remember . . ." Grace's voice is loud and clear. She must have moved toward Michael because it's almost like she's whispering in my ear, she's so close. "Whenever you see one of those monsters, it's on you, Michael. On me, on Shaq, and on you. We created them. Regardless of what the company has done now. If we get into the tower, we get the antidote and the power is back in our hands. We disinfect this place from top to bottom, remove any evidence we were ever here, then we disappear. Nobody else dies, we get the rest of our money, and everything goes back to normal. But to make any of this work, we need that antidote."

Antidote?

It feels like the floor has dropped away. I grip the wooden bars tightly, the walls closing in on me as my head spins. *Just get out . . . make sense of this later . . .*

I take the first couple of steps up. One foot after the other, one hand and then the next . . .

I'm halfway up when the forgotten flashlight, top-heavy and balancing precariously in my elastic waistband, falls. It ricochets off the opposite wall and lands on the floor with a deafening *thud*.

"What the hell was that?" Michael shouts.

I climb like zombies are chasing me. Fast ones.

23

Oh, you bet I move fast.

If they're zombie-creating mad scientists, it won't take them too long to figure out that I'm hiding in the dumb dumbwaiter shaft.

As I reach the upstairs hatch, there's a noise from below. I glance down. No square of light, no shout. They haven't got the door open yet. But they will. I clamber out of the hatch and close it. As if that will make a difference. It's not like they're going to follow me up the shaft; they'll use their evil superbrains and come on up the staircase instead.

I run to the grand staircase, and I'm halfway down when a door slams. I duck. Somewhere downstairs there is movement. *Please don't come this way.* I pause, waiting for running feet, but none come. Got to keep going. If I don't move now, I'll miss my shot.

I scurry down the staircase and sprint toward the basement door. There's a wooden chair propped under the handle and I fling it aside, open the door, and take the steps two at a time.

"We have to go!"

Lily looks up at me. Cam is still in his box-nest.

"Where's everyone else?" I look frantically around the dimly lit basement.

Lily stands up. "You got out of the chute?"

"Yes," I say impatiently. As if this wasn't completely obvious! "Where are the others? We have to go now!"

"Pete said something about a tunnel. Alice and Smitty are playing spin the bottle."

I hear Alice's unmistakable fake giggle coming from behind the wall-curtain. Rage flushes through my body. Here am I, risking life and limb for them, and they're dicking around?

"Get Cam and anything you need," I order Lily. "We leave, now!"

"Where are we going?" Lily calls after me, but I ignore her and head through the wall-curtain. It's an excellent question, but I am not going to waste time answering it now.

Alice and Smitty are sitting cross-legged on the floor. In between them is a bottle.

"Get up," I spit. "Get Pete. We're leaving."

Smitty scrambles to his feet. "What's going on? You heard them?"

I nod grimly. "I heard them all right. They made the zombies. In the tower. I don't know how or why, but they created a drug or something that made everyone turn. Somebody paid them to."

"What?" Smitty is aghast.

"Are you off your rocker?" Alice giggles.

"If you don't believe me, fine. But now they know one of us was listening in, and we have to leave before the *real* bad guys get here, the ones they sold the drug to." I turn and run back into the basement, not bothering to see if I've convinced them.

Lily is still bending over Cam.

"Something's wrong," she mutters. "He won't wake up."

"Carry him!" I shout.

Smitty, Alice, and Pete appear through the wall-curtain.

"What's this about zombie-making in the tower?" Pete says.

"That's what they're doing here?" Lily says.

"And all of this is a huge experiment?" Pete almost looks exhilarated.

"So it would seem. No time to make sense of it now," I say. "There are two Ski-Doos and a sled in the stable through the courtyard. We make a run for it. I take the first Ski-Doo with Cam and Lily on the back." I glare at Smitty and Alice. "Pete drives the other. You're free to fight over who gets to ride in the sled behind."

I'm up the stairs before they can comment, and I'm relieved to find the door still open. Pausing for a second at the end of the corridor while the others line up behind me, I listen. A door slams, somewhere way off, upstairs maybe. Good. Now's our chance.

"This way!" I whisper, and head across the hall to the main door. It's bolted above and below, the way we originally left it. With a glance up at the staircase, I reach for the high bolt while Smitty scrabbles at my feet for the lower one. He's quicker than me, and first to grab the handle and turn.

The door does not open.

"Pull it!" Alice cries, elbowing Smitty out of the way and clasping the handle in her slim hands. It's useless, it's locked. By a key. Another key, a key we don't have.

"Check the basement!" There's a shout from somewhere above. *Michael.*

"Back door," Smitty says firmly.

Alice makes a dash for it and we all follow . . . except Lily and Cam, who are crouching on the floor.

"Come on!" I hiss at them.

"He's sick." Lily looks up at me with big eyes. As if to prove her point, Cam retches, and there's a slosh on the polished floor.

"There's no time, we have to move!" I run toward her, the bitter smell of puke hitting me in the back of the throat.

"Bobby" — Lily's voice is almost begging — "I don't know if we can keep going. Maybe we should just give them what they want. Give them the key to the tower."

"We're not giving them anything," I say.

As I reach for her, I turn and see Shaq standing at the top of the staircase. He's heard everything. He stares down at us. I stare back, frozen, a look of desperate pleading on my face.

"Please," I barely whisper.

He thinks about it.

Then he shouts, "They're here! They're here!"

Bastard. You didn't want to, but you screamed for the Nazis anyway because you need them to like you.

And we're running. Me with the sick Cam in my arms, and Lily all long legs and flailing arms behind me. We reach the kitchen and hear the shouting and the kicking from the mudroom. Smitty, Alice, and Pete are flinging themselves at the back door, which was so very unlocked when I came in through it, but which is now totally and utterly locked and impenetrable.

"There must be another way out!" Pete cries.

"There!" Lily points to the kitchen window, which is still open a crack.

"They're behind us . . ." I dump Cam on the floor beside Lily and rush to the door we just came through, grabbing a wooden chair as I go. I thrust it under the handle. *Oh, I'm a quick learner* . . . Smitty catches on and together we barricade all three doors.

"This won't open any farther!" Lily is up on a chair and trying to force the window. Smitty leaps up beside her and pushes with all his might.

"Break it!" shouts Alice, but it's hopeless. The small-paned, stone-framed, lead-glassed windows that seemed such a plus-point for their anti-zombie appeal are working against us, big-time. Unless Pete can fashion a demolition ball out of some duct tape and a piece of string, those windows are staying intact.

We are utterly trapped.

There's a scratching at one of the doors. Alice screams. The handle turns frantically, then there's thumping. Alice screams again, and I want to thump her. Way to tell them we're still in here.

Then the thumping stops.

"Guys . . ." A low, calm voice. "We're not going to hurt you." It's Grace.

"Like hell you're not!" Alice shouts back. "You're going to turn us into zombies!"

I grab her arm. "Shut up!" I yelp.

"OK," Grace continues from behind the door. "So you heard some stuff. But there're a lot of things you don't know, and the safest thing for you to do is trust us and let us in."

"Did you really create the zombies?" Pete walks toward the door. He's not panicked, just interested, with maybe a touch of I-Was-Right-All-Along. "Was it a virus mutation? Biological warfare? Is this some kind of government experiment? Who are you working for?"

We all freeze.

From the other side of the door, Grace makes a noise, a kind of half sigh, half chuckle. Like she's very, very tired.

"Pete, yes?" she says. "You're the brains, aren't you?" Her voice is soft, seductive even. "Open this door and I'll tell you everything, I promise. You'll be fascinated, believe me."

Pete walks toward the door, and I'm almost about to tackle him to the ground in case he goes for the chair, but then he speaks.

"That's very flattering, Grace," he says. "I'm sure I would be fascinated. All we ever wanted was a few answers."

"Screw answers, I want to go home!" wails Alice.

"I know, Alice, I know," says Grace. "We all do. We want you to be safe, we want everyone to be safe, that was the intention all along." Her voice is creamy, and I imagine her, like a Hollywood goddess, leaning against the door languorously — holding an ax behind her back. She speaks again.

"You should know . . . What's happening here . . . It's not the first time."

OK, she's got our attention. And she knows it.

"People have been turning, all over the world — isolated cases. It's been going on for a while."

"Really?" says Smitty. "Must have missed that on the news."

"It's true." Grace sounds convincing enough. "Naturally, it's been kept quiet by the authorities. Imagine the panic if this got out."

"Imagine." Smitty's voice is thick with sarcasm.

"What's causing it?" says Pete.

Grace clears her throat. "Nobody knows. Our group was tasked to find a solution, an antidote. But then the company that was funding us tricked us. All they really wanted was to discover whatever it was that was turning people so they could use it as a weapon — something they could sell. They fooled us. You know how adults can be."

I roll my eyes. For a smart person, Grace is incredibly stupid if she thinks this Us 'n' Them crap is going to work.

"We created an antidote," she continues. "And it's in the tower. We just need to get it, and we can make everything right." She pauses, and I can almost hear her licking her lips, waiting to see if we'll bite. "Do you want to be the heroes? Help put everything right?"

"Yes," says Lily weakly.

"Wait!" Smitty shouts. "You have an antidote? Then why the hell aren't you out there giving it to people, you cowards?"

"Smitty," Grace's voice purrs, "it's not the final product, just a prototype we're developing. We believe it works, but we can't be sure. We know it doesn't work for people who have already turned, only on those who are in the very early stages of infection."

"So what was the Veggie Juice all about?" Smitty retorts. "Getting some test subjects to lock up in your tower?"

"No! That wasn't our idea!" For a moment, I almost think Grace has lost it. But she quickly gets it back. "That was the company, not us. They started the outbreak as a test, to see how it would spread and how people would react — they even tried to infect us the same way, because we're witnesses. And now we need to get the antidote before they come and take it away for good."

"And exactly what will you do with the antidote once you have it?" Pete asks. It's a good question.

I can hear the grim determination in Grace's voice. "There are people out there who will know what to do with it. For the right reasons."

"And for the right price?" Pete laughs.

"It has never been about the money!" says Grace.

"Bollocks!" yells Smitty.

"But if you're interested . . . ," she intones, "some of that money could be yours. All you have to do is give us the tower key."

"I don't care about money!" screams Lily suddenly. "All I want is to get out of here, and for Cam to get better! We need to get him to a hospital!"

"He's poorly?" Grace says. "I've trained in children's medicine, Lily. I can help him. Open up, give us the key to the tower, and I'll make him all better." Grace can't prevent her voice from trembling. She's not that good an actress. I was more convincing in the school Nativity play as a sheep.

"Sadly, we don't have the key," said Pete. "If we did, we'd give it to you."

"We do have the key." Lily reaches into her pocket and holds it up. "They know we do."

"You've had it all this time?" Alice shouts. She turns to me, like it's all my fault. "You knew about this?"

"Do the right thing, Lily," urges Grace from behind the door.

"Okey-dokey." Smitty walks toward the door. "We'll just do that, then, eh, Grace? And we'll be the heroes. And you'll heal Cam. And give us a big wad of cash."

There's a scream from the window. It's Lily. At first I think she's freaked out under the pressure, but then I see there's a hand reaching through the window, a hand grabbing her hair, pulling her. A zom? No, Shaq. I see the top of a ladder and his dark head behind the glass. Then, in almost the same minute, there's a crash behind the door to the mud-room, a crash and a shout. Michael has come in the back door.

The classic diversion technique: Grace kept us talking; the men crept up from behind. We should have known better.

Chaos breaks out. Cam is screaming; Alice, too. I grab Lily's arm, trying to pull her away from Shaq. Smitty flings himself at the door with Michael on the other side. Grace keeps talking, low and persuasive, dripping poison into Pete's ears. I can hear the dog barking somewhere, then there's a cracking noise and the door splits in two. The door to the mudroom is still in place — barely — but I can see Michael through a gap, his face turnip-purple and full of rage, Smitty trying to hold the pieces of wood together. As I try to wrestle Lily free of Shaq's grasp, there's a silver flash and I see the key spring from her hand and fall to the kitchen floor.

Before I can react, Alice has fallen upon the key. She runs to the tower door and thrusts it into the lock. Both Smitty, Pete, and I yell, "Noooooo!" and I catapult myself across the room, abandoning Lily, trying to reach Alice. She turns the key and opens the door. And then she's inside, and gone, with Pete hot on her heels.

Maybe they're right. Maybe this is our only way? As I make the decision, the door finally gives way and Michael comes barrelling in headfirst, slamming into Smitty, who rolls onto the floor and ends up at my feet. He doesn't stop Michael, who smacks into the kitchen table, whacking his head on the corner. He falls to the floor, dazed, barely moving.

Lily drops to the ground beside Cam. A second later Shaq appears and lets Grace in. She stands there, cow prod in hand. She sees the open tower door and her eyes flash.

Smitty drags himself to his feet and gently pulls me inside the tower. He puts his hand on the door.

"Good," Grace says. "You opened the door. We won't hurt you."

Smitty ignores her. "Lily, get up. Get Cam, come here." His hand is firm on the door, ready to pull it shut.

On the floor by the table, Michael groans.

"Quickly, Lily," Smitty says, pulling the door, narrowing the gap.

Lily crawls to Cam, who is silent and curled into a tight ball, his face in his little hands. "He's dead."

All eyes flick down to Cam.

"He's not dead," says Smitty. "He's ill. Pick him up, come over here."

Everyone holds their breath. On the floor, Cam stirs. Head down, his stubby legs kick out, trying to find some hold on the floor. Lily cries with relief.

"See? He's fine," Smitty says. "Carry him."

A dark shape leaps out from the mudroom door. The dog, barking and snarling, teeth bared and pink gums moist. He goes for Cam, and Lily falls back, startled. The dog stops just short, but his agitation increases and he bounces and smacks his jaws at Cam.

It is Cam and Cam alone who is pissing him off.

"Oh my god," Shaq mutters. "The kid. The kid is infected."

"No!" Lily shouts.

Cam sits up and turns to face her. I see his face and feel a stabbing pain in my stomach. His chubby smile is black and twisted, his mouth oozing.

The dog keeps barking.

"Lily," Smitty says carefully. "Leave him."

"No!" she screams.

There's a scuffle by the table as Michael wakes up suddenly, like someone's thrown a bucket of water over him.

"The kid is infected!" Shaq shouts again, and Michael scuttles away into Grace.

Them on one side, Smitty and me on the other, Lily and Cam and the dog in the middle.

Cam makes an unearthly moan, like a baby buried alive, trying to cry the dirt out of its lungs. He holds out his arms to his sister, black blood running freely from his mouth.

"Cam . . . ," Lily whimpers.

"Lily!" Smitty yells again.

But she holds her arms out to Cam.

Grace screams, "No!"

And as brother and sister embrace, Cam plants his milk teeth into Lily's trembling shoulder.

Michael and Grace leap forward. Smitty pulls me away from the door and slams it shut, locking us in the tower.

24

There is a *thump*ing on the door.

So muffled, it's like we're underwater. Maybe it's because of the thick door, but I feel like I'm floating above myself, spiraling somewhere on the ceiling — or above the ceiling, in the clouds . . .

"Bob. Bob."

Smitty's shaking me lightly — or maybe it's really hard. Again, can't be sure. And then he's taking me by the hand and pulling me up the stairs. Winding stairs that are brightly lit, white, clean. This is not a castle; it's like suddenly we're in a spaceship. The stairs seem to go on forever. With every step I return to my body.

Here comes the dizzy. I sink onto the gleaming stairs.

"We left her."

Smitty crouches by my side. "You saw her get bitten."

I nod.

"Cam was infected." Smitty sounds like he's trying to convince himself, but he doesn't need to convince me. There was no doubt about it. No tiny shred of doubt.

"They're not dead yet." I rub my face with my hands and spring to my feet, head zinging with the rush of blood. "Grace said there's an antidote up there. We should let her in — she might still be able to help Cam and Lily . . ."

"No!" Smitty shakes his head. "She said it didn't work after someone has turned."

"Lily, then!"

"We have no idea if Grace was even telling the truth." He's firm.

"If there is an antidote, I'll go get it myself." I push past him and stomp up the stairs. "I'm not leaving them without trying, even if Cam can't be saved."

"We should have . . ." Smitty's voice sounds small and pained. "*I* should have taken better care of him. Or at least taken notice. Poor little guy."

I stop short and cast him a look over my shoulder in surprise. The Smitty I know doesn't do Broken Down Doll. I don't know whether to be touched or terrified.

"You can't beat yourself up." I risk putting my hand lightly on his arm. Our eyes meet for a second. "He must have been infected before we even met him."

"Lily." Smitty takes a breath, and briefly touches my hand. "There's still a chance the antidote will work on her. It takes different amounts of time for people to turn — Mr. T was almost instantaneous, the drones in the café a few minutes — but Cam took days."

"Then we have to try!" I turn away and am hauling myself up the stairs again before I can think better of it.

I reach the top of the stairs and run through an arched doorway.

The room in front of me is no TARDIS out of *Dr. Who*, but it's a whole lot bigger than I would have guessed. It's circular with a vaulted ceiling and huge, elevated windows. Everything is white and shiny and new-looking, with desks and bookshelves hugging the walls below the windows, and a long slablike table in the center of the room. I think we've found Frankenstein Central.

"You're OK?" Pete's bent over a desk in the corner, manically fiddling with something. "Did you shut the door behind you?"

"No, we left it wide open, you dweeb," mutters Smitty. "Thanks for caring."

"Can they get in? What are we going to do?" Alice shouts from above. She's perching on a broad window ledge that runs almost the full circumference of the room and she's holding a phone up to the window, checking for reception. Heaven only knows which orifice she's been keeping that phone in for the last few hours . . .

I snatch at a cabinet door, then a drawer, flinging the contents on to the floor. "Where would they keep the antidote?" I rake through some shelves. And then I see it: a fridge. That's exactly where I'd be hiding my magic potions. I heave the door open to find shelves full of test tubes and syringes.

"What for?" says Alice.

"Too late," says Smitty, and his words hang in the air like a bad smell.

He points to a cabinet by the doorway. Inside it are six small TV screens. Very much like the office at the Cheery Chomper. Exactly like the office at the Cheery Chomper. I shut the fridge and move toward the screens. There are different views of the courtyard, back and front doors, the main gate. And the kitchen.

Lily is standing facing the camera, swaying softly, as if listening to music. At first I think her eyes are closed, but then I realize her eyeballs have rolled back into her head and all I can see are the whites. There is a single thick string of dark saliva hanging off her chin, and as she sways, the dribble swings, too. Suddenly her arms shoot out at her sides, her wrists flexed and her fingers like claws, almost as if she's playing piano, the music in her head reaching a crescendo.

"What can you see?" Alice shouts from above.

Cam has gone. Everyone has gone. It's just Lily, or what used to be Lily.

"What's happening?" Pete calls from the desk.

My eyes are too dry for tears, and my heart is banging in my chest. And then there's a flash of movement behind Lily, and it's Michael with Smitty's dwarven ax held high above him, moving in on her . . .

"Switch it off!" I cry, and Smitty's hand shoots out and smacks the screen's OFF button. All goes blank.

Smitty punches the cabinet, then he turns on a nearby leather chair, wrestling it to the ground and kicking it across the polished floor.

"What the hell's going on?" Alice is reaching critical level.

"Cam turned and bit Lily," Smitty says quietly, his chest heaving. "She turned, too."

"Oh my god!" Alice wails. "Cam was one of them all along?" She casts the phone down onto the ledge, flings her head back, and *yowls*, sending up some kind of primal scream into the dying light, like every last vestige of hope is leaving her body. It's quite something. She should have got that out of her system a long time ago — like about when puberty hit. It could have made her a much more pleasant person.

I notice the phone she dropped was mine. Never mind. It's not like I was that fond of it anyway.

"I knew it," Pete says. "There was always something off about Cam."

"Really, Snowflake?" There is bitter venom in Smitty's voice. "How sickeningly astute of you."

"What?" Pete counters. "It's not like I'm not sorry or anything. It's horrible."

"At least it was quick." I place a hand on Smitty's shoulder. "Lily, I mean." In reality I don't know if what I've said is true, and Smitty knows it. Cam and Lily could be tortured, in pain, frightened, and half dead, being hacked to pieces by Michael. I dig my nails into my hands and try to banish the thought.

Smitty turns to me and holds my arms just like he did when he kissed me in the coal chute. For a second I wonder if he's going to kiss me again. Probably not appropriate right now.

"We've got to forget it," he urges. "Hold it together and focus on getting ourselves out of here."

I nod, trying to gather myself, to prevent meltdown.

He drops my arms and takes a step back. "Good, good." He's bought it.

I trust myself to breathe again.

"We need to search this place," Smitty says, gritting his teeth. "There's got to be something here that can help us."

"Doing it already," Pete snaps from the corner. "PCs" — he points at the desks — "checking them to see if we can get online."

On each desk unit are a few scattered belongings, like little fragments of personality stamped into place in an otherwise sterile petri dish. On the desk nearest to me there's a tube of lemon-scented hand cream, and a picture of a glamorous blonde wearing sunglasses, her arm around a muscle-bound guy in swim shorts. Grace's desk. Clean and functional.

Smitty turns on the PC and hits a few keys.

A box leaps up: PASSWORD.

Smitty looks up at me. "Any bright ideas?"

He runs to the next desk and turns on that computer. I move to a third desk. The leather chair that Smitty attacked belongs here, and I pick it up and put it back in its place. It's an old-fashioned office swivel chair, worn and cracked, with what looks like horsehair sticking out of a hole in one of the arms. I sit down—it smells familiar somehow, of warm body—and turn to the PC. The hard drive is missing; it's been disconnected.

"Anything?" says Smitty.

I shake my head, halfheartedly fumbling through a cardboard box of belongings on the desk. Nothing useful.

"Pete?" Smitty calls out.

"Negatory," comes the reply.

"Radio!" Alice clambers down from her perch on the window ledge. "Shaq said there was a radio."

She and Smitty begin to plunder the room anew, desperation rising.

"Lies, all lies," Smitty spits, pulling drawers open, rifling through shelves.

I can't bear this. I am so done with the mystery, and the raising and dashing of hopes. I lean heavily against the desk and push the box of belongings to the floor in despair. Something flutters out. *What is that?*

"Oh, kneel down before me because I am Princess of Genius!" Alice has found something. I glance up; it's a laptop. *Great.* Another password not to guess.

My gaze falls again on the glossy rectangle that fell out of the box. *There's something odd . . .* I crouch down beside it. It's a photograph. I hold it up to the light, my heart drumming.

A little girl, four or five years old—no, she's four, I'm sure of it— sitting on a toy tractor, wearing blue shorts and a big grin. A happy summer holiday. A hot day, with a picnic, sticky-ice-cream fingers, and a wasp that flew into the jam . . .

"We're logged in!" Pete shouts. "And there's web!"

I look over to where the three of them are crowded together over the laptop. *Web?* But I'm not sure I can move. I stare at the photograph again. I must be wrong. This makes no sense at all.

"Bob, what's wrong with you!" Smitty yells at me. "We're online!"

There are no easy answers. I shove the photo into a pocket and force myself back into the moment.

"We have Internet?"

"In a sense," says Pete. "However, that's not the end of the story."

I hurry toward him. "Can you contact someone? Do people know what's going on here? Is it happening everywhere?"

"Hold your horses . . ." Pete is typing something furiously. "They would never make it easy for us, would they?"

"What do you mean?" Smitty is hanging over the back of Pete's chair, like it's all he can do to stop launching himself into the screen of the laptop.

Pete pauses, and plays with his head scab. "It's weird. And clever. I've never seen anything quite like it before."

"What?" Smitty bellows in his ear.

Pete smiles up at him. "You know how your parents set controls on your laptop so that you can't look up how to make a bomb out of pipe cleaner or get hooked perving on bimbos?"

"Of course he does," Alice sneers.

"Well" — Pete's smile widens — "that's what they've done here. They've set up restrictions so that we can't access any sites they don't want us to." His smile fades. "Like anything at all, pretty much."

"Nothing?" I ask. "You can't e-mail, either?"

"There's an e-mail server but it's password protected." He hits a few keys. "No web access really, just a browser that won't let me browse. I've checked the history. There's only one website coming up. Something called Xanthro Industries."

Smitty frowns. "What's Xanthro Industries? Sounds like some kind of drug company. Are they the bad guys?"

I feel the room start to undulate softly. For want of anywhere better, I sit down heavily on the floor.

"What's up with you?" Alice says, backing away from me, her eyes wide. "Do I need to get my knife out again? Are you going to turn?"

I shake my head. "No." I snake my hand into my pocket and close my fingers around the photograph. The photograph of Roberta, age four.

Smitty looks down at me closely. "Xanthro Industries. You know what that is, don't you?"

I look up at him.

I nod.

"Xanthro Industries is the company my mother works for."

25

Of course, as soon as I say it, I wish I hadn't. Because now all three of them are scuttling away from me like I'm public enemy number one.

"Your mother?"

Pete is looking at me with extreme disgust, like I've just taken a dump in his mouth. It's almost funny. I feel a giggle well up inside of me, but push it down. Going all fruit-loopy now is not going to help.

My mother. *My mother.*

"Xanthro Industries is a pharmaceutical and biotech company." Pete has one beady green eye on the laptop, the other on me in case I leap up and bite his head off.

"No kidding." Smitty's eyes are fixed on mine. Without a flicker.

Pete nods, reading. "They make drugs. Experimental drugs. Including the contents of Veggie Juice, I'm betting?" He's swaying, quite literally reeling, with shock.

Reel all you like, Pete, you won't touch what's going on inside my head right now. The first feeling is sheer un-frickin'-believable flabbergastery — but the second feeling is even weirder. The feeling that I'm *not surprised.*

Because Xanthro Industries is basically responsible for everything that's wrong in my life. The company kept my mother away from birthdays, school plays, and the umpteen times I had a boo-boo and needed her there to kiss it better. They uprooted us to the US, then worse, dragged us back to the UK. They made my mother work so hard for so long that she — a doctor — never noticed my dad was sick until it was way too late. So, really, the idea that Xanthro Industries should be involved in a zombie apocalypse does not *surprise* me one tiny bit.

But the idea that Mum's involved? Ever since I hit my teens, I've been convinced that my mother was a nightmare, but I put that down to hormones. Hers and mine. It's not like she's über-evil or anything. And yet now it all makes stomach-lurching sense: the long trips away, the tiredness and stress etched into her face. The photograph, her lingering smell on that leather chair. She's been working here, at the castle.

But did she do this? Did she make those monsters?

"What's the story, Bob?" Smitty's voice is calm but serious.

I look at the three pale and angry faces across the room.

"I have no idea what's going on."

Wow, that sounds super-convincing. Actually makes it sound like I masterminded the whole thing.

"Look." I scramble to my feet, and they all take another step backward. "Why on earth would I be here — in the middle of everything — if my mother had been involved in this? Why would she put me in danger?"

"Ha!" Alice snaps. "If you were my daughter, I'd do the same."

"Wrong," I snap back. "As much as things with my mother are . . . difficult, she'd never risk losing me." It's only when I say it out loud that I realize it's true. "Not after last year, not after my dad dying. It would be too much for her." I feel a lump forming in my throat.

Smitty's face softens a little. "Your dad died?"

"Six months ago." My breathing almost stops. It's the only good way to keep those pesky emotions down; just don't breathe and you can fool yourself it doesn't hurt. "He had cancer. Which is kind of ironic, seeing as my mother's an oncology specialist."

"A what?" Alice clearly thinks I'm making this shit up.

"A cancer doctor," Smitty mutters.

Alice shakes her head. "Your dad carked it? Great sob story, you loser."

"Shut it, Malice!" Smitty shouts.

I feel my shoulders inching up around my ears. "My mother researches cures, does clinical trials. But she doesn't grow zombies in a lab."

Pete crouches down on the floor, engrossed with the laptop again. "They were creating a drug here at the castle, for sure. There are some notes, fragments of e-mails. I don't pretend to understand it, but it's something to do with activating dormant antibodies with a chemical stimulant."

Alice finds time to roll her eyes. "Oh, spare us the science bit."

Pete glares at her. "This is *all* the science bit, you ignorant donkey."

"Stand down, Batgirl and Lady Shiva." Smitty walks toward me, then turns back to face Alice and Pete. "Bobby's kosher. So her ma works for some evil drug corporation. Big fat deal. She nearly got chomped good and proper more times than either of you."

I'm grateful, of course. My shoulders drop a little as he stands by my side. I risk a look, and our eyes catch for a second. *Thank you.* Alice sees the shared glance, and groans sarcastically. Smitty ignores her.

"Whatever you believe about Bobby, think about looking after yourselves. Grace said there was some kind of antidote here. We should look for it. At the very least it will give us something to bargain with if the bad guys show up." He strides over to the wall. "Aren't there any lights in here? This spooky shadow crap is getting old."

We look for a switch.

I think he's persuaded them not to kill me — yet.

"Got it!" Alice finds the switch and flicks it.

There's a loud *bang*. I don't so much hear it as feel it; the tower walls shake and the floor vibrates.

"What did you do?" cries Pete at Alice.

"Nothing!"

I shake my head. "That was something outside."

Alice is already scrambling up to the window ledge, with Smitty close behind.

I run across the room to the security camera screens. Smoke is obscuring the pictures, but I can make out people outside, dozens of people — at the gates, at the front door, and many more in the courtyard. My heart leaps. The army! They've found us at last. Guns a-blazing, they've come to rescue us!

Then the wind changes direction and the smoke clears. There's an oil drum burning — that must have been the bang we heard, not army guns. The grainy black-and-white figures are stumbling and clawing the air. Their heads are lolling. The dog is there, too, barking and snapping at the figures agitatedly.

It's not an army.

The hordes have come home.

Alice's screams from the window confirm it.

Smitty, flattened against the glass, cries out, "There's Pube-Face!"

I look at the courtyard screen again. Michael is holding what looks to be a gas can in one hand and a makeshift torch in the other, waving it at the mob.

"Oh my god!" Alice is pressed against the glass beside Smitty. "He is so dead."

"But not Undead." Pete joins me at the TV screens, standing a little farther away than he would have ten minutes ago. "Yet."

As we watch, Shaq emerges from the Ski-Doos' stable. Even with the blurred resolution on the screen, I can read his look of desperation. They can't escape on the Ski-Doos. I feel for the spiky lump in my pocket. I have the keys.

The hordes advance.

Michael looks like he's screaming for Shaq, who has disappeared back into the stables. Or maybe he's shouting for Grace, who is nowhere to be seen. Maybe she's fared better with her cattle prod, or maybe she was standing too close to the oil drum when it went off. Or maybe she's already one of the hungry crowd.

Shaq appears again. But it's not because of Michael's screaming. Cam is clinging to his leg, clinging with arms, legs, and teeth, latched on, immovable. Shaq can't run far with a three-year-old zombie on his leg, and he falls just clear of the door.

The crowd moves in. Michael flings gas wildly from his can, and waves his fiery torch, but the liquid splashes over nobody but him. And then, inevitably, he lights up like a beacon, the flames whipping up over his head. He hurls the torch away from himself, his arms lifted in a useless effort to extinguish the fire, silently dancing a jig on our black-and-white TV screen.

I turn away.

Smitty, who caught the whole episode at the window in Technicolor, turns away, too.

"We have to get out of here, we have to go now!" Alice jumps down from the ledge.

I hit the button to turn the kitchen camera on again. Black smoke oozes thickly from the door leading to the mudroom. What are the chances? Michael's last action was to throw his torch into the castle and set us all on fire.

"We'll burn to death in here!" Alice cries. "What are we going to do?"

And as we all stand there trying to think of a good answer to her question, a phone rings.

26

My first thought — just for a split second — is that the ringing noise is a fire alarm.

But then my brain catches up with reality. It's one of those generic ringtones you get when you first buy a phone, one that only grand-parents and really stupid people actually leave on, because they can't figure out how to change it, or don't even realize they can.

And then I click. It's my phone. I never bothered to change the ring-tone because nobody ever calls me on it, because I am Bobby No-Buddies.

But someone's calling now.

I remember Alice dropping my phone on the window ledge.

I climb onto one of the desks, stick a foot on a shelf, and hoist myself onto the ledge. There's the phone, the screen flashing. I practically fall on it, seeing PRIVATE CALLER displayed on the screen a second before I press the ANSWER button.

"Hello?"

There is silence on the other end. Then a clicking noise as if someone is playing with the buttons. Then silence again.

"Hello!"

Smitty and the rest are panting at my heels, squashed on top of the desk below. I can see they want to climb up to me, tear the phone from my hands—but they're holding back. Because they're scared of me. Scared of my phone.

"Hello? Can you hear me?" I shout. "Who is this?"

I look at the screen. I have reception all right—four bars strong. But only one bar of battery. I tussle with the idea of hanging up and calling the police—anyone!—but there's always the chance that if I hang up, those four bars will mysteriously disappear again.

"Hello!" I try again.

"Hello?" a voice says.

I nearly faint. There's someone there.

"Hi!" I shout. "Can you hear me?"

"Yes, just about . . . Bobby, is that you?"

Tears rush behind my eyes, my ears pop, and the ground feels like it's rushing up toward me. I grab at the window frame to stop myself from falling.

"Mum?"

"Bobby!" My mother's voice cracks. "Are you OK?"

"Yes!" I feel hot tears down my cheeks and I don't care. "I'm here with three of my classmates; we're in the castle!"

"I know, Bobby," my mother says.

"We're in the tower, those things are outside—"

"Don't panic, just listen to me carefully."

"What's going on, Mum?" I scream. "What have you been doing here? I know about it all, the research—Grace and everyone—the dead professor!"

Smitty, Pete, and Alice have joined me on the ledge, unable to hold back any longer.

"Bobby, I want you to do exactly as I say," Mum tells me.

"OK." I wipe the tears away.

"Take deep breaths, remember how Dad used to tell you?"

"Yep," I choke.

"I'll explain everything, but you need to get out of there now. You're in danger," she says slowly.

"You think?" I say. "The zombies are at the door and the castle's on fire, so yuh-huh, we're in danger!"

"You need to come to me." Her voice is clear and calm. "I'm on the island in the middle of the loch."

"What?" I peer into the darkening sky, across the frozen water. I see the island, just about. "Maybe you didn't hear me, Mother" — I grit my teeth — "but there's the small matter of getting out of this castle first."

"Bobby," she reprimands, "you're not listening. There are people coming, dangerous people. They're coming to collect what's theirs, and then destroy the castle. You can't get in their way. Keep calm. I'll help you escape."

"The Xanthro bad guys are on their way?" I look at Smitty, Pete, Alice. Their jaws are slack. Like we needed more incentive to leave.

"But first, you need to go to the refrigerator," my mother tells me. "Quickly. Look for a syringe marked 'Osiris 17.' It's the antidote. We need it to put things right, Bobby! Go now!"

I let out a yelp of frustration, press the button to put her on speaker, and hurry along the ledge until it ends. There's a bookcase below and to the side. I swing myself onto it and climb down, using the shelves like steps, dropping onto the floor beside the fridge.

Now, in an ideal world, there should be just one fluorescent syringe in the fridge with THE ANTIDOTE stamped on it. Instead there are hundreds of syringes and test tubes in dozens of trays. They all have handwritten stickers with long names, serial numbers, and dates.

"Hurry, Bobby," my mother says again.

I search the shelves desperately.

Smitty jumps down from the desk, slaps his hand on the fridge door, and slams it shut. "What in the name of nuts is going on?"

"Get off!" I push his arm and try to open the door, but he's wedged a foot against it. Alice is down, too, and places her hand against the door in solidarity.

"Tell us." Pete arrives, wheezing, and slaps a clammy hand on my shoulder.

"What's the problem, Bobby?" Mum shouts.

I shrug off Pete's hand and turn to face them all. "My mum wants us to get the antidote and bring it to her. Xanthro is coming for it, we need to hurry."

"And there are more of the infected on their way." Mum's voice on speaker is loud enough to reach everyone. "I can see them coming toward the castle. If you don't leave now, you'll be overwhelmed."

"I'm pretty friggin' overwhelmed already, Bobby's ma!" Smitty shouts at the phone. "OK, let's do this!" He flings open the fridge door.

"Find Osiris!" Mum barks. "I'll get you out of there, trust me."

I scan the syringes for names. So. Many. Syringes.

"Osiris 17," my mother says. "Hurry up, Bobby, I mean it. We can't linger here."

"OK, OK." I pull trays out of the fridge and set them on the floor.

There's a bizarre silence as all four of us kneel and sort through the syringes; just the occasional rattle of plastic, a swearword here and there, and my mother's embarrassingly loud breathing coming from the phone. The seconds tick away and sweat drips into my eyes, making me blink. A couple of times the needle covers almost pop off; God knows what kind of hell I'd be unleashing if I accidentally stabbed someone.

"I've got it!"

It's Pete who finds the golden ticket. He holds up a syringe with clear liquid inside. It's labeled OSIRIS 17. He snags what looks like a small beer cooler from one of the shelves, fits the syringe snugly inside, and flings the cooler over his shoulder. "Let's go!"

"You're sure?" Mum says from the floor.

"No doubt," I reply, picking up the phone.

"I've found one, too!" Alice is holding another syringe aloft. I snatch it from her and check the label.

"There's another?" my mother shouts over the speaker.

"Yes, Mum. Now get us out of here!" I scramble to my feet.

"What does the label say exactly?" Her voice is shaky.

I cry out in exasperation, but take another look. "'Osiris Red.' Now we go!"

"Bobby, be very, very careful with that vial," my mother says. "That's the stimulant. Pack it up and bring it with you, but don't, whatever you do, expose the needle, do you hear me?"

I stare at the syringe in my hand. "You mean this is the bad drug? The one that turns people?"

"Yes, Bobby. It's very valuable."

Smitty holds my arm. "That's the zombiefier junk?" He shakes his head. "We leave that here."

"Bobby, I want you to bring it!" my mother yells. "Do as I tell you and get moving! Now!"

I look at the vial, then at Smitty.

Alice is jogging on the spot like she needs to pee. "Whatever you're going to do, do it and let's get out of here!" she shrieks.

"We leave it and the bad guys will get it. So it comes with us."

Smitty hesitates, then he nods. Gently, I place Osiris Red into Pete's cooler next to Osiris 17.

"I can't keep this line open much longer." Mum's cool is beginning to desert her. "Xanthro controls the signal; we're going to be cut off."

"So tell me how to get out already!" I scream at her.

"Make your way down into the cellar, go to the end of the cells, and feel the wall on the left-hand side. There's a control box that opens a door to a passage that will bring you to me. You need a four-digit code to open the door — it's your birthday." She exhales. "Be careful to enter it correctly the first time or it will go into lockdown. Please hurry, Bobby."

There's a *click* from the phone.

"Mum?" I shout.

Nothing.

"Mum!"

She's gone. And my four bars of reception have disappeared.

"Come on!" Smitty shouts, and heads for the stairs.

"Are you smoking crack?" Alice screams at him. "Look!" She's pointing at the security camera screens.

We all look. On the kitchen cam there's movement through the smoke. Bodies packed tight into the room. It's a zombie mosh pit. There's no way out.

"We can get around them," says Smitty.

"No way." Pete's face is grave. "There are too many."

"They're right at the door!" Alice starts to cry.

There's thudding from the bottom of the stairwell. Hands hitting the door, knocking, asking to come in.

"Then there's only one thing we can do," Smitty says. "We let them in."

27

We are all crouching on the high window ledge, in a deadly lineup: me first, then Smitty, Pete, and finally Alice. Candy in a zombie vending machine. Make your selection.

Alice is gripping the window frame, all set to smash through the glass and jump to her certain death below, should the need arise.

"So, explain to me again how this can possibly work?"

"Can't get past them in the kitchen." Smitty is psyching himself up, eyes darting, breath heavy. "But we can in here. We let them up the stairs, they come in, we climb around them." He points across the room. "Along the ledge, onto the bookcase, across to the fridge, jump to the security camera cabinet, and down the stairs. Easy."

"Zombie parkour," I mutter. "Don't think that's been done before. Better film this, Alice, it could go viral."

"Ha. Ha. Ha." Pete's voice shakes.

"*Pardonnez-moi,*" Alice says, "but am I the only one who sees the fatal flaw in this amazing plan?" She leans across to Smitty. "Why are they going to clear a nice space for us by the stairs?"

"We stay on this side of the room, they'll come toward the meat." He sounds sure. "When they're all below us, we move. They can't climb. All we need to do is keep off the ground and it'll be kushti." He gives us a manic grin.

Like it's that simple. But it's a plan, and it's the only one we've got.

"Do it," I say to him. "Do it quickly."

He nods at me, and before Alice can protest or any of us can change our minds, he monkeys down from the ledge, runs across the room, and out onto the stairs. There's no turning back now. The three of us listen to the fading sound of his footsteps as he descends.

"What if there are too many?" Alice gabbles. "What if we can't get around them?"

"Looked like twenty in the kitchen, at a guess." Pete is very quiet. "The fire at the back door should hold the others outside for a while. It's our best shot."

I look across the room and try to imagine it full of twenty zombies. I won't have to imagine for much longer. I trace my escape route out in my head. Timing will be everything; if we go too soon, they'll still be blocking the way to the stairs. We have to wait until they're all in and right on us. It's going to be the biggest game of chicken any of us ever played.

Smitty appears at the doorway, eyes wild.

"We're open for business!" He runs across the room, grabbing a plastic broom leaning against the wall. "Weapon," he pants, throwing the broom up to me. He leaps onto the desk, pulling himself up onto the ledge. "They were waiting for me, all right." He's laughing, pumped up. "Practically fell through the door when I opened it. I had to fly up those stairs!"

Flying. Now there's an idea. Pity I mislaid my wings.

We all watch the doorway.

"What do we do? What do we do?" Alice panics.

"We wait," I answer.

We watch the doorway.

"Where are they?" Alice is already close to tears.

I glance over at the TV screens to see if I can make out movement in the kitchen, but we're too far away to see.

"Shh!" Pete says. "We'll be able to hear them."

We strain our ears.

Nothing.

We should hear them by now; the groaning, the shuffling up the stairs. We can't hear anything—well, except for Alice, who by now is sobbing openly.

"It's OK," I reassure her. "We can do this."

We watch the doorway.

Nothing.

"What's wrong with them?" Smitty leaps down onto the desk again. "The one time you want the morons to chase you, they don't." He makes his way cautiously across the room.

"Maybe the door closed again, with the weight of them pushing?" I try to be helpful.

"Guess I'll have to go and see." Smitty steps into the doorway.

"Careful!" Alice screeches.

"Never knew you cared." He turns to throw her a kiss, and as he does, a bloodied claw appears and swipes at him from behind. Alice, Pete, and I scream in unison.

"Shiz!" Smitty dodges at the last moment, rolling across the floor and out of reach. The freerunning is *on*.

"Hurry!" I scream at him.

He's back up and on the desk. I shoot out an arm for him to grab. He pulls himself up to us again.

"Oh my god oh my god oh my god." Alice's eyes are on the doorway.

The first zombie appears. It's a he. Youngish. Not in bad shape at all. His clothes are shredded, but apart from that you'd just think he was suffering from a really bad hangover.

And he's tall. Seriously tall, with long, dangly arms.

Darn, that sucks.

He stands there, head rolling from side to side, taking in the room.

"Oh my god oh my god oh my god!" Alice's whispers become a cry. Tall Guy turns his head, focuses, and suddenly remembers what he's here for. He starts to stagger toward us.

"Where are the others?" Pete mutters. "Aren't they coming?"

He's right to be worried. For this to work they've all got to come at once.

And then they do.

A wad of zombies appears at the doorway and squeezes into the room, and then there is a flow of bodies, like they were just waiting for the bottleneck to be eased, and now there's nothing holding them back at all. Once they see us, the moans start, building, rhythmical almost. They're on the scent. Behind me, Alice's crying ramps up in response.

Meanwhile, Tall Guy has reached the desk below us. He smells like butt. He looks up at us with blank, cloudy eyes and flails out an arm. As one, we shrink up against the cold glass of the window.

"Nobody. Move," rasps Smitty. "Wait till they're all in the room before we go anywhere."

I hope that the final zombie is kind enough to tell us he's the last guy in. Once we go, there's no turning back. The room fills up disgustingly quickly, and the groans become deafening. I feel stomach acid rise into my throat. *Keep it together.*

Tall Guy has been joined by the fastest of the rest, and they are trying to remember how to climb; one makes it half onto the desk, reaches up, and seizes one of Smitty's feet.

"Here!" I pass Smitty the broom and he thrusts it at the zombie below. What we'd give for his dwarven ax . . .

"That's it!" Pete shouts. "Must be all of them!"

I look toward the doorway. The room is almost full; the flow has stopped.

"We move!" Smitty shoves Tall Guy with his sweeper. "I'll hold them here until you're all clear!"

Dammit. That means I'm trailblazer.

I edge along the ledge. Suddenly, moving is much more difficult. One slip, and it's Game Over. The ledge ends. It's onto the bookcase now. I did it before; it's simple.

It's not simple. Suddenly it's waaay too far.

"Go! Go! Go!" Smitty wrestles with the mass of arms below.

Hands scraping up the wall at me, I slide down and across to the bookshelf. Easy does it. My foot finds a hold. I'm about to leave the safety of the ledge. A hand grasps my ankle. I screech and draw both legs up out of reach, and for a few seconds I'm dangling from the ledge, about to tumble into the sea of monsters.

"Oi, uglies!" Smitty shouts, and bashes the window with his broom. The glass cracks, the zoms are distracted for an instant, and I see my chance. Finding new footholds, I pull myself up and scale the bookcase toward the fridge, kicking the books off into the faces of the ones below, the shelves shaking as I go.

An easy jump away — don't screw this up . . .

Geronimo!

It seems like I'm in the air for a lifetime, then I land on all fours with the biggest *Boom Shakalaka* on top of the fridge. Success. But at a price. Pain shrieks from my left wrist. No time to care, no time to check it.

A body slams into me — it's Pete, gasping for air and as pink as I've ever seen him. He must have raced to reach me this fast. I grab his arm with my good hand and pull him against the wall with me. He mutters thanks.

Back on the ledge, Smitty is still beating them down with his broom. Beyond him there's Alice, pressed against the window.

"Alice!" I yell at her. "Move now!"·

The going's as good as she's going to get; half of the zoms are now distracted by Pete and me on the fridge, the other half by Smitty. But she's crying and shaking her head, and I feel a heaviness in the pit of my stomach because I know the situation's hopeless. One of us should have stayed. Smitty's preoccupied, to say the least, and she's not going to move without some serious intervention.

"Crap!" I look at Pete. "I'm going to have to go back and get Alice."

"No." Pete nods to my left wrist, and I realize I've been gripping it with my other hand. "You're injured."

Before I can argue, he's off, spidering back over the bookcase, kicking out at the hands that grab. I slap the top of the fridge with my good hand.

"Here, you lunkheads!" I shout at the hordes. "Look at me!"

But most of the zoms are on Pete because he's moving faster, or Alice because she's screaming louder. A couple of them have managed to clamber up onto the desk now. Smitty won't hold them for long.

"We have to jump!" he yells at Alice. "We'll go together!"

She moves toward the bookcase, but stops when the ledge does.

"It's too far!" she screams.

Pete reaches up from the top of the bookcase, holding out a hand.

"Jump! I've got you!"

She leans forward ever-so-slightly, and that's all Smitty needs. He bundles her up and practically launches her off the ledge. For a second she's all windmilling arms, and then she lands, somehow Pete catches her, and Smitty catapults himself on top of the two of them, still holding his broom. They made it.

But the bookcase can't hold three. The monsters surge as one toward them, and as they scramble to reach the fridge, the bookcase wobbles threateningly.

"Hurry!" I shout. "It won't take the weight!"

Smitty's clear, thumping down beside me on the fridge.

"I can't!" Alice freezes again, fresh tears running down her face.

"Are you going to let those losers get you?" Smitty yells at her, holding out a hand. "You're better than that, Alice!"

It's the first time he's called her that. Alice sets her jaw — but before she can move, Tall Guy shows up from the maelstrom of Undead, a long Mr. Tickle arm reaching up and clawing at her leg. She squeals and jumps. She hits the fridge hard, her nails scratching at the smooth, round corners like a desperate cat trying to find some grip. We pull her up by the strap of her thong, giving her the ultimate wedgie.

"By the seat of your pants." Smitty grins at her.

"Don't get any ideas, sicko," Alice gulps, and pushes her hair out of her eyes.

There's an almighty crash. The force of Alice's jump rocked the bookcase too much, and it has come away from the wall and hit the floor, squashing a handful of zoms.

The good news is, Pete jumped to safety at the last minute. The bad news is, he jumped back onto the ledge. He looks at us from across the void, all color draining from his face. He's marooned.

"Stay where you are!" Smitty shouts. "We'll find something to help you!"

Like what? We're standing on a fridge. There's nothing in reach. Pete knows he's not going anywhere.

I look at the doorway to the stairs. It is temptingly clear.

"Maybe there'll be something in the kitchen?" I shout. "We could come back up."

"Screw that!" Alice says, snatching the broom from Smitty's hands. With a battle cry worthy of a samurai, she jumps down onto the back of the fallen bookcase and whacks the first couple of monsters in her path. "Get away from us, you stinking dirtbags!" she screams. Wielding the broom like a sledgehammer, she takes out Tall Guy. "I am So! Over! This!"

Pete seizes the moment, leaping down beside Alice. Instantly, Smitty and I are reaching down to pull them up, our two heroes — one pale and panting, the other newly and wonderfully psychotic.

"To the stairs!" Smitty declares, like some kind of musketeer. We leap from fridge to TV cabinet to doorway, leaving the monsters clutching at air.

I lead the charge down the tower stairs, hoping and praying there are no surprises waiting in the kitchen.

28

No surprises. But that's not saying much.

Smoke belches from the mudroom into the kitchen. The fire won't hold the zoms outside for long.

"This way!" Smitty leads us out of the kitchen and we race through rooms until we reach the hall.

"Uh-oh!" Alice yells.

A clutch of Undead are lingering around the globe, batting it with their mangled hands and trying to make it spin. No doubt they're planning world domination.

I grab Alice and pull her toward the basement door after Smitty and Pete.

Down we go, narrowly avoiding the trail of nails Cam left on the stairs, and arrive in the basement.

"Crap a brick sideways!" Smitty stops dead.

It's déjà boo. Half a dozen zoms, standing around with nothing to do. Until they see us.

"Oh my god" — I sound like Alice — "it's Gareth."

No doubt about it. There, in the middle of the group, is our old friend from the gas station at the Cheery Chomper. He's been through the wars.

The nibbled-corn-cob arm has dropped off entirely, and he seems to have lost most of his clothing, but it's him all right. He still has his name tag at least. He looks up at us and snarls.

"Do you think he recognizes us?" I whisper.

"I think he recognizes Smitty," says Pete.

"Oh yes." Smitty licks his lips.

"Let's motor!" Alice goes off raw once more, running down into the cellar. She grabs the handle of the tarp-covered lawn mower and, with an almighty grunt, pushes it at the nearest zom, literally mowing him down. Now there's a path to the wall-curtain. "Come on, slowpokes!" she shouts at us.

We run for it.

Pete and I reach Alice at the wall-curtain, while Smitty hefts up an empty wooden crate and bowls it toward the group, felling two zombies in one glorious shot. But as he grabs another projectile, Zombie Gareth grabs him. With his remaining arm, he hoists Smitty up by the back of his leather jacket. Smitty wriggles like a squid on a fish hook and falls out of his jacket, leaving Gareth holding it up by the collar.

Smitty is nearly with us when he stops.

"Nah. This is not how it's going down." He turns deliberately and stares at Gareth. "Tosser doesn't get to keep the leather."

"Smitty, no!" My scream is useless.

He dashes back to Gareth, dodging the swipe of another monster on the way, snatches the jacket, and executes a perfect roundhouse kick, knocking Gareth onto his zombie butt with a satisfying *crunch*.

Then he sprints back past us, grim-faced. "Lamebrain had that coming since I met him."

We run through the wall-curtain, down into the wine cellar, and out into the corridor past the cells.

"Where is this control panel, then?" Smitty gasps, first to reach the end of the corridor.

"On the left somewhere." I join him, running my hand over the stones.

"I looked before, but I couldn't see anything obvious." Pete is panting.

"Leave it to me." Alice crouches low. "Here!" She presses something, a piece of stone pops out, and there's the control panel.

An eerie groan echoes down the corridor.

"Hurry!" Alice says. "Open the door!"

Smitty's finger is poised to enter in the code.

"Your birthday?"

"April sixteenth — wait!" I stop his hand. "Shit."

"What is it?"

"US or UK?" I rake a hand through my hair. "No!"

Down the corridor the moaning grows louder.

"Enter the code!" Alice screams, trying to force the wall open.

"Which way around?" Pete's eyes are popping out of his head.

"I don't know!" I cry, exasperated.

"What do you even *mean*?" Smitty says, thumping the wall with his fist.

"The date." I stare at him. "If Mum meant the US way, it's month first, day second. If it's the UK way — day first, month second. We had a running joke about it because we could never get it right."

"They're here!" Alice is looking down the corridor.

"So which would she use?" Smitty's finger is poised over the buttons.

I shut my eyes and think.

"Tick-tock, Bobby!" Pete says.

"UK. Day first, month second."

"Are you sure?" Smitty says. "We don't get a second chance."

I nod frantically. "She always said it was more logical. And because, *dammit*" — I roll my eyes — "we're British."

He punches in 1604, I hold my breath, there's a grinding noise, and the wall slides away and disappears into itself. Woulda been nice if it closed up after us, given the circs, but them's the breaks. We'll have to rely on speed.

We run down a wide, barely lit passage, our feet smacking the concrete floor. Down, down, down, the floor slopes and leads us deep underground. Didn't I say this was the School Trip from Hell? Well, now we're going back there.

Eventually the ground levels off. Now it's slippery underfoot. There's a hissing noise, too, and I feel rain on my face, which makes no sense at all, because we're in a tunnel about a mile under the ground. And then I realize: *We're underneath the loch*. I keep running, praying the tunnel doesn't decide to flood. Alice is on rocket fuel and leads the race, Smitty's right by me, and Pete brings up the rear. Got to keep going — they'll eventually catch up, and —

"Aargh!"

My head snaps around. I catch the tail end of Pete in a full-on skid. He goes down hard, his feet twisting under him at speed, chest smacking onto the ground. He lies there in the wetness, arms outstretched, the cooler held up like a rugby ball in a match he'll never play.

We race to him; he's shaking badly.

"Saved it," he wheezes, handing me the cooler. "Need . . . inhaler." He flaps his hands around his chest, looking for a pocket. Smitty crouches in front of him and searches inside his coat.

The cooler has come unzipped. I hold my breath and take a quick look inside.

No broken needles.

"We're good!" I shout.

Smitty has found the inhaler and Pete is blindly sucking on it, desperately, one hand gripping Smitty's arm. I secure the syringes and sling the cooler over my shoulder. Pete leans on Smitty and hauls himself to his feet.

"You can run?" I say.

He nods, shivering.

"Come on!" shouts Alice up ahead. "There's something up here!"

We set off, and Pete buckles on the first step, falling to a trembling heap on the wet floor once again. "My ankle!"

Without discussion, Smitty and I each throw one of his arms over our shoulders, like we did all those years ago when we helped the driver out of the snow and back onto the bus. We limp down the corridor, the cooler bashing my side and my wrist thudding in pain. The tunnel is uphill now. The water that's running from the ceiling and down the smooth walls is beginning to stream past us on the floor.

"It's a dead end!" Alice cries. The way is boarded up with old, rotted planks, daylight showing through the cracks between each one.

"Not for long!" Smitty does the same roundhouse kick he used so successfully on Gareth, and before I know it we're all flinging ourselves at the wood, beating our way through, breaking and pulling off the planks.

We fall out into the open. *Freedom*.

What remains of daylight, and a rush of cold. Bitter, bitter cold, with a vicious, penetrating wind. At least it reminds me I'm alive, for now. I look around, the wind blasting my hair into my eyes and making them sting.

We're on the island. It's about half the size of a football field, but there's nothing here other than a clump of trees. I can see the castle beyond the frozen loch, and snow-laden pine trees with distant blurred hills rising up to meet the sky. The stuff of Christmas cards.

Alice leans into the tunnel entrance in an attempt to get out of the wind. Her blond hair is beginning to form dreads, and her cheerful red miniskirt is now a delicate shade of swamp. No more lip gloss or mascara. I suddenly feel terribly sad.

"So where is your mum?" she says.

Good question.

And then I see her, by the trees, coming toward us. A lean figure striding across the snow determinedly. I don't know whether to run to her, or away.

I stay where I am. As she gets closer, I see she's dressed in a black one-piece snowsuit. She actually looks kinda slick. Not like the mother I know.

"That her?" says Smitty. "Ding-dong."

Oh horror. Gross in extremis. Smitty's hot for my mum. Just when I thought I had kept hope alive.

She breaks into a run. "You're OK?" She clutches at my face with insulated gloves, making me flinch. "Injured? Bitten?"

I shrug her off. "Minor stuff." I hold up my limp wrist and she gives me a look. "Not bitten, sprained," I clarify.

"The rest of you?" She turns to them.

"Pete's ankle's twisted. Other than that, we're spanky," Smitty says, guarded. He may fancy her but he doesn't trust her. Not yet.

"Fine. I have transport." She points to the trees, and now I see a small jetty I didn't spot before. At the end of it I can just make out two ATVs, tethered together on the ice. "We should go before they get here." She nods toward the castle. Does she mean the bad guys or the zoms? Through the last rays of day I can make out shadows shambling out onto the ice from the direction of the castle, arms outstretched, groans building.

"You've got the Osiris vials?" my mother asks.

I hug the cooler to me like a baby. "Yup."

"Good work." She holds her hands out for it.

"I'll carry it."

She tuts impatiently. "OK. Let's go." She turns to lead the way to the jetty, and Smitty and I pick Pete up off the icy ground.

"Um, hello?" Alice grabs my arm. "We just go with her? Evil Scientist Mother?"

The alternative being . . . ?

"We need some answers!" Pete splutters.

"Here." I unload him onto Alice and stomp through the snow after my mother, trying to catch up, just like that little girl in the photo would have.

"Just because we're being chased by the Undead doesn't give you a free pass, you know!" I shout at her. "You were working here! Did you create these zombies?" The wind whips my questions out over the loch. "You owe me an explanation!"

She doesn't stop or even slow down, and at first I don't think she's heard me. But then she turns her head.

"All you need to know for now is that our intentions were good."

"Yep, Grace already sang that tune," I shout at her, struggling to keep pace. "Your little team was re-creating some zombie virus to give to Xanthro."

"We were trying to find a cure!" She stops suddenly and spins around. "The stimulant was a mistake. I tried to hide it from Xanthro. Had I known there was any question of this"—she gestures to the zoms looming toward us on the ice—"I would have refused to be involved!"

I reach her, panting.

"You didn't know about the Veggie Juice?"

She shakes her head. "Of course not. My team sold me out—at least, Grace, Michael, and Shaq did—too young and stupid to know anything else but greed. They gave Xanthro the stimulant. Xanthro made the juice to conduct a controlled outbreak, to see how it would spread. Now that their experiment is over, they're on their way to destroy the evidence."

"Newsflash, *we're* the evidence!" shouts Smitty, catching up to us.

"Precisely," says my mother. "The only thing that will keep us all safe is that antidote." She points to the cooler on my shoulder. "Xanthro doesn't have Osiris 17, and as long as we do, we can bargain with them."

"Some breaking news here, too, you freakazoids!" Alice warns from behind me. "Zombies ahoy!"

I glance back at the tunnel entrance; our basement friends are here. And by the looks of things, they've been joined by others.

"Let's move!" my mother shouts, and we hurry toward the jetty.

"There are hundreds!" Alice is scanning the loch. "Over there!" She points to a different place on the ice where a new mob is heading toward us, shambling and horrible, with bloodied drool and broken, clutching hands. "And there!" She turns to my mother, frantic. "Where are they all coming from?"

My mother doesn't answer, just nods grimly and runs out onto the jetty toward the ATVs.

"Shut the front door." Alice is transfixed. "They're disappearing."

"You seeing things?" Smitty peers through the fading light. Alice is right. Whole groups of Undead are vanishing into the loch. It takes me a moment to realize what's happening.

"Ha-ha!" Smitty laughs, victorious. "They're sinking through the ice! Lard arses! Suh-weet!"

Pete clears his throat. "Er, yeah. And if *they're* too heavy, what about five of us on quad bikes?"

My mother takes charge. "The ice is thickest the way I came." She jabs a gloved finger in the direction away from the castle. "We go now, we make it." She points to a rickety gate at the end of the jetty. "Close that behind you!"

"Amazing," mutters Alice. "Because that will totally do the trick."

"It'll hold them for a few minutes." My mother's bionic hearing is working well. She descends the steps and makes her way across the ice to where the ATVs are parked. "Can you drive one of these?" she shouts up at Smitty. "Accelerator, brake, gear change." She turns keys to fire up the headlights.

"Hakuna Matata." Smitty bundles Pete down onto the ice and deposits him on the bike.

"Oh, give me a break."

At first I think Pete is protesting the idea of riding Girlfriend behind Smitty, but then I see he is squirming on his seat, looking down at the ice around him.

"You might want to check this out!" he adds, lifting his feet high off the ice.

Smitty looks down, incredulous. "No flippin' way."

There, below the ice, like tadpoles in jelly, are the hordes. They might have fallen into the loch, but they've continued on their mission to reach us. They thump at the ice with blue hands, trying to break out. In the shallows, they are crawling, their backs pressing up against the ice, cracking it.

"Could this *be* any more messed up?" Alice is jumping up and down on the jetty. "We! Need! To! Go!"

"Then get your arses down here!" Smitty urges us, mounting the quad bike with Pete on it. "Let's roll!"

As I look at him, there's a massive cracking noise and the bike lurches forward, throwing Pete clear onto the ice. Smitty clings to the handlebars, his face frozen with shock and fear. But it's OK, the ice holds, he's all right. He lets out a relieved laugh.

"Woo-hoo! What a ride —"

A second crack, deafening — like hell itself has opened up — and both bikes are swallowed whole beneath the ice.

"Smitty!"

I run to the edge of the jetty. The bike bobs up in the water, but he doesn't. Pete skitters on the ice toward my mother, and they throw themselves up the steps to safety.

Then I see it. A hand, Smitty's hand, reaching out of a dark patch in the water, clutching the air. And then his head comes up, white and terrified, mouth open and snatching at breath. Head, shoulders, and the other hand, hauling himself out of the frigid water onto the ice.

And then I see the third hand.

Bloated and flabby and blue, rising high above Smitty, clamping down on his head, and pushing him back below again.

I look around desperately — *need something to help!*

Smitty comes up for another breath, launching himself like a breaching whale, high into the air. But not high enough. His arms stretch across the ice, but he slips back. Our eyes meet for a second and I'm filled with the hopelessness of his gaze. And then his face hardens, trying to be brave, trying to make one last effort to be strong — strong enough to save himself, and save me from seeing him slip away into the deep.

The blue hand comes again — and then another and another — grasping for Smitty as he rolls through the water as slippery as an otter, striking out with legs and arms, fighting the good fight with everything he has. But it may not be enough.

There's a coil of rope hanging from the end of the jetty. I grab it; it's frozen into curls and only just better than useless, but it's all I have. Hurriedly abandoning the cooler, I step off the end of the jetty onto the ice.

"Bobby, no!"

I ignore my mother's cries, not quite daring to run but taking giant, sliding strides, urging myself toward Smitty's brave face. He's wedged himself between chunks of the ice to stop them from pulling him below.

"I'm coming!" I shout — so feeble — but he hears me and I see a glint of hope in his eyes. Then fear, fear for me.

"The ice . . . ," he gasps. "Thin . . ."

I know it. I get down onto all fours and slide like a baby giraffe toward him, looking below, looking through the ice to see what it is that is pulling him down. There they are, the people that were, a writhing mess of limbs and grotesque, puffy, gray heads. I pull my gaze away and focus on the hole.

"Here!" I throw the rope. Pathetically. It goes nowhere. I'm going to have to get closer. I scrabble forward, lie flat, and throw again, with more force. Smitty leaps toward it, and he's caught, a prize fish on my line. I edge backward, but it's obvious I can't pull him clear.

"Just hold it!" he cries through a mouthful of ice water. I anchor the rope between my legs and up around my shoulder and lie flat and heavy on it, clenching with both hands. There's a massive wrench as Smitty levers himself up, the hands grabbing after him. I brace myself against the rope and hope it will be enough.

It is.

He is suddenly beside me, wet and gasping like a newborn.

And then Mum's there, gripping my legs, anchoring me as I anchor Smitty.

There is no energy for words. We crawl back to the jetty, helping each other. By the time we're there, Smitty has found his strength again and climbs it first, but my legs buckle at the last impossible hurdle, and I crumple. He reaches down for me, seizes my jacket, and yanks me up, Mum pushing me from below. And then we're there, on solid ground at last.

As we lie panting, I notice that Smitty's jeans are torn away at the knee.

And in the pale of his flesh are three jagged and angry bites.

29

Smitty sits up jerkily and begins to shiver. I pull off my ski jacket and put it around him, feeling tears prick the corners of my eyes.

Alice shakes me. "We have to get out of here—they're at the gate!" She stares down at Smitty, seeing his leg. "Oh, sugarama." Her bottom lip starts to tremble.

"Leave me!" Smitty commands us. "Go!"

"Enough with the martyrdom!" I scream at him. "Get on your feet and get moving!" The tears are running down my face.

"They got me, Bobby. I'm going to turn!"

"Grow a pair!" I clutch his arm and hoist him to his knees. "We're doing this together." I give him my utmost hard-boiled look. "And if you turn, I'll go apeshit on your ass."

"Me, too, you flippin' wuss," sobs Alice.

"Count me in!" shouts Pete. "With knobs on!"

"You're all such total lamers," Smitty snickers, in spite of the shakes wracking his body. "Why did I have to get stuck with you?" He may be freezing to death, but he's not turning yet—he wouldn't dare. He tries to stand but cries out in pain and falls back, his body arching against the ground.

I look up at my mother. "Help me move him!"

Her face is glacial. "Leave him."

I stare at her.

"He's been bitten, Bobby. You know what will happen."

"Help me help him!" I shout at her, thinking frantically. Alice and I will not be able to take Pete and Smitty far without help. "He's fine!"

"He's infected." She refuses to look at him.

"I hate you." The anger fuels my attempts to get Smitty on his feet. But Smitty's not helping.

"Listen to your ma, Bob." His eyes narrow. "We haven't got this far only to have it all go FUBAR now. Scram."

I feel the panic building, like an old wound freshly exposed. I turn on my mother.

"I'm so dumb, aren't I? Why would I expect you to care about Smitty? You never care about anything but your work. You never even cared about Dad."

"Of course I did," my mother says, her voice trembling. "Osiris was about trying to help him."

My heart falls several stories. "What do you mean?"

She pulls my arm. "We don't have time for this!"

"Have to agree!" Pete says.

"Bobby, just go!" Smitty yells at me. "I'm finished!"

And then I remember.

I have the antidote.

"Over my dead body." I shake off Mum's arm and stagger to the cooler where I left it on the jetty.

Mum clocks me. "Bobby, no!"

"I'm saving him, Mum!" I shout at her, unzipping the cooler. I've got the syringe in my freezing fingers. "Don't try and stop me!"

She leaps toward me, arms outstretched, but I dodge out of the way behind Smitty.

"They're *so* completely here, people!" Alice is frozen in place by the jetty gate, and the dozen drooling fiends now pressing against it. The wooden bars are beginning to bend.

My mother takes a step toward me. "That is the only antidote, Bobby. It's indescribably valuable." She moves again, and the two of us dance around Smitty. "It has the potential to save millions of lives!"

"What about Smitty's life?" I shout, holding the syringe out of reach. "I thought you were all about healing people." I shake my head, laughing. "No wonder you couldn't save Dad."

She looks at me as if in sympathy — my own eyes staring back at me from her face, filling with tears.

"He was infected."

The world falls away from me.

"Dad was . . . one of them?"

My mother shakes her head. "No, he was a carrier. One in a million. But then he got sick and nothing could make him better . . ." Her voice cracks.

"Not even this?" I cry, holding up the syringe.

My mother's face crumples. "We ran out of time. It was too late for him."

"Not for Smitty." I push the syringe into Smitty's hand, then rush at my mother in the strangest of embraces, to keep her off him.

Smitty hesitates only a second, then pops the needle free. "Yeah. I'm so much sexier alive. Woo!" He sticks himself in the leg and pushes the plunger. "Rock 'n' Roll!"

"No!" my mother howls, throwing my arms off her.

There's a crash, and the gate that was holding back a dozen zoms is shattered.

"Time's up!" Pete shouts.

"This way!" My mother swallows her tears, the leader again. She pulls Smitty up, and together we all scramble down the steps back onto the ice, moving painfully slowly around the hole thick with hideous zombie soup, not daring to race too fast, not daring to linger. The headlights from the quad bikes still burn bright from their watery graves deep in the loch, illuminating the squirming bodies from below. I don't want to look down. I focus on the other side, blocking out the pain and the cold, blocking out the fear of ice cracking, of grasping hands and sharp teeth. Alice and Pete forge ahead, following the tracks to the far bank, and we follow. It's not too far, but far enough with a drunken Smitty heavy on my shoulder. Mum is under his other arm, and together we heave him across the ice. She wanted to get her hands on the antidote, but I guess not quite like this. Smitty is her precious cargo now.

We reach the other side just as the night finally closes in. My mother leads us to a path through the trees; she seems to know the way in spite of the darkness. I take what I hope is a last look back; the castle is a tiny speck of light in the distance. Who knows what's going on inside there now? Maybe the whole place will burn to the ground before Xanthro arrives.

We emerge through the trees onto a road. I'm gazing into the distance with my thousand-yard stare — and there's something . . . A yellow glow in the distance, hovering. At first I think nothing of it. My mind is fried, I'm probably delusional. But then Alice stops.

"What's that?"

"You see it?" Smitty murmurs.

"I do," Pete says.

Maybe we're all tripping. Or maybe we all actually died back on the loch and this is the light at the end of the tunnel, and our nearest and dearest are waiting to welcome us into heaven. I sink happily to my knees. *I'm going to see Dad again.*

Smitty falls down beside me. He knows it, too. The light gets closer. It's coming toward us. I love it. I can almost feel its warmth. This is the entrance to the afterlife, and I'll finally get some peace. Alice and Pete kneel, too. I hope God won't be miffed that Mum stays on her feet; it's not very respectful of her. Still, he probably knows she's a bit like that. I'll bring him around.

"Stand up!" Mum tries to lift me.

But I'm comfortable here in the snow.

The light's blinding, and there's a rumble on the ground.

"Get up!" Mum screams, pulling me, but I'm stuck here. She runs out in front of the light, arms waving. There's a screeching noise and the light stops just in front of her. *Weird.* She runs back to me and throws her arms around my shoulders. "I've got you! I've got you!"

Great, nearly went to heaven and Mum screwed it up. Typical.

I glance at Smitty. He's squinting into the light. And then he sees something, and a huge grin spreads across his face. His hands shoot up into the air, and he throws his head back, whooping like a madman, double-rainbow crazy.

"It's the bus again," Alice says dully. "It found us."

I pull myself to my feet.

There's a familiar hissing noise of a door opening, and the crunch of feet on snow. And then there's a middle-aged man with a flashlight. Definitely not God.

"Wot you doin' in the middle of the bloody road?" He shines the flashlight in my eyes. "Could have killed the lot of you!"

I shut my eyes and slump into the snow once more. There are plenty of voices now, all around. Bona fide humans. Live ones. *Score.*

"It's going to be all right, Bobby." Mum in my ear again. "I love you, we're going home safe, and you don't need to fight anymore."

And then I feel hands lift me and help me up steps and into the warm bus. Not our bus, of course, but just like it. Dozens of faces are staring at us, eyes wide.

Kids.

On a school trip.

There are the popular girls with the pastel-colored skiwear, there's the rebel at the back with the attitude, and the loner sitting behind the teacher, earbuds in place, wishing she was anywhere else but here.

"Flashback City," says Alice.

"Fresh Meat," says Pete.

"More than enough room for you all," the driver is saying as we troop down the aisle. Someone helps me onto the backseat. "We should be back in civilization in an hour or two if the weather holds off," he continues. "You should have seen it up at Aviemore, talk about a blizzard." His voice is light and easy. "Are you sure you're all OK? I can call ahead for a doctor once my phone starts working again. You're not the first people we've seen out wandering on this road. They didn't seem in great shape, either. What a night to get caught out, eh? Biting cold."

I hear my mother talking to him, spinning a yarn, making it right. Pete and Alice are sitting a row ahead and across the aisle. Alice is already fast asleep, her head resting on Pete's shoulder. And then Smitty is plonked down next to me, his leg wrapped in a makeshift bandage with someone's scarf. A blanket is put over us. I feel the rumble as the bus starts up, and we drive off slowly.

A deluge of tired moves over me. I turn to Smitty before it wins.

"Tell me one thing."

He gives me a drugged-out smile. "Anything."

"Is there a hatch in this bus? And a trapdoor in the floor?"

With great effort he pulls himself up to look down the aisle.

"Yep. Both present and correct."

"Good." I relax into my seat. "Then we'll be OK."

Smitty gives a sleepy chuckle, the bus roars as it ramps up a gear, the driver turns up the radio, and there's some totally tacky song on about how we're all in the sun, and we're so lucky, lucky, lucky. I begin to drift off, and under the blanket I feel Smitty take my hand. I allow myself a smile as I hear his voice in my ear, soft and strong.

"That's right, Bob. We'll be OK."

I snuggle deeper, my body surrendering to the sleepy. But something's digging into my ribs. It's the cooler. I untangle the strap from my shoulder and lower it gently onto the floor. I hope the other syringe will be safe there. To turn another coach-load of kids into zombies — that would just be plain sloppy. As I push the cooler under the seat in front with my feet, I feel something blocking the space. Then the bus jerks and it slides out into the aisle. Leaning across Smitty, I look to see what was in my way.

A rectangular carton.

With an orange cartoon figure on the front.

Opened.

Empty.

CARROT MAN VEGGIE JUICE!
PUT SOME FIRE IN YOUR BELLY!

Adrenaline courses through my body like someone just plunged a needle straight into my heart.

No, no, no . . .

"Smitty! Wake up!" I shake him, my voice rising to a scream. "We need to get off this bus — now!"

ACKNOWLEDGMENTS

Huge thanks to my agent Veronique Baxter for her passion, wisdom, and generally being one cool chick.

A big fat zombie smackeroo to Siobhán McGowan and all the marvellous team at Scholastic, for embracing and championing the book so mightily, and helping Bobby find her home in the USA once more. Many thanks, folks.

To my patient and wonderful editors Imogen Cooper and Rachel Leyshon, and to Barry Cunningham, Rachel Hickman, and all at Chicken House UK for their boundless enthusiasm.

What would I do without my Gripers? My fab fellow writers: Elaine Dimopoulos, Jean Stehle, Sonia Miller, Jane Kohuth, and Laura Woollett. Thank you so much for supporting and inspiring this random Brit through all the revisions and beyond.

A special *holla* goes out to Emma Sear for not letting a little thing like the Atlantic Ocean get in the way, and to my fly girl Jennifer Withers for all the horror I'm ever going to need.

To Keith and Didi McKay, for being right, goddamn it. Love you muchly.

Finally, to John Mawer and Xanthe, for giving me the best reason in the world to survive the zombie apocalypse.

BONUS! A KILLER SNEAK PEEK AT THE SEQUEL, UNFED!

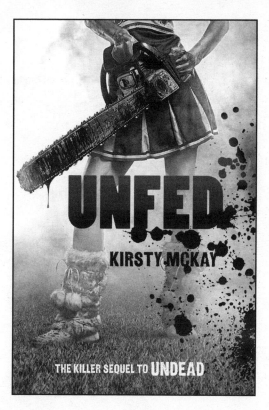

It's the morning after the night of the return of the living dead — or something like that. After running/bus-driving/snowboarding for her life alongside rebel Smitty, geeky Pete, and popular Alice, Bobby thought she'd found the antidote to the veggie juice that had turned the rest of their class into zombies. When Smitty got (*nom, nom*) chomped, Bobby pumped a syringe full of it into him herself. But now Bobby's a prisoner in some hospital of horrors, with no clue how she got there. And Smitty is missing. What if he isn't cured after all? Bobby knows she's got to find him, even if it means facing Scotland's hungry hordes — plus Alice's buckets of snark — again.

Pop. Pop. Pop-pop.

As we head out into the stairwell again, we can hear muffled shots from upstairs somewhere. Sounds like popcorn. I hope they're bagging zoms, not live people. I wonder briefly how many live ones are running scared, like us. For a second I think about if we can help them. Then I remember they're probably Xanthro, which makes them the enemy. They're on their own.

We retrace our steps back to the corridor with the exit sign; my heart is thumping like it's going to burst, but it's only partly the running. It's the hope that hurts. The feeling that we're so close now, but the hardest part may be yet to come. *Please*, I yearn, *please let us make it. It would be so unfair if we didn't after all of this.*

"This way." Russ is first, and fastest.

We round a corner and turn left down a short section of corridor, and suddenly there's stuff underfoot. The momentum keeps us going for a few seconds, and it's like an obstacle course where you have to run through the tires, except we're picking up our feet and skidding and hopping over something much more grisly. As one, we come to a halt and look down at what we're stepping in.

Bodies. And bits of bodies. Adults, children. I see faces, some stretched in pain. Cloudy eyes, skin sucked of color. These people, they have been chopped up. Someone set to and liberated hands from arms, and heads from necks. There is blood everywhere, pooling on the floor, splashed on the walls, dripping from the ceiling. The sharp smell hits me in the back of my throat, and the bright assault of red is blinding to my eyes. It's unspeakable.

Alice starts to hyperventilate. Pete grabs her and tries to talk her down. I lift one foot, mesmerized by the thick, dark red molasses slopping off the sole of my boot. Bloody, bloody hell. It covers the floor, not one single inch of white floor remains. I have never seen so much blood; I didn't know we had that much in us.

"We. Need. To. Keep. Going," Russ gasps through clenched teeth, like you do when you're trying not to be sick. "Don't look," he says. But if we don't look at them, then where do we look? They are everywhere.

"It's OK," says Pete. "They were monsters."

"All of them?" I say, pointing at a glint in the red. A round opal ring is drowning in ooze.

"Martha!" Alice gasps, sinking to her knees.

There's nothing left of her except red, and the ring. I didn't like the fact that she lied to me about my mother being dead, but I wouldn't have wished this on her. I wouldn't wish it on anyone. I pick my way through to Alice, grab her shoulder, pull her with me. We have to go before we sink, before we drown in this sea of red, this nightmare that threatens to overwhelm us.

I can hear the others behind me, but I don't look back. Alice and I reach the end of the corridor, make another turn, and the bodies thin out. We start to run again, slick feet against white floor, no doubt leaving a trail of raspberry jam footprints behind us. We pelt flat out and skitter to a stop in a large room, which is completely empty apart from a circular desk at the far side.

"Where now?" wails Alice.

"There!"

Set into the wall to our right is a pair of huge, steel doors. I run to them, and before I can question the wisdom, smack the UP button on the wall.

"What do you think, Pete? This it?" I'm oh-so-conversational, like we're taking a casual stroll and I'm asking him the way to the park. The smell of blood will stay with me forever now, the iron tang, the bitter and sweet taste in my mouth.

Before he can answer me, the doors open with a *ping*. A bright silver elevator. Without pausing, we run inside — me dragging Alice, Pete and Russ bustling each other in — and I push the button marked SURFACE. Nothing happens.

"Why isn't this thing moving?" I hit the UP button over and over, like that will make a diff.

"Drat it!" Pete points to a circular hole beneath the button. "We need a key. The lift won't work unless we find one."

"What?" I scream, but already I'm running out into the room and heading for the desk. Where else would you keep an elevator key? If not here, then our only option could be to sort through the body parts in the corridor.

And the others know it, too. Pete is searching cubbyholes behind the desk; Russ looking on the floor, underneath potted plants and rugs. Only Alice remains by the elevator, sitting there, sobbing, holding the door open. And then she screams.

A single figure, dressed in black, is coming toward us.

Not Undead, very much alive.

But this is no soldier.

The figure steps into the room, and the light falls on wisps of golden hair that have sneaked out from beneath a black knit hat. The face is young, placid, beautiful — and it breaks into a full-on smile when she sees me.

"Bobby!" she calls. "Thank god I've found you."

My jaw drops.

"They're coming." She moves toward me hurriedly. "We need to get out, now."

I take a big step back, the desk between me and her.

Alice screams again.

Pete shakes his head. "No, no, no, no!"

"Who is this?" Russ straightens up.

I blink. I'm not imagining her.

"This is Grace."

Once I've said it out loud, it sinks in. I make my run for the elevator.

"Who's Grace?" Russ says, running after me.

"The enemy!" Pete gives a choked yell.

"It's OK," Grace calls out. "Bobby, you can't go anywhere, you need a key!"

I get ready to bash at the UP button again.

"Hurry, hurry!" Alice screams beside me.

"Grace," says Russ. "One of the students at the castle? The ones who helped Bobby's mum develop Osiris, and did the dirty on her with the bad guys. That's right, isn't it?" he asks Grace directly, slowly moving toward us, his saw held high in front of him. "I thought Pete told us you died."

"Missing," Pete corrects him. "Shaq was bitten, Michael went up in flames, but we never knew exactly what happened to Grace." He looks at her. "What are you doing here?"

"She sold out to Xanthro, we know that much already," I yell at Pete. "Get in here, Russ!"

"You need a key for the lift, Bobby." Grace takes a step toward us. "You know you do."

"Get away from us, you bitch!" Alice screams, brandishing her drill.

"It's OK, Alice," Grace says calmly. "I'm here to help." She reaches into her jacket pocket and dangles something at me. "And I have the key."

I leap toward her, but she snatches the key out of reach.

"Ah, ah, ah!" she says, shaking her head. "We're going together. I've risked everything coming back here to get you out, Bobby. Now you have to trust me."

"Coming *back* here?" Pete says. "This place is Xanthro, isn't it?"

She smiles at him. "You've always had brains, Peter."

"But you obviously haven't," he bursts out. "Last time we saw you, you wanted to put as much distance between you and Xanthro as possible. You said you knew too much about how they'd caused this outbreak. You said they'd kill you."

"They will." Grace's mouth twitches. "It wasn't my idea to come back. But somebody persuaded me it was in my best interest to be your escape squad."

"Who?" Pete snorts, but I have an awful feeling I already know.

Grace looks at me. "Your mother, Bobby."

"No way!" Pete cries.

"That makes no sense," Russ says. "Why would Bobby's mother trust you?"

"Because she had no option." Grace lifts her chin. "Because she'd tried other means and it hadn't worked, too much time had passed. I was her last hope. I knew the access codes to this place from when we spent time working here, I had a key, I knew my way around. I released the infected as a diversion to bust you out." She looks at me. "It worked."

"Diversion?" Alice screams at her. "You nearly killed us!"

"I'm sorry about that. This batch is different. Xanthro has been experimenting on them, tweaking things to get them to be more efficient killing machines. That way they're more valuable; not only can Xanthro sell the stimulant, now they can sell the ready-made weapon, in human form." Grace takes a step toward us. As one we form a line of weapons at the doorway of the elevator, blocking her way. She steps back again, her hands up in surrender.

"Look," she goes on, "Xanthro is in pieces. The beast is wounded and desperate, and what's happened has only made it more dangerous. They still don't have a cure. And there are factions within the company who will stop at nothing to get their hands on you, Bobby, because you're the ticket to securing your mother, who in all likelihood will produce the cure. I'm your ride out of here. You need to trust me. Besides, you're not getting out without me, look at it that way." She leans forward slightly, her cool eyes fixing me, her voice low. "Let me into that lift, and in a couple of hours you'll be out of the danger zone and with your mum again."

"You know where she is?" I ask her.

She nods. "I do."

"And we're picking Smitty up on the way?"

"Got it in one," she says.

"You don't know where he is." I lean back into the elevator. "My mother wouldn't trust you with that."

"She did." Grace's eyes sparkle. "Didn't you work out the little clues on your phone? He's not too far from here, and he's waiting for you to help him, Bobby. Are you going to leave him for these guys to stumble over? Or shall we go and rescue him now?"

It's my turn to hesitate. Every bone in my body is screaming at me not to trust her, but I believe she's telling the truth. Right now I don't have the luxury of mulling this over. Right now I have to act, and live with the consequences later.

"OK, then." I beckon her in to join us.

She sighs with relief, rolls her eyes in a self-mocking way. "Thought you'd never ask."

There's a *pop*, and a kind of *thud*, and Grace stares at us. I wonder why she isn't moving. A trail of bright red runs out of her hat onto her fore-head and trickles down into her eye, then onto her cheek, then runs off her chin and down onto her coat. Then she crumples and falls forward into the elevator with us.

"No! No! No!" Alice cries.

I don't think. I snatch the key from Grace's warm hand, tossing it up to Pete, who catches it deftly. I haul Grace's legs into the elevator as Pete thrusts the key into its hole and thumps the UP button. Just as the doors close, I catch a glimpse of the soldiers rounding the corner. A masked man holds a rifle.

"Stop!" His voice is gruff and raw. "Stop now!"

It's the same rough voice as the one in the morgue, the third guy who the other two hated.

As if we're going to comply with his wishes.

We lurch as the elevator kicks into action and zooms upward, our ears a-popping, stomachs falling to our feet.

"Grace was shot," Alice mutters. "They shot her. Is she definitely dead?"

"Definitely." Russ has lifted her hat. I don't want to look, but I can't tear my eyes away from the neat hole in her temple.

"Oh god, hurry, hurry, hurry!" Alice slaps the elevator walls.

A pool of blood forms behind Grace's head, growing. I press myself against the wall of the elevator. I don't want it to touch my feet. Russ looks up at me. "We should search her. She may have been carrying something useful." He unzips her jacket.

"I'll do it."

I don't know why, but it feels like less of a violation if it's me. Russ stands aside, and I carefully bend over her. In Grace's inside jacket pocket, my hands close around a single key attached to a fat fob.

"Here." I hold them up for the others to see. "We get outta here, we have transport."

"Think she just parked at the front door?" Pete grimaces.

I check her other pockets, head down, swallowing back tears. She was shot. In front of us. I don't care that she was the enemy; a few seconds ago she was alive, breathing the same air as us, with the same fear and hope in her heart.

"Are there any clues to where she was going to take us?" Russ says.

I shake my head. "Can't find anything." I wipe my hands down my jacket, as if cleaning them of Grace's deadness. "I'm hoping if we find the car, it comes with a dirty great map and instructions."

Alice is sobbing. "Are you . . . going to take . . . her leggings?" She points down to Grace's legs, her face desperate.

"No." I shake my head. "I can't do that." I'd rather look like a cheer-leader than swipe Dead Grace's clothing.

The elevator slows to a stop.

"Be careful, everyone," Russ says. "We don't know what's out there."

We brace ourselves. The doors *ping* and open onto semidarkness and the smell of damp cow. We're in some kind of outhouse.

"What do we do with her?" Pete points at Grace.

I jump over the body, then carefully pull her half out, so that every-thing waist up is still in the elevator. If the doors can't close, the elevator can't move, and that should slow them down some.

"She wanted to help us escape. She got her wish."

this is teen

Want to find more books, authors, and readers to connect with?

Interact with friends and favorite authors, participate in weekly author Q&As, check out event listings, try the book finder, and more!